Still
Love You

By Allie Everhart

Still Love You
By Allie Everhart

CHAPTER ONE

WILLOW

I cannot believe Silas is standing in my dorm room. Driving me home. Back to Berkeley. Where he is now living...and working for my dad! How could my dad hire him? Out of all the people he could've chosen, he had to pick Silas?

What is Silas even doing here? He's supposed to be traveling the world, hiking up mountains, doing volunteer work.

"Willow?" He's standing in front of me now. The door is closed and it's just the two of us. His full lips—the ones I know so well because they've touched every single part of my body—slowly slide up into a smile. "Are you going to say something? Maybe a hello?"

I swallow, my eyes diverting back to his. "Oh, um, yes. Hello. Sorry. I'm just surprised to see you here."

"I thought your parents told you I was moving back."

"Yeah. They did. I just didn't believe them."

His eyes remain on mine. "Why wouldn't you believe them?"

I glance away from him. "Because you have a history of not following through on things."

I shouldn't have said that. He just got here and I don't want to start fighting with him before we even get in the car.

Silas and I used to fight about a lot of things. The fights were intense but short-lived, always ending in a passionate kiss, followed by clothes being ripped off and our bodies colliding. Just the thought of that has me sweating even more in this sweltering hot room.

"They turned the air off," I say, fanning myself. "That's why my room is so hot. I guess they thought we didn't need it since everyone's moving out today."

Spring semester at Camsburg College just ended and half of the girls on my floor have already left for the summer. I was saying goodbye to my friend, Lilly, who lives next door, when Silas appeared. Months ago, my parents told me Silas might be moving back to Berkeley and working on their farm, but I never thought it would actually happen. Silas is a free spirit. He changes his mind all the time. He said he'd be in Europe for two weeks, but ended up being there for two years. I assumed he'd never come back.

My parents were supposed to pick me up today but instead they sent Silas. I'm sure this was all some ploy to get me to be friends with him again, or more than friends. My parents always liked Silas and wanted us to be together. But all good things must come to an end. And they did, the day he left.

"I don't think it's hot in here," he says, "but I spent the past couple years working outside all day in some of the hottest regions on Earth, so this is nothing."

I haven't talked to Silas in two years. When he left, he told me he was going backpacking in Europe, but apparently he only did that for a couple weeks, then spent the rest of the time doing volunteer work. I only know that because my parents told me. They're good friends with Silas' parents.

"So you've been volunteering?" I ask, still fanning myself.

"Yeah. Building houses. Bridges. Planting crops. Mostly physical labor."

I can tell. God, he looks good. All muscle. He was always lean, with defined shoulder and ab muscles that come from surfing. But now? His shoulders are wider, his arms bigger. He

2

looks older, more like a man than the teen boy I remember. His jawline is sharper, more defined, and covered with a thin layer of stubble.

It's feeling even hotter in here. Did they turn on the heat? Or why is it so hot? And why am I the only one sweating? Silas isn't sweating. He seems perfectly comfortable. And he's wearing jeans! Jeans are heavy and hot. I'm wearing a short red cotton sundress with cutouts in the back. I should feel cool. But instead, I'm on fire. Maybe it's early menopause. Maybe this is a hot flash. At 19? Probably not.

I need to face facts. I'm burning up inside because the man I was in love with—the man who turns my insides into hot molten lava—is standing before me, looking even better than I remember.

"Should we get going?" he asks. "The truck is parked right outside."

"Your mom got a truck?" I ask, shocked that his mom would drive something that uses that much gas.

"No, it's mine. It's not brand new. It's a couple years old. Anyway, it's still cool from the air conditioning. I'll get it running again and you could wait out there while I load up your stuff."

"You used the air conditioning?" I ask, shocked again. Silas comes from a family of hippies, as do I. Both our families believe in embracing what nature gives us, which means if it's hot outside, you suck it up. They're always trying to conserve energy, and since air conditioning uses gas, a natural resource that's dwindling in supply, they refuse to use it.

I'm all for conserving energy, but I don't like sweating and feeling like I'm going to pass out, so I have no problem running the air conditioning.

"I know you don't like the heat," Silas says, "so I made sure to cool down the truck before I got here."

"Thanks." I smile.

3

His gaze pauses on my lips. Silas always liked my smile. He said it was what made him want to be friends with me when we met on the first day of second grade.

"No problem," he says.

We both keep staring at each other. It makes sense that I would stare at him. He's changed a lot since I saw him last. But me? I look pretty much the same.

Our eyes meet again. I've always loved Silas' eyes. In fact, I'm jealous of them. They're this rich turquoise blue that doesn't even look real. If I saw them in a photo, I'd think they were doctored to look that color. But no, his eyes are actually that color, surrounded by thick black lashes, which I am also envious of.

I need to stop this. I can't be around him all summer and act like this. I admit there's still something between us. A spark. An energy. An undeniable attraction. But I need to ignore it. We both do.

Silas is the past. It's over between us. We've both moved on.

"So your truck is out that way?" I point to my right.

"The other way. I parked by the side entrance." He turns and walks over to the boxes. "Is there anything breakable in these?"

"No. It's mostly just books and clothes."

"This won't take me long. Do you want to wait in the truck?"

"No. I can help." I'm not the type of girl who sits around and waits for a guy to do things for me. And Silas knows that. He was just being nice, knowing I don't do well in the heat. When it's really hot, like it is today, I don't feel good. Once, I even threw up from the heat, right in front of Silas. It was third grade after we'd been running around all day, but still, I'm sure he doesn't want to witness that again.

I take a box from the stack. Silas lifts up three all at once as if they weigh nothing, even though the ones he picked up are full of heavy textbooks.

"Follow me." He casually walks out to the hall. As I follow behind him, I'm so distracted by how good his ass looks in those jeans that I almost trip and drop the box.

"You okay?" He turns back.

"Yeah. I'm fine."

"You want me to take that?" He nods toward my box.

I adjust my hold on it. "No. I got it."

We go outside and he stops at a shiny black pick-up. It's a really nice truck, with an extended cab and leather interior.

"How'd you get the money for this?"

"I didn't buy it," he says as he sets the boxes in the truck bed. "One of the guys I met overseas gave it to me. He was working at a free medical clinic and we got to be friends. When I told him I was moving back here and working on your dad's farm, he offered me his truck. He's a surgeon from Napa. Said he never used the truck and asked if I wanted it."

Silas holds the door open as we go back inside the dorm.

"He just gave it to you? You're not just borrowing it?"

"It's mine. The paperwork's in my name. The guy has a lot of money. He said he didn't want the hassle of having to sell it and he liked that it'd be used on the farm. He's a big supporter of organic farming."

This shouldn't surprise me. Silas makes friends easily. He has a way of winning people over. He's a great salesman. When he used to work the jewelry booth for his mom at the farmers' market, they always sold out of everything when Silas was there.

I think it's his smile. He has a perfect smile. An easy relaxed smile that draws you in. Not to mention those soft lips and naturally straight white teeth. I had to suffer with braces to get my teeth this straight.

He goes in my room and picks up four boxes. At this rate, we'll be done in ten minutes.

It ends up taking twenty, but only because I had to search my room three times to make sure I got everything. I always worry I'll leave something behind.

Silas watched me during all three searches, leaning against the door with his arms crossed and a slight grin on his face. He finds my somewhat obsessive behaviors to be cute. Most guys find it annoying.

We return to the truck and he opens my door. The truck is high off the ground, making it difficult to get in while wearing a dress.

"Need some help?" he asks as I stand there trying to figure out the best way to do this. My dad has a truck but we only use it on the farm and I don't wear dresses when I'm at the farm.

"I can do it." I go to lift my leg up but find that I can't with this dress on. It's really short and if I lift my leg up that high I'll probably rip the fabric along with exposing myself. Why did I wear this dress? I know why. I wore it because it's unusually hot out today and the dress is lightweight and cool and I thought I'd be riding in the back of my parents' Prius, not a huge pickup truck.

I stand with my hands on my hips, biting my lip as I assess what to do. But before I can make a decision, two large hands reach around my waist and lift me straight up and into the truck, setting me on the seat.

"Silas!" I turn and see his face right in front of me.

He smiles that easy-going smile. "I couldn't wait all day for you to get in the truck." He reaches up and grabs the seatbelt and pulls it down around me, his hand grazing my hip as he clicks it in place. "Safety first." He smiles again, then shuts the door.

I watch him go around the front of the truck. Something about him is different. He seems bolder. More assertive. The old Silas would just offer to help me in the truck, not pick me up and put me there. And the old Silas wouldn't have openly run his eyes over my body when he saw me in this dress. He would've snuck a peek when I wasn't looking.

He's 20 now so maybe he's changing. Growing up. Maybe it's not just his body that's more manly but also his personality.

He's been on his own the past two years, traveling the world, which I'm sure has matured him.

"Why are you wearing a dress?" he asks as he pulls out onto the road that leads away from campus. "Doesn't seem like something you'd wear on moving day."

"All my other clothes were packed. I found this in the back of my drawer. I forgot I had it."

"I like it." He flashes a smile my way. "You should wear it again sometime."

Why is he being so flirty? He knows we're not getting back together. Maybe this is just the new Silas. Maybe he flirts all the time, with *all* girls, not just me. I wonder how many girls he's been with since we broke up. He never had a hard time getting girls. Those eyes and that smile were enough to attract them without him even having to try.

And then that hair. He's got the best hair. I'm jealous of his hair. It's dark brown and wavy yet somehow never frizzes, not even on a rainy day. He doesn't even use any product in it. It's just naturally soft, shiny, and annoyingly sexy. It's long for a guy, hanging just below his jawline.

With that hair, that smile, those eyes and those rock-hard muscles? I'm sure he's been with tons of girls the past couple years.

As for me, I've been with six guys, including Silas. I'm only 19 so some might say that's a lot, but I don't agree. If I were a guy, people would think six is low. I don't know why girls have to be limited to a certain number, or be called sluts for going above that number. I'm a modern woman and refuse to be held to those standards.

My liberal, hippie parents never tried to keep me from having sex. Well, my dad didn't want me to do it, but he knew it would happen. He just hoped it would be with a guy who cared about me, which he told me during one of the many embarrassing conversations my parents had with me about sex. They've always been very open about the topic. They even left condoms in my room when I was fifteen. I didn't use them until

7

I was sixteen. With Silas. He was my first. They say you'll always remember your first time. It's true. I'll never forget that night. And I've never forgotten Silas. But Lord knows I've tried. I've spent the last two years trying to forget about him, and now here I am, sitting right next to him.

"How's college?" he asks.

We've been driving in silence for the past half hour. Silas isn't much of a talker. I guess that's not really true. It's just that compared to me, who talks a lot, it seems like Silas doesn't talk much. But I've been unusually quiet since he showed up because I've been too shocked to speak. I still can't believe he's here.

"It's great," I say. "I like the campus. I like my classes. The professors are good."

I'd normally talk for hours about each one of those things, but right now my mind isn't on school. It's on Silas and how I'm going to survive the summer with him being around me every day.

"That's it?" He glances over at me. "I thought that one question would keep you talking until we got home."

"I guess I'm just tired." I shiver from the cold air blowing on me.

Silas notices and turns it off. "So what else is new? I haven't talked to you forever."

"It's only been two years," I say softly, now regretting it's been so long. It's my fault we haven't talked. Silas called me every day after he left, but I wouldn't answer. I couldn't. It was too hard to hear his voice. Eventually, his calls dwindled to once a week, and I still wouldn't answer. Then it got down to just one call a month, and again, I didn't answer.

"Two years is a long time." His gaze is on the road ahead of us, his hand wrapped around the steering wheel, his thumb lightly tapping it. "Friends shouldn't go two years without talking."

Silas and I were more than friends. So much more. Which is why I couldn't answer his calls.

I pull my seatbelt out enough for me to turn toward him. "Silas, I'm sorry for not returning your calls."

He shrugs his shoulder. "Forget it. It's the past."

"It's not the past. You called just a few weeks ago and...I should've answered."

"So why didn't you?" His thumb continues to tap the steering wheel as his eyes briefly check the side mirror.

"I um..." This is hard to explain. And I don't want to. Telling him why I didn't answer his calls would mean telling him the truth, and I can't do that. It would only lead to us both getting hurt. Again. "I just didn't think it was a good idea...since we're not together anymore."

It's partially true. I knew talking to him would be way too hard, at least for me. I was trying to move on. Trying to get over him. But even without answering his calls, I'm still not over him.

The truth—the real reason I didn't talk to him—is that I still love him. It's been two years since we broke up, but I still love Silas.

CHAPTER TWO

SILAS

I t's been two years. Two years since I've seen her. Two years since I've talked to her. Two years since we had our last kiss. And despite all the days and hours in between that I tried to get over her, the truth is...I still love Willow.

But I can't tell her that. This summer will be hard enough. Living down the street from her. Working for her dad. Seeing her every day. Telling her how I feel would just complicate things even more. Besides, Willow doesn't want that. Us. She made that crystal clear the day she gave me back the engagement ring.

I asked her to marry me the day after I graduated from high school. She's a year younger than me so had just finished her junior year. Our parents are both liberal hippies so had no problem with us getting engaged at such a young age. They knew how in love we were, and to this day, Willow's mom is convinced that Willow and I are soul mates. I think so too. And I know, deep down, even Willow thinks that. But according to her, soul mates can't always be together.

We were engaged for just one week. During that week, we spent every moment together; happy, excited, and talking about our future. But then Willow panicked and called off the engagement. At first I wasn't worried. Willow panics all the time. She's high strung. I'm laid back. It's one of the things that makes us work so well together. We balance each other out. But when she wouldn't talk to me for days after she gave the ring back, I started to get worried. I went to her house but she wouldn't come to the door. I called her but she wouldn't pick up. I texted her but got nothing back. Finally, her parents forced her to talk to me. They sat us in a room and wouldn't let us leave until she'd given me an explanation. And her explanation was that she couldn't see a future with me, at least not the future she wanted.

Willow wants to be CEO of a large corporation someday. She wants to live in a big city in a high-rise apartment and drive a BMW and eat at trendy restaurants. As for me? I'm not entirely sure what my future holds but it's definitely not that. I'd be happy doing whatever odd jobs come my way. Living in a simple house. Driving a pick-up truck.

The only thing I knew for sure about my future is that I wanted Willow to be in it. To be my wife. My best friend. And someday the mother of my children. But that didn't work out, so I need to reevaluate my future, but every time I try, something always seems to be missing. And that something is Willow.

"I called you all those times because I wanted to talk," I say to Willow. "Just as friends."

"I know," she murmurs, her head dropping down.

She seems remorseful, probably wishing she'd answered at least a few of my calls. So why didn't she? The reason she gave me isn't good enough. She couldn't answer because we were broken up? That doesn't matter. We've been friends since we were kids. And friends talk to each other, even after having their hearts broken.

"Are you mad at me?" she asks, her eyes now straight ahead.

"I was," I say, being honest. "But I'm over it."

I can't stay mad at her. I've never been able to. I'm not an angry person. I don't hold grudges. I was more hurt than angry after she gave me the ring back. She was hurt too. In fact, when she told me she couldn't see a future with me, she cried. Sobbed. While I held her in my arms.

11

So how could I be mad at her? Breaking off our engagement hurt her as much as it hurt me. But she felt like she had to do it because she wanted a life that I didn't. I could've gone along with it and lived that life just to be with her, but I knew if I did that, I wouldn't be happy. Willow knows that too, which is why she'd never let me do it.

After we had that talk, I packed my bags and flew to Europe. I couldn't be around Willow. We needed space. I backpacked for two weeks through different countries, taking the train and staying in youth hostels. It was always a dream of mine to do that, but I always thought I'd be doing it with Willow. We talked about it when we first started dating. We said we'd go the summer after I graduated. But then we broke up, so backpacking through Europe without her wasn't so much a dream as a heartache. For those entire two weeks, I couldn't stop thinking about her, wishing she were there with me.

"Hey." I nudge her arm from across the seat. "The past is the past. We're still friends, right?"

She smiles at me but it's a sad smile. "Yeah, of course."

Why is she sad? Because I'm here? I know she doesn't want me here. I could tell by the look on her face when she saw me. I'm sure that's why her parents didn't tell her I'd be working for them this summer. She doesn't want to be faced with the past, which is what I am to her. Just a piece of her past.

Willow doesn't like going backwards. She's always moving forward at lightning speed, which is why I never quite understood why she agreed to go out with me in the first place. She knows I don't rush through life. I take things slow, appreciate the moment, live in the here and now. But Willow? She's always racing ahead, sprinting toward whatever goals she's set for herself. Part of me admires that about her, but the other part of me wishes she wasn't like that, because by doing that, she's missing out on the present. Missing out on the moments she might want to remember someday.

"Silas, look!" Willow perks up, pointing at the next exit. "It's that burger place we love. Do you want to stop?"

"But your parents are making dinner."

She rolls her eyes. "Oh, please. Tofu and vegetables is not dinner. I need real food and this may be my last chance to have it. Can we stop? Please?"

I smile at her. "Only if you split a milkshake with me. And an extra large fry."

"Yes. To all of it." She sighs and reclines back in her seat. "God, that sounds good. They have the best fries. I haven't been to this place since...well, since you left."

She says it as though I wanted to leave. Like I had a choice in the matter. Did she really expect me to stick around? See her all summer without being able to touch her? Kiss her? Put my arms around her? Tell her I love her? It would've been torture to not be able to do those things. And it's not like I could've avoided her. She lives just a few houses down from me. We had the same friends. Hung out at the same places.

But as hard as it would've been, I would've stayed if she'd told me to. If I thought there was any chance we might get back together, I never would've left. But that's not what happened.

When I told Willow I was leaving, she told me to go. And when I told her I might stay in Europe and not come back, she didn't try to stop me. She made it clear we were done and that she was moving on without me. But based on her comment just now, it seems that she remembers things differently. Or maybe it's easier on her if she pretends that I left her. That I'm the one who ended things, not her.

I park in front of Bobbi's Burger Shack. It's one of those places where you can park and order from your car. Or you can order at the window and eat at the picnic tables scattered out front.

Willow and I used to come here all the time. Our parents, who are strict vegans, wouldn't approve of us eating burgers, which is why we never told them we came here. But one day, my mom found a Bobbi's Burger Shack cup in my car. I found it in the garbage later and knew she put it there. When she saw me, she just shook her head and mooed. I laughed and gave her

13

a hug and told her she's an awesome mom. Because she is. She doesn't get angry over little stuff, like her son sneaking out to eat a burger, even though she's vehemently opposed to eating meat herself. She raised me to be who I am, not who she wants me to be. Willow's parents are the same way. We both got lucky that way.

"Wait there," I tell Willow, then I go around the truck and open her door. Before she can attempt to get out, I reach around her tiny waist and lower her to the ground. She's only 5'4 and this truck sits high off the ground. I didn't want her falling out of it. I also might've wanted an excuse to touch her.

She's wearing this red dress that had my blood pumping the moment I saw her. It's a short cotton sundress that's open in the back, showing off her soft skin that has a hint of color from the sun. My blood is still pumping hard, diverting to places it shouldn't be going. Not now, while I'm standing in the parking lot of Bobbi's Burger Shack in front of the girl I'm only supposed to be friends with.

But it's extremely hard to control that part of me when she looks so damn good. Her dark silky hair only hit her shoulders the last time I saw her. Now it's several inches longer and sexy as hell. Her deep brown eyes still draw me in with their intensity. And those lips. I still remember how they feel, how they moved over mine when I kissed her, how they parted to let me taste her.

"Are we going or what?" Willow's standing there, waiting for me to move. I got so caught up in her that I forgot where we were for a moment.

"Yeah, let's go." I instinctively take her hand.

"What are you doing?" She looks down at our hands.

"Sorry." I let her go. "Habit."

We always used to hold hands, even before we dated. It was just a thing we did as friends. But now she won't even let me hold her hand? Guess that just proves that what we had is over. I knew it was, and yet I held out a small glimmer of hope that maybe she'd see me again and change her mind about us.

Wishful thinking. When Willow makes a decision, she sticks to it. She's stubborn as a mule.

I go up to the order window and say, "We'll have two cheeseburgers, one with everything, the other one with a squirt of mustard, two squirts of ketchup, four pickle slices, and one very thin slice of tomato."

The teenage girl at the window stares at me like she thinks I was joking. I wasn't. That's how Willow likes her burger. She's very particular and she knows what she wants.

"You might want to write that down." I give the girl my famous Silas smile and her annoyed expression turns to a flirtatious grin combined with a head tilt.

She holds her pen above her order pad. "Could you repeat that, please?"

"Sure." I repeat the order as the girl scribbles it down while keeping her eyes on me.

I hear Willow clearing her throat behind me, then feel a sharp jab in my side. "Don't forget the fries. And the shake."

What was the jab for? Is Willow jealous that I'm flirting with the girl at the counter? I did it for her benefit. Just wanted to make sure she got her burger the way she wanted it. Or maybe, just maybe, I wanted to see if she'd get jealous. Willow is the jealous type. If you told her that, she'd forcefully deny it, but we both know it's true.

"We'll also take an extra large fry and a large chocolate shake," I say, getting my wallet out.

"With two cups," Willow adds. "And two straws."

After all Willow and I have done together, I don't know why she cares about sharing a straw with me. My mouth has been all over her body, and hers on mine. Just the thought of that causes blood to rush to that place it shouldn't be going.

"I can pay." Willow sets a twenty on the counter.

I slide it back to her, my eyes on the girl taking the order. "How much?"

"It's $12.85."

I hand her a ten and a five. "Keep the change."

"What's your name?" she asks, her fingers purposely sliding over mine as she takes the money.

Willow coughs, then clears her throat.

"Silas," I say, flashing that smile again.

The girl writes my name on the order slip, then writes something else on the back of the receipt and hands it to me. "Your food will be out in a minute."

The twenty Willow left is still sitting there so I take it and walk back to the table we always used to sit at. It's around the side of the building facing an empty lot. It isn't great in terms of atmosphere but that's why we chose it. Nobody ever wanted to sit here so we always got the table. It also gave us privacy, which we needed because sometimes our PDA got a little out of control. When Willow and I were dating, we couldn't take our hands off each other. Or our lips. Our tongues. I need to stop thinking about that. It's causing an uncomfortable throbbing below the belt, and is inappropriate given that Willow and I are just friends and have no hope of being anything more.

"Why were you flirting with her?" Willow asks as she slams a stack of napkins down on the table. By her tone and forceful handling of the napkins, I can tell she's jealous. I'm just not sure why. I'm not hers. She has no reason to be jealous. Unless...I chuckle.

"What's so funny?" She sits across from me instead of beside me like she used to do.

"Nothing." I take a couple napkins from the tall stack. "That's a lot of napkins. Your mom would not be happy. A tree had to lose its life for all those."

"Don't start. I'll get enough of that this summer."

Our parents are staunch environmentalists. They use almost no paper products. Only cloth napkins are allowed and Willow's mom makes her use the same cloth napkin for the entire day, unless it's a messy meal that really dirties the napkin.

"Here." I reach across the table and pick up Willow's hand and place the twenty dollar bill in it, letting my fingers graze her palm. She inhales sharply at my touch, then quickly fists her hand around the money and pulls it back from me. She used to love it when I'd run my fingers over her skin. Not just her palm, but all of her. She said I had magic fingers, able to cause a response in her with just the slightest touch.

"You didn't have to pay," she says, shoving the money in her wallet.

"And you didn't have to jab my side when I was giving that girl our order."

"I didn't jab your side." She takes the stack of napkins and evenly distributes them between her and me. She likes things to be even. It's part of her need to have order. Disorder drives her crazy, which makes living with her parents a challenge.

"You jabbed me so hard I think you bruised my ribs." I lift up my shirt and her eyes go straight to my abs. Her gaze lingers there a moment, then she quickly glances away.

"I didn't bruise you. You look...fine." She sits up straighter and looks out toward the small road that goes by the restaurant, watching as a cyclist goes by. "So why were you flirting with her? You don't live here. It's not like you could date her."

"I wasn't flirting. I was just giving her my order." I stretch my legs out under the table, letting them brush against Willow's.

She crosses her legs and turns to me. "You were giving her the Silas smile. No girl can resist that and you know it. You were definitely flirting."

"Why do you care?" I nudge her leg with mine and keep it there. I know I shouldn't keep touching her but I can't help it. I haven't seen her forever and now that she's here, I have this need to touch her, even in just an innocent way. I'm a very tactile person. Touch is a way I communicate, sometimes without even knowing it.

"I *don't* care," she says in a tone that implies the opposite. "Do what you want. I just don't think you should flirt with some girl you have no intention of asking out. You're leading her on."

"A person can flirt without having it go anywhere."

"Then what's the purpose?"

17

Typical Willow logic at work. She has to have an answer to everything. An answer that makes sense to her.

"There doesn't have to be a purpose." I know that comment will get her going, but I put it out there anyway.

"Of course there does. You can't just do something for no reason."

"Fine." I lean across the table and give her that Silas smile she was referring to. "I flirted with her so she'd get your order correct. I'm sure they're not used to having to follow such specific guidelines for making a burger. I was just making sure they got it right."

She sighs. "I appreciate your efforts but you don't have to resort to selling your body just to get my order correct."

I laugh and sit back. "I wasn't selling my body. It was just a smile."

"I think that girl would like more than that." Willow holds up the receipt, which has a phone number written on back with the words 'call me.'

"Huh. I wondered what she wrote on there." I take the receipt and shove it in my pocket.

"You're keeping it?" Willow looks disgusted with me.

I shrug. "You never know."

"Never know *what?*"

Before I can answer, our food arrives, delivered by a short, scrawny kid who doesn't look legally old enough to work. He's probably the little brother of the girl at the register. They look similar.

"Wait." Willow stops him before he leaves. "Could you get us another cup for the milkshake? And another straw?"

He nods and walks off.

I set the basket of fries between us as Willow inspects her burger, lifting the top of the bun.

"Is it the way you wanted it?" I ask.

"Yes. It's perfect." She puts the bun back in place. "But your flirting trick didn't completely work. She forgot the cup and the straw."

"That's because *you* asked for that, not me." I smile, then take a big bite of my burger.

"Whatever," she mumbles, picking up a fry.

She eats fries one at a time, whereas I grab several and eat them all at once. That's why we always shared an order. It would take Willow forever to finish a basket of fries on her own, eating them one at a time like that.

I wonder if she shares her fries when she goes out with other guys. I try not to think about that. Thinking about her with another guy makes me angry and I never get angry. Except when it comes to Willow. She brings out all my emotions. The good, the bad, the in-between. This girl gets to me the way no one else can.

When I left two years ago, I wasn't sure I'd ever see her again, and now, working for her parents, I'll see her every day.

This is going to be a very interesting summer.

CHAPTER THREE

WILLOW

How am I going to survive the summer? I've been with Silas for all of two hours and I'm already a complete and utter mess. For the past two years, I've been so put together, my emotions kept in check, my sole focus on my career. I've avoided any type of long term relationships, knowing that getting serious with a guy will only lead me to the same place I ended up with Silas; having a conversation about how we're heading down different paths and therefore need to break up. I know exactly what I want for my life and I'm not going to change my plans for some guy.

But that doesn't mean I don't date. Last year at college, I went to a lot of parties, did my fair share of flirting, and went on a decent number of dates. I just didn't let those dates lead to anything serious. Even if I wanted a serious relationship with a guy, it wouldn't be with any of the guys I've dated since Silas left.

I hate to admit this, but being with Silas ruined me for all other guys. Now I expect every guy I date to make me feel like I did when I was with Silas, which isn't fair. Nobody will make me feel that way again. Silas was my first love and there's something special about that. The feelings I had for him just aren't going to happen with someone else, so I need to accept that, but so far I haven't.

"I don't think that kid's ever bringing an extra cup," I say, setting my burger down. I've devoured half of it within a matter of minutes, which is fast for me. I'm usually a slow eater.

These burgers are the best I've ever had and this one is especially good because they made it exactly the way I asked, or the way *Silas* asked, with that famous smile of his. He flashes that easygoing smile and I swear, girls go into some kind of trance and do whatever he asks.

Watching that girl flirt with him got to me in a way I didn't expect. I was actually mad, to the point I was about ready to punch her if she didn't back away. Hence why I said I'm a complete and utter mess. I don't punch girls. I don't punch anyone. I get angry, but I don't take it out on people. Except Silas. He has a way of bringing out all my emotions. Maybe that's why I felt so angry. Seeing him flirt to get his way irritated me, or maybe it was just seeing him flirt, period, with someone other than me.

Wait—I can't be jealous. He's not mine anymore. He's free to date whoever he wants. I just need to get used to that idea. He took off right after we broke up so I never had to watch him date other girls. But I'm sure I'll witness that this summer so I need to start getting used to it.

Silas slides the milkshake over to his side of the table and takes a big slurp.

"Silas! What are you doing? I need to get a cup and another straw."

"Why?" he asks casually. "Why can't we just share?"

"Because..." I'm flustered, trying to find the right words. Why does this keep happening? I've been lost for words ever since he showed up at my door. I've also been nervous, agitated, frustrated. My emotions are all over the place and yet he seems calm and collected. It's irritating.

"Because why?" He stands up and goes around the table and casually takes a seat next to me on the bench. He slides the milkshake back over to what is now *our* side of the table and

21

takes another sip. "It's good. You should try it." He moves it in front of me.

I move it back. "I can't, now that you drank out it."

"Afraid you'll get germs?" He takes another sip.

"Yes. It's unsanitary."

"I don't think you need to worry." He leans down by my ear. "In case you forgot, my mouth has been all over your body. Every square inch of it." His lips brush against my ear and a shiver shoots down my spine. "And my tongue has—"

"Yeah. Got it." I scoot over, needing to put some distance between us before I accidentally kiss him, or do more than that.

His little reminder of our past has me so hot and bothered I'm about ready to do him right now on this bench. Sex with Silas was the best I've ever had but I don't need those memories creeping back in my head. It's bad enough they fill my dreams. I can't control what happens in my sleep, but I *can* control my thoughts when I'm awake. I take a deep breath and clear my mind of all things Silas.

That lasts for about a second, until I feel his hand on my back as he pushes the milkshake toward me again. "Here. I wiped the straw off for you."

Why did I have to wear a dress with an open back? The feel of his hand pressed against my bare skin has my mind returning to those memories I'm trying to forget. Memories of Silas' hands moving over my skin. And his fingers. Those magic fingers. I even used to call them that. His fingers ran over my palm earlier when he gave me my twenty back and I know it was on purpose. A tingling heat coursed through my body when he did it, making my breath quicken. He noticed, but luckily didn't say anything.

I take a sip of the milkshake.

"Good, isn't it?" he asks.

"Yeah, just like I remembered."

"Do you want the rest of it?" He chuckles. "I don't want to contaminate it again."

"It's fine." I slide it between us. "We can share. I was overreacting."

"You? Overreact?"

I laugh and jab his side like I did earlier.

"Hey! That's my bruised side."

"You're not bruised." I sip the milkshake and watch as he lifts his shirt up. I bite down hard on my straw. Holy shit, his abs are amazing! He had decent abs before, but now? His abs—his whole body, really—is in a whole different league. The league with the hot men you see on calendars or underwear ads. I was never really into guys with big muscles, but Silas with big muscles? I feel the need to fan myself, despite the cool breeze blowing past us.

"There'll be a bruise there by tomorrow." He lowers his shirt and picks up a wad of fries, stuffing them in his mouth. He's even sexy when he eats. How is that possible?

"You can finish it." I offer him the milkshake as I eat the rest of my burger. "I'm getting full."

"So what should we do tonight?" He wads up his burger wrapper and tosses it, landing it in the trash bin.

"What do you mean?"

"Do you want to see a movie? Or we could go to the park. The outdoor movies have started for the summer. They're showing old black-and-white horror films this year."

I stare at him. "Silas. We're not going out."

"I know we're not going out as in *going out*, but that doesn't mean we can't hang out as friends."

I'd love to just hang out with him like we used to, but I can't. It's too hard to be around him.

"I can't," I say, but then quickly regret it. I feel bad turning him down. He's trying to make an effort here. Trying to be friends again, even after I broke his heart.

"You can't *tonight*? Or ever?" I hear the sadness in his voice.

"I don't think it's a good idea for us to hang out." I grab a napkin and wipe my hands.

"Do you have other plans?"

"No."

"So you're just going to sit at home all night with your parents?"

I hadn't really thought about what I'd be doing tonight. I guess I should be going out, but I haven't stayed in touch with my friends from high school. I'd feel kind of strange just calling them up after all this time and asking them if they wanted to do something.

"I'll probably just go to bed early," I say.

He nods, like he's accepted my lame excuse, but then says, "We're going out." He gathers up our remaining trash and takes it to the garbage can.

"You can't just decide that for me."

"You can't sit at home all night on your first night back from college. And I'm bored. I want to get out."

"Why don't you go out with Trent?"

Trent was his friend from high school. They didn't go to the same school. Trent went to *my* high school, a public school, and Silas went to private school. It was really more like home school, taught in a house by a lady who used to teach public school but didn't like their teaching methods so left and started her own school.

I went there when I was younger. That's how I met Silas. I called it hippie school because there were no rules. You learned at your own pace, and if you wanted to play outside all day, you could. The lack of structure drove me crazy, so the summer before my freshman year, I convinced my parents to let me go to public school. I was a cheerleader in high school and Silas used to come to the football games and we'd go to parties afterward. That's when he met Trent, who was a linebacker until he got injured during his senior year. Silas and Trent hit it off and became good friends.

"Trent's got a new girl," Silas says. "She's taking up all his time."

"He just got home from college. How'd he get a girl so fast?"

"He's been home for a week. He met her last week when he was at the park for the outdoor movie. He said the place was crawling with single girls."

So if Silas goes there alone tonight, he'll probably meet someone. Some other girl. Dammit. I'm not ready for that. I'm not ready to see him with someone else. I thought I was, but the sick feeling in my stomach right now is telling me I'm not at all ready for that.

"Okay, I'll go," I say, getting up from the table.

He grins. "What changed your mind?"

"Nothing. It just sounds fun. I like outdoor movies. We used to go to them all the time."

"Except we never actually watched the movie." His grin remains as he takes my hand and begins walking back to the truck. It's so true. The movie was just a place for us to make out without our parents around.

"You can't keep doing this." I hold up our joined hands.

"Why not? When we were friends we held hands."

"We were also seven years old at the time."

"We were older than seven. We held hands all through grade school and middle school."

It's true, but we stopped holding hands once I went to a different school. After that, I didn't see Silas much until we started dating.

Switching schools was a turning point in my life. That's when I decided I'd had enough of my parents' hippie lifestyle and was not going to follow in their footsteps. The hippie clothes? The vegan diet? It's just not me. And I have no desire to take over the family business someday. I admire my parents for running an organic farm. It's their passion and something they believe in. But it's not what I want to do.

I'm a type A personality and I want to run a company someday. A large corporation, probably in the financial sector. I want to be a CEO. I decided this years ago and my first step in getting to my goal was to go to a normal school. Colleges don't want students who grew up going to hippie school. Employers don't either.

I'm still holding Silas' hand. I didn't let go because I like holding his hand. It's familiar. Comforting. When I hold some other guy's hand, it doesn't fit right with mine. Something always feels off.

But holding Silas' hand is like coming home. It brings back the memories I keep trying to forget. Those feelings I keep trying to bury. And those urges to do more than just hold his hand.

"See?" He squeezes my hand, then lets it go. "That wasn't so bad." He opens the passenger door.

"Don't—" Before I can get the words out, he's already hoisted me up and into the truck. "I got it," I say as he reaches up for the seat belt. I don't want him putting it on me again. The last time he did that, my heart went into overdrive the second his hand pressed into my hip as he secured the belt in place.

"I won't do that every time," Silas says as he starts the truck.

"Do what?"

"Lift you into the trunk. I only did that because you have a dress on and I didn't want you giving the whole parking lot a show."

"I could get in without giving anyone a show," I insist.

"Oh, really?" He smiles. "I'd like to see you try. I'll stand behind you just in case."

"In case what?"

"In case you fall backward. Or your dress rips."

"That won't be necessary. I won't need to get in the truck again. We're almost home."

"We're taking it tonight when we go out."

"Then I'll change into shorts."

My phone rings and I almost don't answer when I see it's my mom. I'm mad at her for doing this. I know she purposely sent Silas to get me, hoping we'll end up together.

"Hey, Mom," I answer.

"Hi, honey. Did Silas get there on time?"

"Yes, but why didn't you tell me he was coming to pick me up?"

"We asked him at the last minute. We were all ready to drive down and get you but then your father wasn't feeling well so I called Silas. Make sure to thank him. He had to miss his last hour of class in order to do this for us. If I knew he had class I never would've asked him, but he insisted on helping us out."

"What's wrong with dad?"

"He felt sick to his stomach. I don't think it's the flu. I think it was something he ate. He's resting now."

My parents don't like to waste food so my dad will eat most anything to avoid tossing it out, even if it has mold on it. He'll just eat around the mold.

"Are you two almost here?" she asks.

"We're about ten minutes away. We'll be there soon."

"Silas has sure grown up, hasn't he?" she says in her matchmaking tone.

"Mom," I say, urging her to butt out.

"See you soon, honey," she says in a cheery voice before hanging up.

"You should've told me my dad was sick," I say to Silas.

"He told me not to. He knows how you worry."

"I wonder what it was this time. Moldy bread. Moldy cheese. Expired milk. That man needs to stop eating food that's gone bad."

"He's been doing that forever. You can't change him now."

"People can change." I swipe through my phone, checking messages, then stop as I remember what my mom said. "So what class are you taking?"

He hesitates like he doesn't want me to know. "Introductory accounting."

I turn to him, shocked. "Are you serious?"

"Yeah. Why?"

"Silas Sparks is taking an accounting class? You hate math."

27

"Not if it's useful. I didn't find geometry useful which is why I never did well in it. I don't put effort into things I'm not interested in."

"Why is accounting useful? You don't want to be an accountant."

"No, but maybe someday I'll have my own business. It'd be good to have some basic business knowledge."

"Wait." I shake my head really fast. "Who are you and what did you do with Silas?"

"What do you mean?"

"You want your own business? A business is a lot of work, Silas. You don't even like getting out of bed in the morning."

He shrugs. "Like you said, people change. I spent the past two years working fifteen, sixteen hour days and I actually didn't mind it. I was making a difference. Putting a roof over someone's head. Planting enough food to feed a village. Digging trenches to help get water to people. If I'm making a difference, then I don't mind working hard."

"I didn't mean you don't work hard. I know how much you've helped your mom with her jewelry business. I just didn't know you wanted to go into business yourself."

"I don't know if I will. I'm still exploring my options."

"So does that mean you're staying here? You're not going back overseas?"

"That depends." He gets off at the exit that takes us to our neighborhood.

"Depends on what?"

"On how this summer goes."

How this summer goes? What does that mean? Is he talking about me? Us? Is he trying to get back together with me?

He's quiet as he drives down our street. My curiosity is killing me. I have to ask.

"Are you going to explain what you meant by that?"

"No," he says simply. We're in my parents' driveway now and he smiles at me. "Would you like help getting out?"

"No. I can do it." I open my door and notice how far up I am from the ground. It would be a bad idea to jump in these sandals I'm wearing. I'd probably break a toe or twist my ankle.

"You sure you don't want some help?" Silas is now standing by my door, watching me.

"Maybe a little," I mumble.

He lets out a laugh as he picks me up and lowers me to the ground.

"You need different tires on this thing," I say. "It's too high up."

"Tires are expensive. I'm not changing them. You'll just have to figure out a way to get yourself in and out." He nods toward the house. "You can go inside. I'll get your stuff."

He turns to walk away but I catch his hand. "Hey."

He looks back. "Yeah?"

"Thanks for picking me up today. And helping me move all my stuff."

"Sure." He walks to the back of the truck.

I follow him. "I'm sorry you had to miss part of your class. If you need help catching up on whatever you missed, I'm pretty good at accounting. I've had two semesters now."

He lowers the tailgate. "You're offering to be my tutor?"

"Only if you need one." I watch his arm muscles flex as he lifts up three heavy boxes.

"I'll keep that in mind." He glances at the front door. "Your mom's coming."

"Willow!" She races toward me and gives me a hug. I haven't been home since spring break and my parents have been so busy with the farm that they haven't had a chance to drive down to see me.

"Hi, Mom." I give her a tight squeeze. My mom drives me crazy, but I love her and think she's the greatest mom ever, despite her hippie ways. And today she's in full hippie attire; a tie-dye dress in pastel colors, white Birkenstock sandals, and a long blue scarf tied loosely around her neck.

We go inside the house and my jaw drops when I see the living room. I used to call it the rainbow room because my parents painted each wall a different color; red, blue, yellow, green. But now it's all one color, a light sea foam green, and we have actual furniture instead of an assorted mix of bean bags and butterfly chairs. They've been replaced by a dark gray couch and matching loveseat. Bright orange throw pillows are scattered over them, but that's nothing compared to the crazy mix of colors I'm used to.

"What happened in here?" I ask.

My mom hangs her arm around my shoulder. "Your father and I redecorated. Do you like it?"

"Yeah. It looks great."

And yet I kind of miss how it used to look. I despised it for years, but now that's it's gone I almost wish it were back.

I thought I'd go home for the summer and everything would be the same. But I'm getting the feeling I'm in for a lot more changes than just the wall color in the living room.

CHAPTER FOUR

SILAS

"**D**oes anyone want dessert?" Candace asks, holding out a plate of flat pale discs. I think they're supposed to be cookies.

"No, thank you," Willow and I say at the same time.

Candace invited me for dinner, but given that Willow and I just splurged on burgers and fries, we weren't really hungry. But we managed to eat a few bites since her mom went to the trouble of making dinner, which consisted of steamed tofu smothered in some kind of sauce and served with lumpy mashed potatoes. The meal was pretty bad and dessert will be even worse.

Willow's mom is a horrible cook. She's also a horrible baker. But in her defense, she can only do so much when she's limited to organic, dairy-free, gluten-free ingredients.

"Then I guess I'll save these for later." She winks at Willow. "It's a new recipe. Your father loves them."

"I think I heard my name." Carl appears, wearing pajama pants and his long blue robe, his curly brown hair a mess from sleeping on it. "There's my girl." He goes up to Willow. "Welcome home, honey."

"Hey, Dad." She hugs him. "Are you feeling better?"

"Much." He stands back and rubs his stomach. "It must've been those strawberries. They were starting to get pretty moldy."

"Dad, you need to stop eating that stuff."

"Nonsense." He kisses her cheek. "Mold is a product of nature. I just had a sensitive stomach today. So Silas, any problem with the move?"

"No. Willow had everything packed and ready to go."

"She's always so organized." He stands next to Candace, taking one of the cookies from the tray she's holding. "Are you kids going out tonight?"

He acts like we're dating again. Like Candace, Carl would love to see his daughter end up with me. He didn't used to be like that. He used to try to keep us from dating, but back then he didn't want *any* boy dating his daughter. His liberal values turned conservative when it came to Willow. Candace was the opposite. She thought Willow should be allowed to explore her sexuality, which she did. With me. Many, many times.

But before I could even date her, her dad made me take a quiz. An actual quiz he'd written and printed out. I had to sit at the kitchen table and take it while he watched, as if I could somehow cheat on it. The quiz had all these questions about Willow's likes and dislikes, including her favorite colors, foods, movies, and bands. Then I had to make a top ten list of things I like about her. That was followed by an essay about why I wanted to date her. It took over an hour to finish the quiz and I ended up getting an A minus on it. Carl said I had her favorite foods wrong but I actually had them right. Willow pretends to like their vegan health food but she's a junk food girl all the way. And she loves meat, as evidenced by how fast she ate that burger today.

"We're going to the park for the outdoor movie," I say to Carl.

"I'll go change." Willow takes off for her room.

Carl sits across from me and lowers his voice. "You didn't tell her, right?"

"No. But it's going to be impossible to keep this from her."

"I need you to do this for me, Silas. I don't want her knowing until I've exhausted all my options."

"Can you get another bank loan?"

He shakes his head. "The bank won't loan us another dime. We've already given them the house as collateral. We have nothing else to offer them."

"Use my truck."

"We're not doing that. You're already doing more for us than you should."

"You guys are like family. I'll do whatever I can. I'll get to work earlier and stay later. I was thinking of planting some flowers in the space where the broccoli didn't grow. People pay more for flowers than broccoli."

"We should try that," Candace says, sitting next to Carl.

He nods. "It's a good idea, but it's not going to be enough."

"Dan will give you a loan," I say. "I know he will. I just haven't been able to reach him."

Dan is the guy who gave me the truck. He's worth millions. I haven't been able to call him because he's doing medical aid in a remote part of India where there's no phone service.

"That man doesn't even know us," Carl says. "He's not going to give us a loan. He'd get almost no return on his investment."

"That's not true. We can make this work. I know we—"

"Shh." Carl's eyes dart to the hall.

"Ready?" I hear Willow behind me.

I turn and see she's changed into white shorts and a navy blue fitted t-shirt that shows off her round perky breasts. I need to keep my eyes off those tonight or I'll end up with the problem I had earlier.

"Yeah, I'm ready." I get up from the table.

"Do you two want some snacks to take with?" Candace asks. Her snacks are either wheat-free crackers that taste like cardboard or these sesame chips she buys that look like bird food. By now, Candace has to know that Willow doesn't like these foods and yet she keeps offering them to her. Maybe she's hoping her daughter will like them eventually.

"No, thanks," Willow says. "We won't be out long."

"There's no rush to get home." She gives her a quick hug. "Have fun tonight."

Willow and I go out to the truck and this time she's able to hoist herself into it. I caught a glimpse of her ass as she did it. Her shorts have always been a favorite of mine. She likes the short ones. For her it's a fashion thing, but for me it's the view they provide when she bends over.

I get in the driver's side. "What do you think? Chips or candy?"

"Let's splurge and have both." She pulls her seatbelt on. "I'm actually excited about this. I haven't been to an outdoor movie since...well, since you and I went. Cami kept inviting me to go senior year but I just never got around to it."

Cami was one of her friends from high school. I was gone during Willow's senior year but I heard through the grapevine a little about what she was up to that year. Trent was my main source of information. He's my age so he was in college when Willow was a senior but he had some friends in her class. I used to always ask him if she was dating anyone. He wouldn't give me names, but he did say she dated one of the football players and a guy from the basketball team. As a super hot cheerleader, Willow could've had her pick of any of the athletes in school. I'm sure she went out with more than two.

"I need to stop and grab some blankets," I say, pulling up to my house. It's just down the street from Willow's. I park and go around to her side to see if she needs help getting out. She hops out and stumbles, but then straightens up and holds her arms out like a gymnast does at the end of a routine.

"Nice landing," I say, laughing at her.

"Thank you." She smiles.

I hold the door open for her and hear my mom yell, "Willow! You're back!"

"Diane! I've missed you."

The two of them hug, then my mom whisks Willow off to the living room. My mom loves Willow like a daughter. Our families are good friends, especially our moms.

While Willow and my mom are off talking, I go to the kitchen to find some snacks. I can't afford to buy any. I'm really short on cash and working for free all summer is going to make my financial situation even worse. But I'm not doing this to make money. I'm doing it to help Carl and Candace...and Willow.

I rummage through the bin of snacks I keep in the pantry. My mom is a health freak like Willow's mom, but Martin and I like our junk food so we keep stashes of it just for us.

"Going out tonight?" Martin opens the fridge behind me.

"Willow and I are going to the outdoor movie. I'm bringing some snacks."

He closes the fridge. "Toss me a candy bar. Diane made me eat tempeh tonight and I'm starving."

I toss him a Snickers. "I had steamed tofu. It was pretty bad."

Martin laughs. "Well, hopefully we'll live longer eating this way. Have fun tonight."

"See ya later."

Martin is my stepdad. Not officially, because he's not actually married to my mom. But he's been with her for twelve years so he's like a dad. I've never met my real dad. My mom had sex with him at a concert and never saw him again.

Martin is an English professor at UC-Berkeley. He's a quiet, laid-back guy who spends most of his time reading. He's ten years older than my mom and never been married. He's asked my mom to marry him at least three times but she keeps turning him down. She loves him, but sees no need to get married. She said a piece of paper wouldn't change anything so why bother?

I see her point, but as for me? I want to get married someday, which is why I proposed to Willow two years ago. And even though she broke off our engagement, when I think about getting married someday, I can still only picture myself with Willow.

"I let her borrow my sweater," my mom says as she walks in the kitchen, her arm around Willow. "I didn't want her to get cold. It's supposed to cool off tonight."

Willow smiles at me as she holds one of my mom's hand knit creations. I know she wants to laugh, but she won't because she doesn't want to hurt my mom's feelings.

"Your mom just finished it," Willow says, holding it up so I can see.

It's hideous. My mom is terrible at knitting. The sleeves of the sweater don't match up and the bottom hem isn't straight. The yarn she used is a mix of neon pink, army green, and dirt brown. It might be the worst sweater she's ever made.

"Isn't it cute?" my mom asks, standing back to admire it. "I know the sleeves aren't perfect but I think it gives it character and a modern flare. It's very youthful. You can have it, Willow, if you'd like."

"Oh, no. I don't want to take your sweater. I'll just wear it tonight."

She'll never wear that sweater. Even if she was freezing, she wouldn't wear it. She'd let *me* warm her up before she'd ever wear that hideous sweater.

"Thanks, Mom." I kiss her cheek. "Willow and I need to get going. The movie's starting soon."

"Have fun!" She smiles at us both. "It's so good having you two home." My mom wants us to get back together, just like Willow's parents do. As we're leaving, I hear her talking to Martin. "Marty, are you eating a candy bar?"

Willow laughs as she goes outside. "She should just let him eat what he wants."

"She would, but he has high cholesterol and high blood pressure so she's trying to keep him alive by feeding him that healthy stuff."

"At least he still gets to have junk food once in a while."

"Speaking of junk food." I hold up the reusable grocery sack, which is the only kind we have. My mom refuses to use plastic sacks. "I loaded it up with your favorites. Chips, candy bars, licorice. We didn't have any soda but they sell it at the park."

"Thanks!" She smiles, then climbs into the truck, still clutching that horrible sweater.

"You're not actually going to wear that, are you?" I point to the sweater which is now sitting between us as we drive to the park.

She shrugs. "It depends on how cold it gets. It'll be dark out soon so no one will see."

"Maybe you could spill something on it so she has to throw it out. I don't even want my mom wearing that."

Willow laughs. "I know. It's pretty bad. Your mom should stick to making jewelry." She holds her arm out toward me. "See? I still have it."

She's wearing the bracelet I gave her as a goodbye gift before I left for Europe.

"My mom didn't make that. *I* did."

"I know." She lowers her arm back by her side. "But your mom taught you how."

My mom makes jewelry and sells it online and at craft fairs and farmers' markets. She makes decent money doing it, as much, if not more, than she'd make at a regular job. She didn't go to college so I don't know what she'd be doing if she didn't have her business. Making jewelry is her passion. I can't imagine her not doing that for a living.

"I love this bracelet," Willow says softly, almost to herself. I glance over and see her looking at it. "I wear it almost every day."

"Really?" I'm seriously shocked by that. I knew she liked it but I assumed she stashed it in a drawer after I left and never wore it. Wearing it would remind her of me and I didn't think she'd want that reminder, especially every day.

"I like the charm you made and the beads you picked out."

The bracelet is a black leather cord that has beads that surround a flat metal charm. The beads are a swirled mix of black, white, and gray. I picked them because I thought those colors would go with most anything she'd wear. The charm is an oval shaped piece of thin metal that I stamped with the infinity symbol. The symbol was meant to let Willow know that I'll always love her, even though we were broken up when I gave her that bracelet. I wanted her to know that I'd love her for all of eternity. No matter what, she'd always have a place in my heart, even if I never saw her again.

"I'm glad you like it," I say, glancing at her. "Maybe I'll make you another one."

"You don't have to." Her eyes are still on the charm, her finger tracing over the design.

"I want to. Besides, I need to practice. I haven't made one of those since I made that one."

"Are you making jewelry this summer?"

The answer is no because I won't have time with all the effort I need to put into helping Willow's parents, but she can't know that so I say, "Yeah. I told my mom I'd make a few pieces. You know how the ladies like a Silas original." I smile at her.

I say it kiddingly but it's actually true. When I used to make jewelry, my stuff always sold out before my mom's did. My mom's designs look like something an older woman would wear. My designs are more youthful, with leather cords, dark beads, and my handmade metal charms. The college kids would buy them up within an hour, even the guys. I made stuff for guys too.

"You should make more than a few pieces. You're really talented, Silas. You should be making jewelry this summer instead of working on my parents' farm. You'd make way more money."

If she only knew how much more. I'd make more doing anything other than working on the farm, given that I'm doing it for free.

"The jewelry was just a hobby. It's not a job."

"But it *could* be. Silas, your designs are awesome. That's why they sold out so fast. And people loved those charms you made.

38

You could just sell the charms separately and people would buy them. They're like a work of art."

Willow is always the first to offer a compliment when it's deserved, which is something I've always liked about her. Most people can easily criticize but can't give a compliment to save their life. But Willow appreciates talent and hard work and she'll let you know when you do a good job. She'll even compliment people she doesn't like. It's not about the person, but about a job well done. That's why she's a good leader and will someday make a great CEO.

"Thanks," I tell her. "But I think I'll stick to farming, at least for the summer."

"I'm serious, Silas. Why are you wasting your time working on a farm when you could be designing jewelry? You'd make so much more money."

"Not everything's about money, Willow."

Sometimes I think that's the only reason she's so obsessed with becoming a CEO one day. Because of the money. She could be the CEO of a non-profit or a small company, but instead she wants to run a large corporation. She wants to make a lot of money, live in an expensive apartment, buy an expensive car. I don't understand it. That's not how she was raised and she's never been materialistic. So maybe it's not about the money. Maybe it's something else.

"I know you don't care about the money," she says, "but I also know that you like making jewelry. You like designing new pieces."

"Willow, I've already committed to working on the farm. And it's what I want to do."

"Are you sure?"

"I'm positive." I reach over and wrap my hand over her wrist, touching the bracelet. "But I'm still going to make you another one of these. You shouldn't have to wear the same one every day."

She just nods, her eyes on my hand, which has now slipped down around hers. I know she said not to, but if she's not pulling away then I'm going to hold her hand.

She's my friend, and I love her, and if I can't have her, then I'm at least going to hold her hand.

CHAPTER FIVE

WILLOW

Silas and I are driving to the park when my phone rings. It's Lilly, my friend from college who lived in the room next to mine. Lilly is a Kensington, as in the daughter of Pearce Kensington, one of the richest men in America. But if you met her you'd never know she was wealthy, unless you saw her car, which is a top-of-the-line BMW.

"Hey, Lilly," I answer. "How's your party?"

Lilly's family had a welcome home party for her at their house in Santa Barbara.

"It was great! It's wrapping up now. Jade and Garret are leaving soon. They have to get the kids to bed. So what are you doing tonight?"

"Going to a movie at the park."

"With who?" She laughs. "The hot guy who showed up at your door?"

Lilly knows all about Silas. I talked about him a lot last year. For some reason, I kept bringing him up in conversation.

"Yeah," I say. "How'd you guess?"

"Are you guys back together?" she asks in an excited tone. She'd never met him before today and yet she thinks we belong together. Probably because I couldn't stop talking about him.

"No." I don't elaborate. I can't tell her about Silas when he's in the car, although there's really nothing to say. We're just two friends going to a movie.

"He's really hot. I thought he was hot in that photo you showed me, but he looks even hotter now."

My eyes wander over to the driver's seat. Silas has his window down, his muscular forearm resting there, his other arm casually draped over the steering wheel. The breeze is blowing his dark wavy hair and he glances over at me and smiles that perfect Silas smile.

"Willow?"

"Yeah, I'm here." I was so distracted by Silas I forgot to respond to her comment. I switch topics. "So have you talked to Reed?"

"Yeah. He made it home. He's out with his dad right now, having a late dinner. Hey, Garret's leaving. I have to say goodbye to my nieces and nephews. We'll talk later. Have fun on your date!"

"It's not a—" I stop when I realize she hung up.

"Who was that?" Silas asks.

"My friend, Lilly. You met her when you picked me up."

"Oh, yeah. She seemed nice."

"She is. We're good friends."

"Does she have a boyfriend?"

"Yes!" I yell it, then realize how crazy that must've sounded. But having Silas show interest in my friend made me crazy. It shouldn't, but it did.

"Why are you yelling?" he asks.

"I didn't mean to. Sorry. So um, why did you ask if she has a boyfriend?"

"I heard you ask her about someone named Reed. I just wondered if that's her boyfriend."

That's why he asked? And here I thought he wanted to date her. What is wrong with me?

"Yes," I say. "Reed was her boyfriend all last year."

"Did *you* have a boyfriend last year?" he asks in a casual tone, as if the answer doesn't matter, even though I know it does. He doesn't want to think about me dating someone else. And yet he hides it with that casual tone. I don't know how he does it. If I asked *him* who he'd dated the past year, I'd sound nervous, giving away the fact that I was desperate for the answer to be no one.

"I dated, but I didn't have a boyfriend," I say.

"And you don't now?"

"No. How about you?" At least I didn't sound nervous when I asked. Maybe I'm getting better at hiding it.

"Yeah."

"Yeah, what?" That sounded nervous, because I *am* now that I heard his answer. My heart's racing and I'm feeling kind of sick.

"I had a girlfriend."

"What was her name?"

"The last one was Lisa."

"*Last one?* How many did you have?"

"Three."

"Three?" I'm yelling again. Dammit. I clear my throat. "You had three girlfriends?"

He chuckles. "Not all at the same time."

"Well, yeah, I know that. I'm just surprised you had three girlfriends in two years."

"That was last year. I actually had two before that."

Anger and jealousy course through me, which makes no sense. Silas hasn't been my boyfriend for two years. I told him we had no future together, so he had every right to date other girls, or...five other girls.

"Where did you meet them?"

"At the projects I was working on. The non-profit I worked for recruited a lot of college students who were willing to take a semester off to do volunteer work. We'd all arrive to a project at the same time and go through training together. Spending all that time together you really got to know each other. People tended to hook up the first week or two."

Hook up? As in have sex? Why am I surprised? Of course he had sex with his girlfriend, which means he had sex with five girls since we broke up. Maybe more than that. Now I really feel sick. I know I had sex with other guys, but still. I liked living in this fantasy world in which Silas never had sex again.

"Willow, let's not talk about this. I don't like talking about other girls with you." He pauses. "And I really don't want to hear about the other guys you dated."

I nod, and keep quiet until we reach the park.

The place is packed with people, mostly people our age. These outdoor movies are really just a place to meet up with friends. Then ten minutes into the movie, you leave and go do something else. Or you find someone to hook up with and go...hook up. I can't even think those words without imagining Silas with a girl. Why did he have so many girls? Did he get a new one at every new country he went to?

"Does this work?" Silas has the blanket laid out on the grass. We're far away from the screen but the front spots were already taken.

"Yeah, that works."

He sets down our snacks. "You want to walk around? See if there's anyone here we know? Trent's here somewhere but we may never find him in this crowd."

He takes my hand but I pull it away. "We probably shouldn't do that here. If we see people we know, they'll start rumors that we're going out again."

He smiles. "What's wrong with that?"

He's right. I don't care if people think we're going out. It's not like I'm hoping to attract a guy tonight. I don't want a boyfriend this summer. I'm fine being single. I can date again when I go back to school in the fall.

"Come on." I push him ahead and he leads us through the crowds.

"Silas!" someone yells. I recognize the voice but can't see him. He must be sitting down.

"Hey, Trent." Silas walks toward him and I follow behind.

I finally see Trent, sitting on a blanket with a blond girl in his lap. He's always had a thing for blondes. He'd love my friend, Lilly. She has gorgeous blond hair. People always think she colored it that way, but nope. It's all natural.

"Shit," I hear Trent mumble.

I look to his right and see a girl walking toward him. Actually, she's walking toward Silas.

"Hi, Silas." She hugs him. "Good to see you again."

"You too. How've you been?"

"Great! Back from college."

"UCLA?"

She smiles and flips her hair. "I'm surprised you remembered that."

I think I know this girl. She looks familiar. Medium brown hair cut in chunky layers with blond highlights. Dark brown eyes. Short. Petite frame with not much of a chest.

"Hey, Willow." Trent motions his girl to move off him and the two of them stand up. "Welcome home." He hugs me.

"Thanks. It's good to be back."

Trent is usually laid-back but right now he seems anxious, his eyes darting between Silas, me, and the girl I'm sure I know from somewhere.

"Willow, you remember Kristy, right?"

Kristy. Now I remember. Kristy Callahan. She went to my high school but was a year ahead of me, in Trent's class. She was a star gymnast, almost made the Olympics. I didn't know her that well in high school but she always seemed like a nice person.

"Hi, Willow." She smiles at me.

"Hi. Are you here for the movie?" I feel my face heating up. Why did I ask such a dumb question? Of course she's here for the movie! Everyone's staring at me like I've lost my mind, which I have thanks to Silas' recent admission that he's been with five girls in two years. "What I meant was, are you here with friends?"

She gives a sideways glance to Trent, then says, "Um, yeah. I came here with Trent and Haley."

Trent brought another girl on his date? That's odd.

"Hi, I'm Haley." The blond girl extends her hand to me.

I shake her hand. "Hi. Nice to meet you."

Kristy seems uncomfortable, twisting her hair around her finger as she stares at Silas and me. Finally, she says, "Are you two still dating?"

Silas looks at me to answer. "No. We're not dating."

I hear Trent mumble "shit" again.

Kristy looks at Silas. "So you're home for the summer?"

"Yeah. I'm working for Willow's dad."

"Do you maybe want to go get something to eat?" She smiles. "We could come back here later if you want."

She's asking him out? Was this all a set-up? Did Trent know Silas would be here so he found him a date? Did Silas know about this?

Now I'm mad. Silas and I may not be together but I don't need him to flaunt his dates in front of me. I'm also mad at Trent. Of all the girls he could've set Silas up with, he picks a gymnast? Every man's fantasy?

"I'm gonna go." I fake a smile. "It was good seeing all of you." I turn and walk away as fast as possible.

"Willow, wait!" I hear Silas behind me.

I keep walking. I don't want to talk to him. I understand he's going to date other girls, but he doesn't have to parade them in front of me. That's just rude.

"Willow!"

I'm almost back at our spot when he finally catches up to me.

"Willow, stop." He grabs my arm.

I yank it away. "I'm going home."

"Willow, I didn't do this. I had no idea she would be here."

I'm not sure if I believe him. This doesn't seem like something Silas would do, but maybe he's changed.

"Would you please just sit down?" he asks.

I glance down at the blanket he brought. It's the same one we used when we were dating and would come here for movie night. He even brought a pillow, because sometimes I'd fall asleep midway through the movie and he wanted me to be comfortable. And the snacks. He brought all my favorites. I wonder if he stocked up on them before I came back to town. Stupid Silas. He always does all these nice things that make it nearly impossible to be mad at him.

"Willow?" he asks.

I nod. "Let's sit down."

"Why don't we move back there?" He motions to the far end of the park where there aren't any people around. I help him pick everything up and we find a quiet, secluded spot.

Once we're seated, I say, "You can go out with her. My mom could probably come pick me up." I pluck a blade of grass from the lawn and run it between my fingers, focusing on its smooth texture to distract myself from the hurt I'm feeling right now.

"I don't want to go out with Kristy. I told you, I had no idea she'd even be here."

"She came with Trent. She was obviously here because of you." I toss the blade of grass aside and lie down on the blanket, knees bent, my eyes on the bright moon above us.

"But I didn't know that until just now. When I talked to Trent earlier, he didn't say he was bringing Kristy here tonight. He shouldn't have done that. He thought he was helping me, but..."

"Helping you?" I sigh. "Silas, you've never needed help getting a date."

"That's not what I meant." He lies next to me, propped up on his side. "He was trying to make me feel better. Trying to get my mind off things."

"What things?"

He looks down and pauses for so long that I think he's not going to answer, but then says, "Today was really hard."

"Why? What do you mean?" I think I already know why but I want to hear his answer.

"It was hard seeing you again." He looks up at me. "It's not that I didn't want to see you. I did. I've been wanting to see you for two years. It's just that...once I did, I wanted things to go back to how they used to be and...I know they can't."

I feel wetness in the corners of my eyes because I can feel the hurt in his voice and I can see it in his face. And because I feel the same way. As soon as I saw him, I wanted to go back to how things were. The moment he appeared at my door, I wanted to run up and hug him and tell him how much I missed him.

"So Trent was trying to get you to move on?" I ask.

"In his own idiotic way, yes."

"Maybe you should. Move on." I choke on the words because it's not what I want. But I love Silas, and I want him to be happy, and in order to do that, he needs to move on.

A long pause lingers between us.

"Is that really what you want?" he asks. "For me to move on?"

I swallow past the lump in my throat. "Yes."

"If you wanted me to move on, then why did you get so upset when Kristy asked me to go out with her?"

"I was angry because you invited me here and then a girl showed up. It was just a misunderstanding."

"You know I'd never do that to you. I would never plan some elaborate scheme in order to try to make you jealous."

"I know," I whisper.

He brushes the back of his hand over my cheek. "Willow, I need you to be honest with me. I need you to tell me how you really feel. What you really want."

I don't answer so he continues.

"I need to know if there's any hope for us. If you'd even consider the idea of us getting back together."

God, this is so hard. Being around him makes me want to go back to how things were, but eventually I'd have to break up with him. I already did that once and it was hard enough back then. I can't do it again. I don't want to have to close that door a second time.

"We're older now, Willow. We've both changed. Maybe we could make this work. I'm willing to try if you are."

A tear slips down my cheek. Luckily, it's dark so he can't see it. But I'm afraid to talk because my voice might crack. I don't want him knowing how much this is killing me. If I do, he'll think there's hope for us, and I can't give him that. Because there *is* no hope. We want different things in life. That hasn't changed. So as much as it hurts, the cold, hard truth is that we can't be together.

"Willow." He turns my face to his, forcing our eyes to meet. "I can't move on unless you tell me for sure that this is over."

More tears spill out and I shut my eyes trying to hold them back. I slowly nod. "It's over. You need to move on. We both do." My voice was shaky. Dammit.

His hand is cupping the side of my face and his thumb sweeps over my cheek, feeling the wetness.

"One last kiss?" he asks.

I open my eyes and see that the hurt on his face is gone. He almost looks relieved. Is it because I gave him an answer? It wasn't the answer he wanted, but at least it was an answer. Now he can find someone else. Someone who's better than me. Someone who can make him happy.

I never answered him about the kiss, and before I can, he leans down and presses his lips to mine. And I'm instantly reminded why no guy has ever compared to Silas. There's something between us—a spark, chemistry, some unexplainable force—that makes my body come alive whenever we're together like this. And that's just from a kiss. Sex with him is even more amazing.

No wonder his flirting affected me so much today. My body craves him. His kisses, his touch, the feel of him.

His tongue slips past my parted lips and I tug him closer, begging for more. Begging for this to never end. I just want to stay in this moment and not think about the future or our different paths or saying goodbye. I want to live in this moment, for just a little longer.

But then it ends. He slowly pulls back, his eyes on mine. "I love you, Willow."

I bite down on my lip, trying to keep myself from saying it back. I want to. I really do. But that will just take us down a road we can't be on.

He smiles. "We're still really good at that."

"Good at what?"

"Kissing."

I smile back. "Yeah, we were always good at that."

"Among other things." There's a sexiness to his tone. A flirtatious vibe that makes me wonder if he didn't accept my answer just now. Is he still going to try to date me? Try to kiss me again? Or do more than that? At this point, I'd agree to it. I'm weak after that kiss and desperate for more of Silas.

But that would be a bad decision. A very bad decision.

I quickly sit up. "Should we go watch the movie?"

"Nah. I'd rather stay out here." He sits up, facing me. He picks up our bag of snacks. "Any requests? Or should I surprise you?"

"Surprise me."

He reaches in the bag and pulls out a bag of Skittles. I used to eat Skittles when I was sad. The bright colors made me feel better.

"Thanks." I take the bag.

He leans back on his hands. "So tell me about college. I want to hear all about it."

"Okay, but first I need to get my sweater." I reach over to grab it.

"You cannot wear that."

I laugh. "I need something over my arms. It's starting to get cold."

"Sorry, but I can't let you wear that sweater." He scoots back, leaning against the tree. "Come here."

He brings his knees up, making a spot for me between his legs. I sit in front of him and he pulls me closer until my back is up against his warm chest. Then he covers my arms with his.

"Is that better?" he asks.

"Yeah. I'm warmer already." Although part of that is because I'm so turned on being this close to him, feeling his body pressed into mine.

"So back to college," he says. "Tell me about your classes."

We remain there for a couple hours, just talking and eating candy. It's just like when we were kids. We'd sit outside and talk and eat candy that Silas took from his junk food stash.

The movie ends and we wait for everyone to clear out of the park and the line of cars to leave. Then Silas takes me home, walking me to the door.

"Goodnight," he says, kissing my cheek.

"Goodnight."

He leaves, and I already miss him. Just one day home. One day with Silas. And I already miss him when he's gone.

CHAPTER SIX

SILAS

"What the hell were you thinking?" I ask Trent when I call him the next day. I couldn't get ahold of him until noon. Before that he texted me that he was "busy," meaning he had Haley in his bed. It was the first time she'd spent the night.

Unlike me, Trent has his own place. It's not really his. It's his uncle's but his uncle isn't there. He's a professor so he's spending the summer traveling and Trent is housesitting.

"How was I supposed to know you were going to bring Willow with you?"

"Like you really thought I'd show up alone to the movie?"

"I thought you'd get there and find Haley and me and sit with us."

"And watch you two make out all night?" I roll my eyes. "Yeah, that sounds like something I would do."

"That's why I invited Kristy. It was supposed to be a double date, although I think Kristy wanted you all to herself."

"Yeah. That was obvious. To everyone. Including Willow."

"Hey, I was just trying to help. I thought you'd be all depressed after seeing her so I was trying to cheer you up."

"Next time, tell me what you're planning. No more surprises."

"So why was Willow there? I thought you were just going to drop her off at her house."

"Things were going well so I invited her to the movie."

"Was this a date?"

"No. It was just two friends hanging out."

"She seemed really pissed when Kristy showed up. If you're just friends, why the hell did she storm off like that?"

"Because she still has feelings for me. She just won't admit it."

"That's Willow. Freaking stubborn. Is she still planning to run the world someday?"

I chuckle, imagining that. "She wants to run a company, not the world."

"Whatever. The point is, as long as she has that idea in her head, she'll keep pushing you away."

"Well, I can't change her mind. It's what she wants to do."

"Does she know what you're doing for her parents?"

"No. And she's not going to find out, so don't say anything."

"If she knew, I bet she'd get back together with you."

"I don't want that to be the reason. That's not why I'm doing it."

"I'm just saying if she knew how much you were giving up to do this, she'd—"

"I don't want her getting back together with me because she feels guilty or thinks she owes me. It'll never last if that's the reason. She has to want this, more than she wants the life she's already planned for herself, and I don't know if that's ever going to happen."

"Why doesn't someone just tell her that being a workaholic CEO is not going to make her happy? Why does everyone keep encouraging this? Even her parents are going along with it, and they think corporations are the devil. They're letting their daughter work for the devil."

"Her parents will always support her in whatever she wants to do, even if they don't agree with it. You know that."

"Yeah, but in this case she's wasting time going after something that isn't right for her. It's just like with cheerleading.

She wasn't the cheerleader type but she still did it and we both know how much she hated it."

I smile. "But she was damn hot in that uniform."

He chuckles. "Can't argue with that. Those legs, that ass, her—"

"Shut the hell up. You're not supposed to be thinking about her that way."

"Every guy thought about her that way. She's hot. And she's even hotter now than she was in high school. She's filled out in all the right places. Which means she'll have her pick of guys this summer. She'll probably have someone by next week."

"Is this your way of making me feel better?" I ask, my muscles tensing up at the thought of some guy going out with Willow.

"It's my way of telling you not to get your hopes up when it comes to her. And don't be surprised if she goes out with someone else."

"She's not going to start something with some guy, knowing she's leaving in September."

"Why wouldn't she? She's obviously not looking for a longterm relationship or she'd still be with you. She just needs a guy to take care of her needs."

"Okay, seriously? Not helping. And for the record, I'd be more than happy to take care of her needs. And she knows that."

"Yeah, but with you there's all this emotion involved. Too much history. If she just wants a summer fling, she'll find someone else."

"She's not going to do that."

"Did you ask her if she wants to get back together with you?"

I keep quiet, choosing not to answer him.

"You did, didn't you? You asked her and she said no."

"She just needs more time."

He sighs. "Silas, I know you want Willow back, but if she wanted that, she would've told you that last night."

"I knew she'd say no. I only asked her to see how she'd react. And she was freaking crying when she told me we can't get back together. That says a lot, Trent."

"Maybe. Or maybe it says she hasn't changed her mind from two years ago. She may still love you, but if she can't see a future with you, she's not going to get back together with you. And if she does, it won't last. She won't stay with you."

"That's your opinion. Not mine."

"Silas, please tell me you are not going to waste your whole summer going after her."

"It's not a waste. I told you, Willow still has feelings for me. She's just not ready to admit it."

"Yeah, great. So she'll date you for a couple months, then break up with you before she goes back to college."

"You're really starting to piss me off. I'm hanging up now."

"I'm just being honest with you. I'm trying to help."

"Well, stop trying. I don't need help. I can figure this out on my own."

"Fine. Whatever." I hear him pop open a can. "Shit. Damn soda just sprayed all over my shirt."

"So what's up with you and this new girl? Must be serious if she spent the night."

"That was more for convenience. I was too tired to drive her home."

Trent doesn't date girls for very long. Two weeks is about all he can handle and then he's ready to move on to someone else.

"You should try a relationship sometime," I tell him. "It'd be good for you."

"I'm not a relationship type of guy. Maybe that'll change when I'm older, but for now I'm playing the field. Enjoying my options. Moving on when things get boring. And there are plenty of girls out there who want the same thing."

I get the feeling he's implying Willow is one of those girls. And maybe she is. She said she hasn't had a boyfriend in two years but that she still went on dates. So does that mean she'd go out with someone like Trent? Someone just to have sex with? Shit, I hope not.

"I've gotta go," I say, grabbing my keys and heading downstairs. "I told Carl I'd be over there by now."

"When you see Willow, tell her I said hello." He says it like he's interested in her.

"Don't even think of asking her out. I'll freaking strangle you."

"Relax. I know she's yours." And then he mumbles, "Even though she's not."

I go out to my truck. "Why are we friends again?"

He laughs. "Because you love me. And I'm the only one who tells you the truth."

"Bye, Trent." I hang up and pull out of the driveway and head to the farm. It's a few miles outside of town. I was going to get there at seven this morning but Carl told me to wait until after lunch. It's Sunday, and he doesn't want me working weekends, but I insisted so he told me I could work a half day.

In order to get everything done, we should both be working sixteen hour days, seven days a week. The farm isn't huge, but it's still a lot of work and Carl had to let some of his workers go because he couldn't afford to pay them.

Willow's parents have had financial problems for the past year. I don't know all the details or how it all started. I just know that they haven't been able to keep up with their bills and now they're in serious debt and may lose the farm.

Carl told me he's depleted his savings account and can't get any more loans from the bank. The only money he has left, which he refuses to touch, is Willow's college fund. That's why we can't tell her what's going on. If she knew, she'd insist on taking time off from college or switching to a cheaper school, and her parents don't want her doing that. I don't want her to either. She's always wanted to go to Camsburg and now that she's there, I'd hate to see it taken away from her or have her not be able to go to college at all.

"Hi, Carl." I walk into the trailer, which he uses as an office. It's not much. There's a desk and a few chairs and a small table where he eats his lunch.

"Hello, Silas." He gives me a wide grin. From his cheerful demeanor, you'd never know he's on the verge of losing his farm and maybe his house. That's just how he is. Candace is the same way. They're eternal optimists, choosing to believe things will somehow work out. And if they don't, at least they have their family and their health. That's all that matters to them.

"Gorgeous day, today." Carl stands at the window, looking out at the fields. "Full sun and not a cloud in the sky."

I stand next to him, taking in the view; rows of green-topped vegetables neatly lined up, the sun shining down on them. Being here at sunset is even better. The colors light up the sky and there's nobody around. It's peaceful. Quiet. Simple.

That's what I like. The simple things, like a beautiful sunset. Or the way a carrot tastes fresh out of the ground. Or the way it feels to connect with someone through a kiss. Like last night, with Willow.

Last night didn't go how I'd planned. Actually, there was no plan. I thought we were just going to the movie. But then the whole incident with Kristy sent the evening down a different course. Willow was jealous, extremely jealous, and I had to know why.

I needed to know if Willow still had feelings for me. I hadn't planned to spill my heart out like that, telling her I love her and that I wanted to try again, but I never think straight when I'm with her. My emotions take over and I say things I didn't mean to say.

Willow told me to move on. That we weren't getting back together. But I knew she was lying. That's not what she wants. Her words said one thing, but her body said another. The way she responded when I kissed her? It's like she never wanted it to end. She kept pulling me closer, and when I made even the slightest attempt to back away, she held on, like she wanted to keep me there.

Kissing her was just like I remembered. We have more than just chemistry. When we kiss, we express how we feel about each other. And last night, the moment my lips touched hers, it was as if the past two years never happened. Like nothing had changed. I could feel how much she still cared about me, wanted me, wanted what we used to have.

I wanted to keep the kiss going but I needed to end it because if I push her too far, she'll revert back to the Willow I left when I took off for Europe. When we said goodbye before I went to the airport, she was closed-off, distant, almost like a stranger. I saw a glimpse of that Willow again when I arrived at her dorm yesterday. But then I lifted her up and put her in my truck, and the playful, sweet Willow I know and love started peeking through.

As the day wore on, more of it peeked through. And last night, when we shared that kiss, I could feel the old Willow desperate to break loose. Desperate to tell me how she really feels and what she really wants. But she wouldn't let herself say those words. Instead she told me to let her go. To find someone else.

It was her tears that convinced me she was lying. She doesn't want me to be with someone else. She wants us to be together. To have what we used to have. And knowing that gave me hope. In fact, hearing her shaky voice when she told me to move on, and feeling her wet cheeks, made my heart spring to life. For the first time in two years, I felt like Willow and I have another chance at having a future together.

"Where do you want me to start?" I ask Carl. "The lettuce rows?"

He turns to me, releasing a long exhale. "Silas, why are you doing this? Is it to prove something to my daughter? If so, I need to be honest and tell you that it's unlikely she'll want to continue what you two had together. She's got her mind set on a certain future and she's determined to make it happen."

"This isn't about Willow. This is about helping people I care about and doing something I believe in." I gaze out at the fields.

"This farm may not generate a lot of money but you're doing something important. Working the land without polluting it. Growing food that isn't coated in chemicals. Providing jobs for guys that have very little education. I don't want to see all that end and have this land sold to some rich developer who'll end up turning it into another strip mall."

"This far out of town, it'll probably be a housing development."

"Either way, that's not what it's meant to be. This is *your* land. And you love doing this, so this is what you should do." I pause. "As for Willow and me, I'm not sure what will happen with us but I'm not ready to give up on her. I'd never stop her from going after her dreams. I just want to make sure that dream is really what she wants."

He pats my back. "You're a good kid, Silas."

I look over and see his grin is back. "Thanks."

"If I were able to pick who my daughter would end up with someday, you'd be my first choice."

I smile. "I would hope so after that quiz you gave me. You had me sweating bullets taking that thing."

"At least you got the important questions right." He motions to the water cooler in the corner. "Fill up some bottles, then let's head out to the fields."

Carl and I spend the rest of the day weeding and thinning out the new seedlings. The sun is hot, and by six, I'm drenched in sweat. I took my shirt off and could ring it out it's so wet.

We're done for the day so I go to the hose and lean over and run the cold water over my head and down the back of my neck. I instantly feel better. Now I just need food and a hot shower and I'll sleep like a baby.

"You want to join us for dinner tonight?" Carl yells from a few feet away. He's winding up one of the hoses.

"No, thanks. I think I'll just grab something on the way home."

He walks over to me. "Or you could go home, clean up, order a pizza and see if a certain girl would like to join you."

I smile. "Are you trying to play matchmaker, Carl? After that speech you gave me about me not having a chance with your daughter?"

"I never said you didn't have a chance. I was just telling you what you're up against. But even if you and Willow end up going your separate ways, it's not happening right now." He grins. "What do I always say?"

"To live in the moment." He said that to Willow and me all the time when we were kids and in a hurry to grow up. We'd roll our eyes, not really sure what he meant, but assuming it was just something dads say.

"Live in the moment, Silas. Just enjoy the time you have with each other. Don't waste it." He glances behind me. "Looks like my ride is here." He points to the Prius driving up.

Willow's parents only have one car so if Candace needs it, she has to drop Carl off and pick him up. There's an old truck on the farm he can use if he needs to, but it doesn't run well so you wouldn't want to drive it too far.

"Hey, Dad." It's not Candace. It's Willow.

Carl walks over to her. "Hi, honey."

Willow's standing by the car, wearing khaki shorts, a white tank top, and flip-flops, her hair in a ponytail. She's got that cute, girl next door look that always turns me on. I feel movement in my jeans and try to mentally stop it, but it's not working.

If I'd known she was coming here, I would've tried to clean myself up a little. Instead, she sees me when I'm sweaty and drenched with the water I just hosed myself down with.

But she must not be too disgusted. She hasn't looked away.

CHAPTER SEVEN

WILLOW

Holy freaking mother of—

My steamy hot, totally inappropriate thoughts of Silas are interrupted by my dad.

"Honey, I forgot something in the trailer. I'll be right back."

He leaves and I'm left with that perfect specimen of a man. Shirtless, wearing worn jeans that hang low on his hips. He's wet. Drenched, like he just ran a hose over himself. His hair looks darker when it's wet. It's tousled, pieces of his natural waves curling up in places. His skin, a rich golden brown from the sun, looks even better dripping with water. Carved muscles line his torso, and despite my best efforts, my eyes keep drifting to his six-pack abs.

"Hey, Willow," he says, walking to his truck. "I was just heading home."

I'm too speechless to say hello back, my eyes now focused on his back, which is pure muscle. How the hell did he get his body like that? What kind of volunteer work was he doing the past two years?

"Silas," my dad says. "Eight tomorrow?"

"Six," he calls back.

"Silas, you don't have to—"

"I like to start early." He gets in his truck.

My dad turns to me. "He's worked hard today. Why don't you go offer to buy him dinner? Order a pizza. It's on me. Your mom's making tofu tonight. I'm sure you'd rather have pizza."

I bite my lip, watching Silas as he dries his head off with a towel he must've had in the truck. I *would* like to have dinner with him, but I don't want to lead him on.

My dad gets in the Prius as Silas starts backing up.

"Silas, wait!" I run over to him.

"Yeah?" He gives me that Silas smile that melts my heart and turns me on at the same time. That smile is dangerous. It makes me want to do things my head is telling me not to.

"Do you want to have dinner with me tonight? We could order a pizza."

He glances at my dad. Why is he looking at my dad? He laughs a little, then looks at me. "Sure. Just let me clean up, then I'll give you a call."

He drives off and I notice how fast my heart is going. Must've been that ridiculous smile of his. Or maybe the beads of water glistening off his bare chest.

"You getting in?" my dad asks. He has the car pulled up next to me. I hadn't even noticed it was there.

"Yeah. Sorry." I get in the passenger's seat. "Silas wants to have pizza so I guess it's just you and Mom for the tofu." I tried to sound casual but I must've failed because my dad's smiling.

"It's nice to have Silas back, isn't it?" My dad is so obvious. Trying to get information out of me about my feelings for Silas. It's not going to happen.

"I guess."

"He's a nice young man." My dad rolls his window down, letting the breeze blow in. "He's matured a lot after all that time away from home."

"He had five girlfriends while he was gone," I say, letting my dad know Silas isn't as perfect as he seems.

"What's wrong with that?"

"Dad! Five girls? In two years?"

He shrugs. "When I was his age, I had more than that."

"You did?" I can't imagine my dad getting that many girls.

"It wasn't anything serious. I'd meet a girl, we'd date for a while, then move on. At that age I was still figuring out who I was and what I wanted out of life. When I was a freshman in college, I thought I'd be a—" He smiles. "Why don't you take a guess? What do you think I wanted to do for a career?"

"I don't know. Something having to do with agriculture or the environment?"

He shakes his head. "No. I thought I'd be a lawyer."

"A lawyer? You hate lawyers."

"I do now, but back then I wanted to be one."

"Why?"

"I was 18 and had to pick a career so that's what I picked. I used to watch a lot of those legal shows on TV."

"So what happened? Why didn't you become a lawyer?"

"Because it wasn't for me. I worked at a law firm freshman year and watched the other lawyers, saw what they did all day, and realized that wasn't what I wanted to do. Sitting at a desk? Working a hundred hours a week? Writing and rewriting contracts? Arguing with people? That wasn't me at all. I don't know what I was thinking."

"Is there a reason you're telling me this?"

"I just want you to consider all your options."

"I have, and I know this is what I want to do. I know you think all corporations are evil and out to destroy the world, but I don't agree."

"I've only said that about a few companies, not all of them. I'm not trying to talk you out of going into business. I just want you to be happy. I don't want you spending every waking moment at work."

"You spend all your time at the farm."

"Yes, but it's my passion. I love being there. And I always had your mom and you there with me. My job didn't take me away from my family. Honey, what I'm trying to say is to explore your options. Talk to people who are in those executive positions you want to be in someday. Interview a CEO. Ask him or her what a typical day is like. I have no doubt you could run a company someday and be very successful. But I also want you to be happy."

"I got it, Dad."

He pats my knee. "Lecture over." He turns the radio up and listens to one of his talk radio programs until we get home. As he parks in the driveway, he says, "You should go in and tell your mom you won't be joining us for dinner."

When I get inside, she's already making the tofu. She has all these different tofu recipes and they're all disgusting.

"I'm eating with Silas tonight," I say, then rush to my room so she won't ask me any questions. I got enough questions from my dad, as well as a lecture.

Why was he saying all that stuff to me? He never gives me advice on school or my career. He and my mom say you should let a child find their own path in life and not interfere. So does my dad think I'm on the wrong path? Did he change his mind about interfering?

Sometimes I think I *am* on the wrong path. I know I want to work in business, but I'm not a hundred percent sure I want to work for a huge corporation and eventually run it. I've never told anyone this, but I'd really like to start my own company. I'm just too afraid to do it. Too afraid I'd fail. So I'm taking the safe route; getting an entry level job at a large corporation and working my way to the top. It sounds boring when I think about it. It doesn't excite me at all, but I'm sure it will once I actually have a job.

My phone rings and I yank it out of my pocket and see it's Silas calling. I answer it. "Hey, that was fast."

"I had to hurry. I'm starving. And I want to see you."

He's flirting again. Did he not hear me last night? I told him to move on. This is not moving on. But I'll play along. In fact, I'm going to flirt right back.

"I can't wait to see you too."

"Then get your ass down here."

A flutter of excitement skitters through me. His flirting should not get to me like this, but it does. I hang up and stash my phone in my pocket on my way out of my room.

I pass my parents in the living room. "Bye, Dad. Bye, Mom."

"Willow, wait." My dad meets me at the door and hands me a twenty. "Have fun tonight." He kisses my head.

"I will. Thanks."

When I get to Silas' house, his mom greets me at the door. "Hi, honey. Silas is upstairs in his room."

"I forgot your sweater," I tell her. "I'll drop it off later."

"Keep it. It looks cuter on you than me. And your friends at college will love it."

I hurry past her and race up the stairs. The image of me wearing that sweater at school has me laughing and I didn't want Diane to see. I'm sure she worked hard to make it.

"Are you decent?" I yell outside Silas' door.

"Depends on how you define that." He yells back.

I open the door and see him standing there in jeans, but shirtless, just like he was on the farm. His hair is wet but now it's because he just showered. He smells good. Clean and fresh with a hint of cologne.

"You gonna put on a shirt?" I ask.

"I'm still hot from being outside so I thought I'd just leave it off." He grins. "Is that a problem?"

He's evil. No girl can resist a hot shirtless man fresh from the shower. Except me. I'm stronger than most. I can resist him.

"Not a problem at all, although it seems unsanitary to eat without a shirt, hence the no-shirt, no-service rule at restaurants."

"We're not at a restaurant. And it's not unsanitary. I just showered. I'm even cleaner than you."

I huff. "That's not true! I showered this morning. I'm very clean."

"Let me see." He steps up to me, his hands grasping my waist as he bends his head down to my neck. His lips graze my skin as he inhales, making me shiver.

"What are you doing?"

He exhales his warm breath over my neck. "You smell good."

"Thanks. Now will you move, please?"

I was tempted to turn my head and kiss him but I didn't. Excellent self control. Score one for Willow.

He slowly backs away.

"I really think you should put a shirt on." It's a lie. I don't want him covering up those incredible abs, but my self-control is winning out, keeping me from doing something I shouldn't.

He gives me a smug smile, then walks over to his dresser and pulls out a white t-shirt. Damn. I'm a sucker for jeans and a white t-shirt, which he knows. He takes his time pulling the shirt over his head, the movement causing his ab muscles to flex. Holy crap, that's hot.

"Is this better?" He stands there, his arms at his sides, looking completely irresistible.

"Sure. Whatever." I turn away from him and get my phone out. "What kind of pizza do you want?"

"Sausage and pepperoni. I'm craving meat."

"No green peppers? Mushrooms?"

"Add whatever you want. Just not anchovies."

"Gross. I hate anchovies." I call the pizza place, but get a message that the number is no longer in service. "Silas, is Pizza Village closed?"

"Yeah. It closed last month." I feel him come up behind me, his arms going around me, brushing against my chest as he takes my phone and types in a number. "This place is good."

I order the pizza, then turn around and face him. "You could've just given me the number."

He smiles. "I could've."

He's taking this flirting up a notch. Time to give it right back.

I slip my hands under his shirt, along his abs, and give him a flirtatious smile. "So, what should we do while we wait?"

He chuckles. "I know what you're doing."

"I don't know what you're talking about."

"It's not going to work." He grasps me around the waist. "It'll just make me do this all the more."

"Do what?"

He leans down and kisses me. A bold, assertive kiss. A kiss that buckles my knees and leaves me breathless. Then he pulls away, waits a moment, then says, "Would you like me to take the shirt off? It seems to be in your way."

I look down and see my hands are now halfway up his shirt, my fingers splayed out over his chest. I quickly yank them away.

"Sorry. I didn't mean to do that."

"No problem." That smug grin appears again. "Maybe we should eat out back. Otherwise it'll smell like pizza in here for a week. Doesn't make for the greatest atmosphere."

"Why do you care about the atmosphere? Are you having people over?"

"Just one." He kisses my cheek, then takes my hand, tugging me out of his room and down the hall.

"You're being very strange."

"Good. I'd hate to be normal. Normal is boring."

I like this new Silas even better than old one, and that's saying a lot because I really liked the old one. But the new one is way more assertive, in a good way. A sexy way.

He grabs a couple sodas from the fridge. His mom lets him have soda. My mom refuses to buy it.

"Right this way." He holds the door open for me and we go in the back yard. It's a small yard but has trees and bushes around the perimeter, giving it privacy.

"You have a fire pit? When did you get that?"

"They got it last year sometime. Martin surprised my mom with it. She always wanted one."

"Can we light it later tonight?" As soon as I say it, I realize I just told him I'd be sticking around after dinner. I assumed he knew that, but maybe not. "Unless you have somewhere you need to be."

"We'll light it after dinner." He hands me my soda and I sit down on one of the patio chairs. He sits beside me and laces his hand with mine, looking out at the yard. "I need to move. I shouldn't still be living with my parents."

"Where would you go?"

"That's the thing. I checked rent prices and they're ridiculous. Even if I got a roommate, it'd still be too much."

"It's not that bad living here."

"I know. I'd just like more privacy."

Why does he need privacy? Is he planning to bring girls here? Or is he referring to *us* needing privacy?

When we were dating, his mom almost walked in on us doing it. We didn't hear her come home, but luckily we heard her walking up the stairs and stopped what we were doing before she got to his room. At least his parents' bedroom is on the main floor so he has *some* privacy being the only one upstairs.

Our pizza arrives, and after we eat, he lights the fire pit and we sit around it and talk until almost midnight. Then he walks me home.

"I had fun tonight," I say as I stand outside the door.

"Can you come over tomorrow? I'll probably be done with work around seven."

"Silas, I can't come over every night. We can't do this. We're not dating."

"I was just going to ask if you could help me with accounting. I haven't had much time to study and I have a quiz next week."

"Oh. Yeah. Of course. Just call me and I'll be over."

"Thanks." He give me a hug. "Goodnight."

He turns and walks away. He's so confusing. He started out the night being all flirty and now he's back to acting like we're just friends.

The next morning I wake up to noise in the kitchen. It sounds like someone dropped a pan. It's six-thirty so my mom's probably making breakfast. She and my dad usually head to the farm around seven. My mom helps out in the mornings, then comes back here in the afternoons to make calls and do paperwork. She runs the business side of things; tracking sales, paying bills, managing the retail accounts, and coordinating when and where stuff needs to be delivered. She doesn't have a business degree so she always says that what she's doing isn't business, but it is and I tell her that all that time. In fact, both my parents refuse to think of themselves as business people. They just say they're farmers trying to make a difference. But in reality they're thriving entrepreneurs, which is what made me want to go into business.

I stumble out of bed and into the kitchen. My mom is there, filling her coffee mug.

"Where's Dad?"

"I already dropped him off." She's talking fast and her smile seems forced. I open my sleepy eyes more and notice she's wearing a skirt. A normal skirt, not one of her long, flowing hippie skirts. And she has a blouse on. A beige button-up blouse like you'd wear to an office. This is odd. I've never seen her dressed like this. I didn't even know she owned those types of clothes.

"Why are you dressed like that?" I ask.

"I'm going to work." She wipes the counter with a dish towel. "I have to leave in a few minutes."

"Work? You're wearing that to the farm?"

"I'm not going to the farm. I'm going to the office." She sets the dish cloth down by the sink. "I didn't get a chance to tell you that I got a job. I'm a receptionist at a real estate company."

"What? Why would you work at a real estate company?"

"You're away at college now so I felt it was time to get a job."

"You already have a job. Managing the farm with Dad."

"I'll still be doing that, but I'm doing this as well." She comes over and gives me a hug. "Have a good day. Do you have any plans?"

"Mom. Back up. What's going on here? Why did you get a job?"

69

"I just told you why. Now that you're all grown up, it's time for me to go back to work."

"You've worked my whole childhood."

"That wasn't work. That was helping your father out."

"You both own the farm. And you weren't just helping out. You were managing the whole business. You still do."

"Honey, I really need to go. We'll talk later." She grabs her purse and heads to the door.

"What time will you be home?"

"Around six. Don't worry about dinner. I have leftover tofu from last night."

She leaves before I can ask any more. This doesn't make sense. My mom has never had an office job. I don't think she's had *any* job other than managing the farm with my dad. And now she decides to be a receptionist at a real estate company? I can't imagine her sitting at a desk all day, typing and answering phones. That's not her at all. And those clothes? She didn't even look like my mom. She normally dresses like a hippie, with long flowing skirts, peasant blouses, and a scarf tied around her head. I used to be so embarrassed to be seen with her dressed like that, but it's her, so I eventually got over my embarrassment. She looked nice today, but that's not my mom. It doesn't fit her bright and colorful personality.

What's going on with her? Did she really just want a new job or is it something else? It can't be about money. The farm is doing great. My parents deliver our products to some of the best restaurants in town and they always sell a lot at the farmers' markets.

I don't know what's going on but I don't like it. Something doesn't feel right.

CHAPTER EIGHT

SILAS

I'm exhausted. I was up all night thinking about Willow. Thinking about what will happen if Carl is forced to use Willow's college fund to save the business. Willow would have to drop out of school, live with her parents, and get a job until she could save up enough money to go back to college. If that ends up happening, it'll change her life, her plan for her future.

"We're breaking for lunch," Ricco says. He's one of the workers, a guy around 30 with a wife and two kids. He used to do construction but hasn't been able to find work the past few months so ended up here.

"I think I'll just work through it, but thanks."

He nods and walks off. The other guys are already seated at the picnic tables having lunch.

It's a lot cooler today and cloudy. I've been digging up carrots all morning and now I'm planting onions. I keep telling Carl he needs to change what he grows. People aren't willing to pay much for carrots and onions, even organic ones. And they're even cheaper at the grocery store so he's had to lower his prices to compete. I've suggested he try growing more unusual varieties you can't get in the store so he could charge more, but he's stubborn like his daughter so it's hard to get him to make changes. I also keep telling him to plant flowers, which people pay a lot of money for, but he says you can't eat flowers and his farm is meant to feed people.

"Hey, Silas." I hear Willow's voice and feel my lips rise. Just the sound of her voice makes me smile.

I stand up and wipe my dirty hands on my jeans. "Hey. What are you doing here?"

"I brought sandwiches. I gave one to my dad and I brought a couple for you. I thought you might want more than one after working out here all morning."

"You made me sandwiches?" I smile wider.

"If you don't want them, it's okay. One of the other guys might want them."

"They're not getting my lunch. Where are these sandwiches?"

"In the car." She glances back at the red Honda Civic. "I had to borrow your mom's car. My mom took the Prius to her new job."

So Willow knows about the job, but her mom must not have told her why she took it.

"Silas. Did you hear me? My mom got a job! An office job. At a real estate company!" She grabs my hand. "Come on. Let's go have lunch. I've been dying to talk to you about this."

"Why me?"

She rolls her eyes. "Because you're my friend, that's why. I tell you everything."

"You haven't talked to me in two years," I say as we walk through the field.

"Yeah, well, that was a mistake. I should've talked to you. I told you I was sorry."

We reach the picnic tables where all the workers are sitting.

Willow leans over to me and quietly says, "Could we have lunch in your truck?"

"Sure. I'll meet you over there. I need to wash up." I go over to the hose and scrub my hands with the liquid soap Carl keeps out here. When I get to my truck, I see Willow has lowered the tailgate and is sitting at the edge of the truck bed, her feet dangling down. She's wearing the red cowboy boots she keeps out here on the farm. She changes into them when she walks through the fields. I love those boots. They give her a sexy cowgirl look. Her long brown hair is in a loose braid with wispy strands blowing around her face. And she's wearing denim shorts and a sleeveless blue plaid, button-up shirt.

That's a smoking hot outfit. Sexy cowgirl all the way. I just wish she was *my* cowgirl.

"Here." She hands me a sandwich. "It's almond butter and mashed strawberries. It's all I could find."

"Sounds good." I lean over and kiss her cheek. "Thanks. You look really hot, by the way."

She looks down, her legs swinging back and forth. "It's just shorts and a shirt."

"Believe me." I eye her up and down. "It's more than that. You look like a sexy cowgirl. Make sure to wear that to my house tonight."

She smiles. "I'm going there to help you study so I was planning to wear my sexy school girl outfit."

She's torturing me with this on-and-off flirting. I'm doing the same thing, but she can more easily hide the effects it has on her. I can't. If she got a good look at my jeans right now she'd know what her little comment did to me.

"Sexy school girl," I say. "Cowgirl. Either one works for me."

"I got you some water." Just like that, the flirting ends and she's back to being my friend, nothing more. It's frustrating. She reaches behind us and grabs two metal water bottles. Her parents won't buy water in plastic bottles. Mine won't either. "This is all we had for chips." She hands me a bag of sesame kale chips.

"I think I'll pass, but thanks."

She tosses them behind us. "So anyway, what do you think is up with my mom? Why would she get an office job?"

I want to tell her the truth. All of it. But I can't. I promised her parents I wouldn't. They want to be the ones to tell her and they want to wait until the time is right. Hopefully that's soon because lying to her is next to impossible. I've always been honest with her.

"Maybe she wanted to try something new. A lot of parents do that when their kid goes to college. They reevaluate their lives and decide to do something different."

"I guess, but an office job is so unlike her." She holds onto my arm just as I was about to lift my sandwich to my mouth. "You should've seen what she was wearing. A skirt and a blouse! And not her typical hippie skirt and blouse, but a black pencil skirt and one of those polyester-blend blouses in a beige color. Beige! My mother has never worn beige. I about fell over when I saw her. I've never seen her dress that way."

"She can't show up to an office in her other clothes. She was just following the dress code."

"You don't seem to be getting the bigger picture here. My mom has an office job!" She lets go of my arm. "This makes no sense." She continues to talk while I eat my sandwich. "I mean, it would make sense if they needed the money, but they don't. The farm makes good money. We have all these new customers." She motions to the handful of workers sitting at the picnic tables. "And my dad has obviously found ways to be more efficient, cutting his labor costs. We used to have twice that many guys."

He *needs* twice that many guys. He just can't afford them.

"So I don't know what the deal is." She leans back on her hands. "Maybe you're right. Maybe my mom's just going through some kind of mid-life crisis. Feeling the need to try something new. Maybe that's why she redecorated the living room. I'm still not used to walking in the house and not being hit with a rainbow of color. She even repainted their bedroom. The same pale green color as the living room. And they have a dresser instead of just tossing their clothes in baskets all over the floor." She pauses. "You know what's weird?"

"What?" I gulp down some water.

"I always hated the way they decorated. The bright colors that didn't go together. The furniture that didn't match. The

74

way everything was so cluttered and disorganized. But now?" She straightens her legs, staring down at her boots.

"Yeah?"

"I kind of miss it." She drops her legs and swings them back and forth again. "Is that strange?"

"No. You grew up with the house the way it used to be and now that it's changed, it's like that part of your life is gone."

"Yes! Exactly!" She turns to me. "As dumb as it sounds, I feel like a piece of my childhood is gone and now all I have are the memories." She lifts her leg up on the truck, bending her knee and resting her chin on it. "And now my mom is working a regular job. She won't even be home until six." She sighs. "Why do things have to change?"

"Because *people* change. They grow and change and decide they want different things out of life."

I feel like this conversation has suddenly become about us. And her.

Willow's eyes lift to mine. "A person can want different things without changing."

"But sometimes those different things end up changing the person. Remember when you changed schools and became a cheerleader? Didn't you feel like that changed you?"

"I guess so. Do you think it did?"

"Definitely. That's when your obsessive need to succeed took over and you did just about every extracurricular activity at school. I had to date you just to give you a break from all that."

She tilts her head. "That's the only reason you dated me?"

I lean down and kiss her on the lips. "I dated you because I love you. I always have, even when we were kids, and I didn't want anyone else to have the girl I love."

Telling her that just now? That was an example of doing as her dad said and living in the moment. I laid it all out there. Told her how I felt. She already knows it, but I said it anyway because I only have a few short months with her and after that I may never see her again. Even if I'm still living here next summer, she could have someone else by then, and if she does,

75

he won't want her hanging out with her ex. So I'm just going to be honest with her so she knows how I feel. I don't want to live my life with regrets, wishing I'd done or said something, especially when it comes to Willow.

She bites her lip, her eyes watery. I didn't think what I said would make her so emotional. But the fact that it did is just another clue that she's not over us. That there's still a chance.

"I need to get back to work." I jump down from the truck, then lift her up into my arms and hug her, letting her feet dangle down. "Thanks again for lunch." I set her down.

"Silas, you got dirt all over me." She brushes it off the front of her shorts.

I grin. "Then I guess you'll have to change into the naughty school girl outfit for tonight."

She laughs. "Nobody said she was naughty."

"I know this girl, and trust me, she can be very naughty." I swat her ass then walk away.

At the end of the work day, as everyone's packing to leave, I go up to Carl. "Willow was asking me questions today about why Candace has a job and why you guys redecorated."

"What did you tell her?"

"Not much. I didn't know what to say. Why don't you just tell her?"

"Because I'm still hoping I can save it. If we sell the house that'll free up a lot of cash."

"Which you'll have to use for rent. And how are you going to explain to Willow why you're selling the house?"

"We'll come up with something." He rubs his hand over his jaw.

"If you don't tell her, she'll put the pieces together herself."

He sighs heavily. "I'm sorry, Silas, but her mother and I just aren't ready to tell her about this. She just got home and we don't want to ruin her summer. We have enough money to keep the farm going a few more months."

"And then what? What if you end up having to take her college money? Are you going to pull her out of school in the middle of the semester?"

"Taking her college money is a last resort. We're not at that point yet and I'm hoping we never will be."

"You have a lot of debt. If you can't make the payments, you'll have to take money from her account."

He sets his hand on my shoulder. "Listen, Silas, I know you're concerned about Willow, but telling her this isn't going to make anything better. The best thing you can do right now is just be her friend."

"I'm trying to."

"Well, you must be doing something right because I haven't seen her smile this much since you two were dating. Are you seeing her tonight?"

"Yeah, she's going to help me with accounting. I have a quiz this week."

"I think it's great you're taking that class. You should be taking more instead of working here for free."

"Don't start. We've been through this a million times. I'm helping you whether you like it or not."

He nods. "Well, if you decide to get that business degree, maybe I'll end up working for *you* someday."

"I don't think so. If anything, I'll be going to *you* for advice. You've learned more working here than I could ever learn in college."

He frowns. "I'm afraid all I could teach you is how to run a business into the ground."

"That's not true. This wasn't your fault. There were forces you couldn't control." I look at the fields, then back at Carl. "Did you give any thought about what you're going to plant in that open part of the field?"

"Probably some pumpkins for the fall."

"They take forever to grow and take up a lot of space. What about flowers instead?"

He laughs. "You and your flowers. You sound just like Candace."

"I'm not kidding. Flowers grow fast and you can charge a lot for them."

"People can buy flowers anywhere."

"Yes, but they like buying them at farmers' markets. I don't know why. They just do. You always see people walking around with flowers. Would you just let me try it?"

He smiles. "Fine. Go ahead and plant your flowers. Take the seed catalog home and figure out what you want. I'll put the order in this week."

"Thanks. I better get going. I need to get cleaned up. Maybe I can convince Willow to eat dinner with me again."

"Given how much her face lit up when she saw you at lunch, I think it's safe to say she'd agree to that."

I tell him goodbye, then take off, the seed catalog in hand. When I get home, my mom is there, cooking her famous vegan goulash. And by famous, I mean famous for being the worst-tasting, most horrible-smelling meal ever created.

"Silas, I made your favorite," my mom says as she sees me walk by. She's being sarcastic.

"Can't wait to eat it," I say as I run up the stairs.

"I made extra just for you," I hear her yell, then laugh to herself.

As soon as I'm in my room, I call Willow. "Hey. What are you doing?"

"Reading. Why? What's up?"

"I just got home. I need to clean up. But after that, I need to get out of here. My mom's cooking goulash."

"Oh, God. Sorry." Willow has experienced the goulash. Both the taste and the smell.

"Let's go out to eat. I'll come by and pick you up."

"I thought we were studying."

"We'll do that later. For now, I have to get out of the house before I throw up from the smell. If it still stinks later, we'll have to study somewhere else. I'll be there in twenty minutes."

78

"I didn't say yes."

"Willow, seriously? You're not going to help a friend out in his time of need? This is goulash we're talking about. Goulash!"

She laughs. "Okay. I'll be ready. See you soon."

When I get to her house, she's waiting for me on the front steps, wearing a short red-and-black plaid skirt and a tiny white t-shirt. Holy shit, she looks hot. It's going to be tough to keep my hands off her. She stands up and looks even hotter, showing off her tan legs which lead to a pair of bright white sneakers.

"Like the outfit?" she asks as she climbs in my truck. I was going to help her get in but she was too fast. But I got a glimpse of her black string bikinis when she lifted her leg up into the truck.

"The outfit is..." I eye her. "Definitely something you should wear again. But just for me. No one else." I shut her door and go around to the other side.

"You can't restrict what I wear," she says as I yank my seatbelt on. "We're not dating. And even if we were, I wouldn't let you tell me what to wear." I notice she's wearing the bracelet I made her. I love that she wears it every day.

"Then the same goes for me." I pull out of the driveway.

"I doubt you'll be wearing this."

"Yeah, you're funny. What I meant is that maybe I'll just start walking around shirtless. You seemed to like it, which means other girls will too."

"Are you saying you're looking for a girlfriend?"

"Do you think I should?"

I see her tense up. "You're single. You can do what you want."

"It wouldn't bother you?"

"Why would it bother me?"

"Because you love me." I flash her a Silas smile.

"I don't—" She sighs in annoyance. She can't say she doesn't love me because the truth is she *does* love me. She may not see a future with me, but she still loves me. "If you love me you shouldn't be dating other girls."

"I don't have much of a choice when the girl I love refuses to date me, now or in the future."

"I'm on a date with you right now!" she yells, then scowls for doing so, like she's mad at herself.

Willow can turn from hot to cold in seconds and I love that about her. She's always surprising me. I never know how she's going to react. When I picked her up at her dorm, she was more even-keeled, trying to hide any and all emotion. But after just a few hours with me, she was back to the Willow I know, with her outbursts that come out of nowhere. It's funny how I bring that out in her, even after all this time.

As we're sitting at a stoplight, I say, "So if this is a date, then can I call you my girlfriend?"

"No," she blurts out.

"Why not?"

She crosses her arms. "Because it's inappropriate. We're friends. That's it."

"Friends who go on dates. And kiss. And wear sexy outfits upon request." I chuckle. "That's my kind of friend."

Her lips turn up just slightly. "Fine. Call me your girlfriend. For one night. That's it."

"If I'm calling you my girlfriend, then I'm going to treat you like my girlfriend." I reach over and put my hand on her exposed thigh. "And just so you know, I'm very affectionate with my girlfriends."

Her leg twitched when I touched it, but then relaxed. Now she's breathing fast, but trying to hide it by looking out the side window. She hasn't removed my hand from her leg so I leave it there as I drive.

So Willow is my girlfriend for the night. This should be fun.

CHAPTER NINE

WILLOW

"You smell like goulash," I say as we wait in line to be seated at our favorite Chinese restaurant in downtown Berkeley.

Silas lifts his t-shirt to his nose. "I do not smell like freaking goulash."

"You do." He doesn't, but I needed an excuse to get closer to him. "Come here." He leans down and I sniff his neck, inhaling the clean fresh scent of his cologne mixed with the scent that is uniquely Silas. God, I love that smell. I could live in that smell.

"So? Do you smell it?"

I lift my head up to look at him. "No. I guess I was wrong."

"You're nuts." His arms go around me and he squeezes me into his chest, where I get another whiff of that intoxicating scent. He keeps me held against him as we wait in line.

"Two for Sparks," he says to the hostess.

"It'll be about ten minutes," I hear her say.

"Ten minutes," he says to me, then kisses the top of my head. "Hmm...what could we do in ten minutes?"

I laugh, my head shooting up from against his chest. "We are not doing that. Absolutely not."

I'm referring to the one and only time we had sex outside in a public place. Okay, not the only time, but the one and only time we did it while waiting for a table. We were at an Italian place and it was late and dark outside and we had a ten-minute wait to be seated, so we snuck out to the alley and did it against the building. It was completely inappropriate but also really hot, in a way that still gets me aroused when I think about it.

Silas whispers by my ear. "We could go behind the building. No one would see us. And this skirt you're wearing is perfect for—"

"No," I say, sounding breathless. I push him back and smooth my skirt. "Let's just wait for the table."

He smiles and spins me around, hugging my back to his chest. I always loved it when he held me like this. His arms wrapped around me in a protective hold, letting the world know I was his.

"You hungry?" he asks.

"Starving." I tilt my head back on his chest.

"Me too." He kisses my forehead.

I shouldn't let him take me out for dinner like this. I'm sure he has little to no money. My dad can't afford to pay his workers very much. Instead he gives them bonuses throughout the year. But Silas just started so he hasn't received a bonus. And he didn't get paid for his volunteer work the past couple years, other than getting free room and board.

We're seated a few minutes later and order our favorite dishes; beef and broccoli for me and Kung Pao chicken for him. Sitting here having dinner, talking and laughing, it feels like we're boyfriend and girlfriend again. I know it's wrong to pretend that we are, knowing we don't have a future together, but I can't seem to stop myself. When I'm with Silas, I want to be *with* him, as in be his girlfriend. Hold his hand. Hug him. Kiss him.

Two years ago, I told myself it was over and that Silas and I would never be together again. I didn't even think I'd see him again. And now? All I can think about is how much I want to be with him. Even today, when I was home and he was working on the farm, I missed him and wanted to go see him.

"Do you think it's safe to go back to your house?" I kid, as Silas pulls out of the parking lot. We just finished dinner and are leaving the restaurant.

"I don't want to risk it. Why don't we find a coffee shop instead?"

"Okay." I laugh. "Maybe the goulash was your mom's way of making us go out tonight. I think she wants us to get back together."

"Did she tell you that?"

"No, but she acts like she does. Did my parents say anything to *you*? About us getting back together?"

"No. Well, I guess your dad did. He basically told me I had no chance with you."

"He did?" I'm a little shocked by that, given how much my dad likes Silas. "Did he say *why*?"

"He said your mind is set on what you want for your future, implying that your future doesn't include me."

I keep quiet because I don't know what to say. It's true. The life I have planned for myself is not the life Silas wants, so he can't be part of it. It's as simple as that, and yet it hurts my heart to admit that, even to myself.

"Your dad's right," he says. "If you decide you're going to do something, you do it, even if it's not really what you want to do. You're very stubborn."

I jab his arm. "I am not stubborn."

"You're one of the most stubborn people I've ever met. You're also obsessive. Compulsive. Unpredictable. And have a bad temper." He puts his hand on my leg and smiles. "And yet I still love you."

"I am not any of those things. You make me sound like a crazy person."

He parks in front of the coffee shop, turns the truck off, unhooks his seatbelt, and looks at me. "You searched every square inch of your dorm room three times before we left Camsburg. Everything was packed, and yet you still had to search your entire room three times."

"Because I didn't want to leave anything behind. That's not being obsessive."

"You labeled each and every box with the contents. Instead of just writing 'desk stuff' you listed every single item that was in the box. In alphabetical order. That's obsessive."

I huff. "You have flaws too, you know."

He smiles. "So what are they?"

I knew he'd ask that. Now I have to think of some. "You squeeze the toothpaste from the middle."

"And why is that a problem?"

"Are you kidding? Silas, everyone knows you squeeze from the bottom and work your way up."

"There aren't any rules to squeezing toothpaste."

"Of course there are. If there weren't, everyone would be tossing out half empty tubes and that's just wasteful."

"What else do I do?" He's watching me, smiling.

"You rip the sheets off the bed when you sleep. Specifically, the fitted sheet, which doesn't make sense because it has rounded corners and elastic to keep it held to the mattress."

"I move around a lot at night."

"And rip the sheets off?"

"How do you know I do this?"

"Because I've seen your bed when I've come over in the morning. It's a disaster. I can't even look at it. I just want to put it back together." I bite my lip, feeling anxious just thinking about his disaster of a bed. "The strange thing is, the night I slept over you didn't do it. We woke up and the sheets were still in place."

That was the night both our parents went out of town for an organic foods expo. They assumed Silas and I were having sex so they didn't feel the need to stay home and keep watch over us.

"Then I guess the only way to fix that problem is to have you in my bed."

"That's not what I—" I'm interrupted by a kiss.

He undoes my seatbelt. "Let's go inside."

We spend the next hour at the coffee shop, going over his accounting homework. It's an introductory class and way easier than the one I had at Camsburg. My classes there are even harder than I thought they'd be, but it's good. I find I learn more when I'm being challenged.

After the coffee shop, I assumed we'd go home but instead he drives the opposite direction.

"Where are we going?"

"Someplace quiet."

He turns down a small dirt road. "The farm?"

"Yeah. We can look at the stars."

It's something we always used to do together. We'd lay out on a sleeping bag in the back yard. When we were dating, we'd take the sleeping bag to the beach or the park. We did more making out than stargazing. And one of those nights, we had sex. It was my first time. We didn't plan it. It just happened.

"Aren't you tired of being here?" I ask. "You spent all day here."

"I like it at night." He stops and parks at the edge of the field. Then he jumps out, grabs a sleeping bag from behind his seat, and lays it in the truck bed. I meet him back there and he helps me into the truck. Then we lie there, looking up at the bright stars lighting up the dark sky.

"Nice, huh?" he asks.

"Yeah." I sound sad and I'm not sure why.

I have so many conflicting thoughts racing through my head right now. So many conflicting emotions. There's this part of me that wants the life that Silas wants. A life that isn't spent racing a million miles an hour, trying to keep up with the competition, trying to make it to the top. A life that's slower, simpler, and leaves time for things like stargazing on a clear summer night like tonight.

Then there's the other part of me that wants the high-powered job at a big corporation. That life will mean giving up my free time, spending all my time at work. It'll involve sacrifices, like having to move, possibly far away from my family. It'll mean giving up weekends to go into the office or travel for work. It may even mean I won't have time to have a family of my own. I know all this, and yet I've decided this is what I want to do. I want to work hard and be a success, and that means making sacrifices.

But then I lie here looking up at the stars with Silas beside me, and it makes me question everything. I don't like questioning myself. I like to make a decision and stick to it.

"Silas?"

"Yeah?"

"Do you ever worry about making the wrong decision?"

"About what?"

"Anything."

"No."

"Why not?"

"Because I know I'll make plenty of wrong decisions in my life. Everyone does. So why worry about it?"

"One wrong decision can change your entire life. It can set you down a completely different path."

"True, but maybe that path was the one you were supposed to be on."

"Then it wouldn't be a wrong decision."

"Depends on how you define 'wrong.' Think about my mom. Some people would say she made the wrong decision by sleeping with some guy she met at a concert after knowing him for less than an hour. She ended up getting pregnant with me, which changed her life from that point forward, but I'm sure if you asked her she wouldn't say she regrets the decision she made that night."

"But what if things don't turn out that well? What if you make the wrong decision and you *do* regret it?"

"Then you make whatever changes you need to in order to move on. You always have options, Willow."

"I know. I just don't like screwing up. I want to be sure I'm doing the right thing."

He turns on his side, facing me. "Is there a certain thing we're talking about here?"

I think he already knows the answer to that so I'm not going to come out and say it.

"I'm just talking in general." I gaze up at the sky. "The stars are so bright tonight. They're beautiful."

"So are you." He leans down and presses his lips to mine.

I kiss him back, ignoring my brain, which keeps telling me to stop.

He parts my lips with his tongue and takes the kiss deeper as his hand moves up my thigh, under my short skirt. My heart races in anticipation, wanting this more than anything. Any doubts are shoved aside as my urge to be with him wins out. I tug his shirt up. He quickly yanks it off, then kisses me again, his hand returning to my inner thigh and gently squeezing. My body is pleading for him to continue but then a thought pops in my head, telling me to stop. To end this before it gets too far. I quickly shove that thought aside. This feels too good to stop.

His hand moves to the edge of my panties, outlining them with his thumb. Silas likes to take things slow, teasing me until the point I can't take it anymore. I both love and hate this about him. I love that he takes his time and doesn't rush, but I hate waiting, wondering when he'll relieve the throbbing need to feel him inside me.

Finally, he gently, and expertly, slips his hand under my panties. My breath hitches as I feel his fingers slide over my wetness. His magic fingers, as I used to call them. They're still magic, maybe even more so now than before, because within mere minutes, I'm coming undone, breathing hard, grasping the sleeping bag, yelling his name.

I reach down and undo his belt, but in my hurried attempt it gets stuck, so he does it himself, then yanks his jeans down along with his boxer briefs. I kick off my shoes, then shiver as I feel his warm hands on my legs, tugging my panties off.

He lies over me, kissing my neck, then my cheek, then my lips.

"What are we doing?" I whisper, dragging my fingers down his back, loving the feel of his warm body pressed against mine.

"Making one of those wrong decisions," he says between kisses. "But damn, it feels right."

"It does, doesn't it?" I gulp down a breath as he nudges my legs apart.

"I don't have a condom," he whispers, as I feel the tip of him touching me. "Are you still on the pill?"

"Yeah," I whisper back.

He kisses me and then I feel him slowly sink inside me. My mind goes blank as I surrender to the moment, forgetting about the future, about what's right or wrong, about all my doubts and fears. I just immerse myself in this moment and how it feels to be with Silas again. He was my first, and no one has ever compared to him.

When it's over, I feel no regrets. I should, but I don't. I love Silas, so what we did just now doesn't feel wrong. Maybe I'll feel differently tomorrow when my mind starts analyzing the aftereffects of what we did, but right now, as I lie tucked inside his arms, nothing about this feels wrong.

His arm tightens around me and he kisses my head. "I love you."

I wish he wouldn't say that. I know he loves me, but it's hard to hear those words, knowing there's no future with us.

But Silas has always been that way. He puts it all out there. His feelings. His thoughts. He's always been honest with me. He doesn't play games like some guys do. He's made it clear he wants me back, but he also openly acknowledges that it's probably not going to happen.

I admire him for being so open, so honest. Very few people can do that. I certainly can't. If I were being open and honest, I'd tell him how much I still love him. How I've thought about him every day we were apart. How I've never allowed myself to get emotionally attached to any other guy because my heart won't allow it. It still belongs to Silas, so giving my heart to someone else would feel like a betrayal. That's something I need to get past in order to move on, but I haven't been able to do it yet.

"I wish we could stay here all night," I hear Silas say. We're wrapped in the sleeping bag and I'm all comfy and warm, my body pressed against his, my head on his shoulder.

"If we did, our parents would start planning the wedding."

He laughs. "They'd assume we're back together, but I don't think they'd be planning a wedding. My mom doesn't even believe in marriage."

"Do you?"

"Willow, I proposed to you. I gave you a ring."

"I know, but we were younger then. Maybe you only proposed in order to make sure we didn't break up when I went to college."

"I proposed because you're my best friend and I loved you and wanted to spend the rest of my life with you. I still do."

My eyes tear up and I squeeze them shut. "Silas, you need to stop saying that stuff."

"Why? I'm just telling you how I feel."

"I'd just rather not hear it, okay?"

He doesn't answer, and I wonder if I hurt his feelings by saying that. I hope not. I don't want to hurt him. It's just hard for me to hear him say those things.

Minutes go by. Long, quiet minutes.

I finally break the silence. "We should probably go home. You have to be at work early."

"Yeah." He slips his arm out from under me and sits up. I get up, too, and we find our clothes and get dressed.

On the drive back, Silas says nothing. Back at my house, he walks me to the door and gives me a hug.

"Goodnight, Willow." He releases me and walks away.

"Silas, wait." I run to catch up to him in the driveway.

"Yeah?" He sounds sad and I know I'm the reason for that.

"I need you to know that I don't regret what we did. I don't think it was a mistake. Or a wrong decision. I wanted it. I wanted to be with you like that again."

He looks at me a moment, then kisses my cheek. "Goodnight."

He gets in the truck and drives away. Why was he acting like that? So closed off? So quiet? Reserved? He's always so open, but just now he wasn't.

Maybe tonight *was* a mistake. Maybe we shouldn't have crossed that line in our friendship. But is that all this is? Or are we becoming more than that?

CHAPTER TEN

SILAS

I don't know what we're doing. Willow and me. Are we friends? Or more than that? I want to be more than that but she won't allow it, as evidenced by the fact that she told me to stop telling her I love her.

It hurt when she said that. More than it should have. I know Willow wants to pretend there's nothing between us anymore, but she knows it's a lie. She also knows that I've always been open with her. I tell her what I'm feeling. I don't hold back. And she knows I'm only this way with her.

It's not easy being that open, but I do it because I trust her and because we're friends and because I love her. So to have her cut me off like that, telling me she doesn't want to know how I feel, really bothered me. Maybe because she said it right after we'd just had sex.

What Willow and I did tonight was more than just sex. More than just our bodies coming together. It was us reconnecting after two very long years. Us telling each other how we felt without relying on words. It was intense, both physically and emotionally, and when we were done, there was this moment where I felt she was finally realizing that what we have together is too good to give up. That we'll never find it again with someone else so we need to find a way to make this work.

But instead of saying that, she shut me out. I poured my heart out to her, even admitted I still want to marry her, and she told me she didn't want to hear it.

If I didn't love Willow so much, I'd accept what she said tonight and stop trying to get her back. I'd do as she asked and stop telling her how I feel. But I know that what she's asking for is not what she really wants. It's just her way of avoiding the truth, avoiding having to admit that she feels the same way I do. Because admitting that might mess up the orderly plan she's mapped out for her life.

Willow is all about order and structure. Being with me is too messy and unpredictable, even though I know deep down she craves the excitement that comes with the unexpected.

When she asked me about making wrong decisions, I had this glimmer of hope that I was starting to get through to her. Making her question whether that plan of hers is really what she wants. If that's really what will make her happy. But then when she told me to stop saying I love her, it was clear she was still committed to her plan.

The next day I get to work early and pick out flower seeds from the catalog Carl gave me. I know almost nothing about flowers, but I've spent years at the farmers' market helping my mom at her booth and I've seen what flowers people buy the most. I list those on the order form, then add some daisies because Willow likes daisies. She also likes roses but those are too hard to grow. I need easy, fast-growing plants.

At lunch, I'm not surprised that Willow doesn't show up. She said she might, but after what we did last night she needs time to analyze the million thoughts now running through her head. She'll try to apply logic to what happened, which won't work, so then she'll call one of her friends and try to talk it out. Eventually, she'll come to some kind of conclusion as to why we had sex and then she'll show up at my door and tell me what she's concluded. I know her so well that I can predict this will happen, just like I predicted she wouldn't show up for lunch.

I'm eating a slice of cold, leftover pizza from the other night when my phone rings. It's Trent.

"Hey, what's up?" I swig my soda.

"I broke up with what's her name."

"You don't even know her name?"

"I do. I just forgot."

"You went out with her for almost two weeks."

"Don't give me shit. I'm not good with names."

"Her name is Haley."

"That's right. You've got a good memory."

"You're pathetic."

"So since Haley's not around, you want to do something tonight?"

I'm sure I won't be seeing Willow so I say, "Sure. What do you want to do?"

"Let's play some hoops. I've got energy to burn."

"Your post break-up high?"

That's what he calls it. Most people get depressed after a break-up, but Trent finds it exhilarating. Sometimes I think he only dates girls for the high he feels after the break-up.

"You guessed it," he says. "I'm a free man. So you want to meet at the park? Maybe around six? We could grab a burger when we're done."

"I work until six. Make it six-thirty."

"Sounds good. See ya then."

I finish the day, not hearing a word from Willow. I'm late meeting Trent because of traffic. He's already on the court, shooting baskets. He gets off work at four. He has a summer job maintaining the golf course at a country club. He basically rides around on a lawn mower all day and flirts with the rich girls who are members. It's the perfect job for him. Easy, low stress, and daytime hours, leaving his nights free to party.

To some people, Trent and I seem like unlikely friends. He was a popular football player at a large high school and I went to a very small private school. He's loud and likes being the center of attention whereas I'm more of a laid-back observer.

93

I could go on and on about our differences, but the thing we have in common is that we don't bullshit. That's why we're friends. He doesn't pretend to be someone else or say what he knows you want to hear. He's honest to the point it turns some people off, but it's what I like best about him. Even with girls, he doesn't put on a phony act. He tells them up front that he's not looking for a relationship and yet he finds plenty of girls who still want to date him.

"You're late," he says, tossing me the ball.

"Yeah? So?" I shoot and miss. I'm not great at basketball. Surfing is my sport, but I haven't been able to get in the water since being back in town. All my time has been spent working or hanging out with Willow.

"It's freaking hot today." Trent rips his shirt off. He's got the start of a beer gut forming after spending two years at college. He goes to UC-Santa Barbara, studying communications. I have no idea why he picked that for a major. He doesn't know either. He just had to pick something. He wants to go into sales, so he really didn't need a college degree but his parents are making him go.

It *does* feel hot. I take my shirt off.

"What the hell?" he says, pointing at me. "You been working out twenty-four hours a day?"

"It's called physical labor. Gets you more in shape than any gym workout will."

"I would've worked construction this summer if I'd known I'd look like that."

"It's not too late."

"Nah. I like the country club. Surrounded by money. Hot girls. Fancy cars. And I get all the free golf I want." He shoots and the ball hits the backboard but doesn't go in. "You should golf with me sometime. I can get you a free round."

"Sounds good. Just let me know when." I don't golf, but it's free so why not? It's something to do.

That's a perk of being friends with Trent. He always gets stuff for free. He knows a lot of people and makes friends wherever he goes and they're always hooking him up with free stuff.

He throws me the ball as two girls walk by. He's staring at them, not caring if they notice. They're tall and thin, wearing bikini tops and cutoff shorts. And they're blond, which is Trent's preferred hair color on women.

"Hey, ladies," he says, smiling at them. "Care to join us?"

They saunter over to us.

"I'm Tess," the one girl says. She has bigger breasts than the other girl and they're spilling out of her top. "And this is Tana."

"Nice to meet you, Tess and Tana," Trent says, eyeing them like he wants them both. "I'm Trent and this is my friend, Silas."

"Hi, Silas," Tess says with a flirtatious smile, her gaze slowly moving down my body.

I say hi back but I'm not sure she heard me. Tana is also checking me out. I almost laugh when I see the irritated look on Trent's face.

"So what are you ladies up to tonight?" he asks.

"We're going dancing at a club," Tana says.

"Need some company?" he asks.

"It's girls' night. No boys allowed," Tess says, her eyes moving back up to my face. "Can I see your phone?"

"It's in my truck."

She lays her palm on my chest and smiles. "You have a truck? I love a guy with a truck."

"I have an SUV," Trent says.

She ignores him and takes out her phone. "Give me your number and I'll call you so you have mine."

"I have a girlfriend," I lie. Trent shoots me an irritated look. "But Trent's single."

"And would love to get to know you girls better," he says, sucking his gut in as Tana looks him over.

He takes his phone out and Tana puts her number in, then says, "I put Tess' number in there too, in case Silas breaks up with his girlfriend." She winks at me, then the two of them walk off.

When they're gone, Trent says, "What the hell? You don't have a girlfriend. Did you see that chick? Freaking hot, and she was practically begging you to have sex with her."

"I have Willow."

He sighs and shakes his head. "For the last time, Willow is not your girlfriend. I know you love her but the girl has moved on. It's time to give up, bro."

"I had sex with her last night."

"No shit?" He grabs the basketball from me and tosses it aside. "I gotta hear about this." We go sit on the bench. "How did it happen?"

"I didn't plan on it. We went to dinner, then out for coffee, and on the way home I decided to stop by the farm."

"You did the look-at-the-stars trick, didn't you?" He nods knowingly. "Girls fall for that every time. I don't get it. What's so sexy about staring at the sky?"

"We didn't even get a chance to look at the sky. As soon as we got there, I kissed her and we couldn't stop. God, I wanted her so bad. Things heated up fast and I thought she'd tell me to stop, but she didn't. She wanted it as much as I did."

"And how was it?"

"Even better than I remembered. I swear, the two of us are made for each other, in every possible way."

"What happened when it was over?"

"I told her I love her and that I still want to spend the rest of my life with her."

He hits my arm. "You're such a girl. What guy says that shit?"

"A guy who's in love. You'd know that if you'd get in a real relationship."

"Relationships are too much work."

"And finding a new girl every week isn't?"

"Obviously not." He smiles and holds his phone up. "Or I wouldn't have got two phone numbers just now."

"That might've been because of me," I say, smiling.

He hits me again. "Shut up, asshole. You don't have to rub it in." He pats his belly. "I'll work this thing off in a couple weeks."

"The way you drink? I doubt it."

"So now what happens? Are you and Willow dating?"

"Probably not. She's not ready to agree to that. But I wouldn't be surprised if we had sex again. She may refuse to date me but I think she's going to want to repeat what we did last night."

"That good, huh?" He leans back on the bench, stretching his legs out.

"It's always good with her. Best sex I've ever had."

"And exactly how much sex have you had since you guys broke up?"

"I don't know. I wasn't keeping track."

He kicks the side of my foot. "Come on. You can tell me. You know I won't tell Willow. How many girls did you hook up with?"

"I'm not giving you numbers. At the time I thought for sure I'd never see her again so I let myself be with a lot of girls, especially right after Willow broke up with me. I was trying to move on, trying to forget about her. But hooking up with other girls just made me realize how much I wanted her back. I even called out her name while I was with another girl."

He chuckles. "Shit, that's bad. What'd the girl do?"

"She didn't know it was a name. She thought I was just yelling out some random word. She actually liked it. She said it sounded sexy, so next time we had sex she kept telling me to say it, so I did."

He laughs. "That's messed up, but freaking hilarious."

"I shouldn't have done it. It just made me think of Willow, which wasn't fair to Jen. That was her name." I hit him. "See? It's been over a year and I still remember the girl's name and you can't remember the name of the girl you were with last night."

He pauses to think. "Miley? Cami? Help me out here."

I roll my eyes. "Haley."

"Haley. Miley. Close enough."

"I can't believe you get girls to sleep with you."

He points to himself. "Between this body and my witty charm, girls can't resist me."

"Yeah, you're real charming. And that beer gut's real attractive."

"So going back to you and Willow, I think you need to put an end to this before she destroys you again."

"She didn't destroy me."

"You quit college before you even started, then disappeared for two years."

Willow doesn't know I'd planned to go to college. I was going to tell her the day she broke up with me. Before I dated Willow, I never even thought about going to college. I was a laid-back surfer who didn't worry about what I'd be doing tomorrow or next week or next year. I took one day at a time and didn't think about stuff like car payments and rent because I didn't have to. I lived at home and drove my mom's car.

But as things got more serious between Willow and me, I started to think more about the future. I knew I wanted to marry her, which meant I needed to start thinking like an adult who would soon have adult responsibilities, like paying for rent and insurance and car payments. Suddenly I was forced to think about the future and make some decisions, one of which was whether or not to go to college. I decided to go, thinking I'd need to in order to get a decent-paying job. It was too late to apply to a four year college so I enrolled at the community college. I was going to work all summer to save money to get my own apartment, then start school in the fall.

I had a future planned out. A future I was excited about and couldn't wait to share with Willow. The day she agreed to marry me was the happiest day of my life. I felt like everything was coming together.

But then a week later, she broke off the engagement, saying she couldn't see a future with me. She was still in high school but had already figured out the plan for her life—a plan that didn't involve me. She told me about wanting to be a CEO someday and how making it to the top would mean putting all her focus on school, and her future job. She said she wouldn't have time for me.

I told her we'd work it out and that I'd support her in whatever she wanted to do. I knew she wanted to go to Camsburg, so I did some research and found a community college nearby that I could transfer to when Willow started her freshman year. We'd get an apartment and life would be great.

But she said it would never work. That I would never be happy in the life she'd planned for herself. I kept trying to convince her we could make it work, but I knew that no matter what I said, she was still breaking up with me.

After that, I packed up and left on the trip that Willow and I were supposed to take together, backpacking across Europe. It was a graduation gift from my mom and Martin. The plane tickets were already bought and paid for, so I went without her. And after my two weeks were up, I stayed there. While backpacking, I met some people who connected me with a foreign aid organization and I ended up on a project in Turkey, building houses for the poor.

Whenever I had access to phone service, I called Willow. She wouldn't pick up but I kept calling. It cost a freaking fortune just to leave a message but I did it anyway. Luckily, my mom didn't complain about the phone bills, probably because she was hoping my calls would make Willow change her mind. She knew how much I loved Willow and wanted to be with her.

A few weeks after I left, I called Trent and he said Willow was telling people I stayed in Europe to continue backpacking. She never knew about my plans for college or for getting a job that summer. She assumed I had no interest in things like school or work but would rather roam the world with no real responsibilities. I told Trent to just let her think that. That maybe it would be easier for her to move on if she did.

"You can't let that girl fuck with your life again," Trent says.

"She's not. I'm back home and I'm going to school."

"You only have one class, which is all you can take because you're spending all your time helping her dad. You wouldn't be doing that if it weren't for Willow."

"I'm doing it to help save their business. Carl has always been like a dad to me and I owe him. This isn't about Willow."

"That's bullshit and you know it. This is you and me, Silas. We don't bullshit each other. You need to admit the real reason you're doing this so you can see this for what it is. An attempt to get Willow back."

"That's not what it is. She doesn't even know I'm doing it." I turn toward him. "You need to shut up about Willow and me. If I want to go out with her, I will."

"You're going to get your ass kicked, Silas. And you're going to get your heart broken. Again. She's going to spend the summer hanging out with you, probably having sex with you, and then in three months she's going to tell you to get lost. She'll go back to her fancy college and find some new guy and you're going to be left with nothing. You won't even have any money saved because you're working for her dad for free."

"She's not going to do that."

"I can almost guarantee that's what will happen. And if she finds out about the farm and the fact that you knew about it and hid it from her, she'll never talk to you again."

That *is* something I'm worried about, but I'm hoping she'll understand. I wasn't exactly given a choice. Carl asked me not to tell her and I'm respecting his request.

Trent stands up. "Let's get out of here. I'm starving."

"We didn't even play ball."

"We'll do it some other time. We need to eat and then I'm going to call Tana and see if she'll tell us what club they're at."

"I'm not going with you."

"You're just going to sit at home waiting for Willow to call? I'm sorry, but that's pathetic."

"That's not what I'm doing. I need to study. I have a quiz on Saturday and some homework to do."

He grins. "Look at you, all serious about school. You might actually make something of yourself."

"You're an ass."

"I'm just joking," he says as we walk to the parking lot. "I didn't mean it as an insult. I've always admired you for not taking life so seriously. I'd like to do the same, but I've got my parents constantly riding my ass, telling me to get my shit together because they're done supporting me the second I graduate."

We leave the park and get a burger at a sports bar. He calls Tana but she won't tell him the name of the club. But she does agree to meet up with him later, which is all he wanted anyway. A quick hook-up. Nothing serious. If he keeps this up, he's going to end up with an STD, if he doesn't already have one.

I do some studying, then look through the course catalog for the fall. I'm going to keep taking classes and eventually graduate. Even if I have no future with Willow, I still want a future for myself. I'm not sure what that is yet, but college is at least a start in the right direction.

CHAPTER ELEVEN

WILLOW

It's eight and I just finished cleaning up the kitchen. My mom had to work late and didn't get home until seven. She was exhausted so I made dinner, and after we ate I offered to clean up. Now she's catching up on processing orders for the farm. I'm going to have to take over some of her responsibilities. It's too much for her and I don't mind doing it. I don't have a job this summer other than helping in the fields, like I always do. But I don't do that every day. Just a few days a week, usually picking berries because the workers hate doing it and I actually like it.

I haven't talked to Silas since last night. I've spent today trying to figure out what to do. How we move forward from here. I'm desperate to talk to someone but I can't call any of my friends here in town. For one, I haven't kept in touch with them so I feel weird just calling them up after not talking for over a year. And two, if I talk to someone here, whatever I say might get back to Silas.

I decide to call Lilly, my friend from college. She knows about Silas but doesn't actually know him so won't tell him what I say.

Her phone rings several times before she picks up. "Willow, I was just going to call you. How's it going?"

"I slept with Silas," I blurt out.

"What?"

"I slept with Silas." I say it slower.

"Yeah, I heard you the first time. I'm just surprised. I thought you said—"

"I know. I promised myself it wouldn't happen, but we've been spending all this time together and we were lying in the back of his truck and it was dark and...well, it happened. And the worst thing is? I don't regret it. Not even a tiny bit. In fact, I practically begged him to do it."

"How was it?"

"Even better than it used to be. I'm not exaggerating. Maybe I was just really turned on last night or maybe it's because I haven't had sex for months."

"Or maybe it's because you're in love with Silas."

"Yeah, that too."

"Wait—what? You're admitting to being in love with Silas? Last year you denied it like a million times."

I sigh. "Well, I can't deny it anymore. I love Silas." I slap my palm against my forehead. "Ugh. I can't believe I just admitted it out loud. You know how long it's taken me to convince myself I was no longer in love with him?"

"I don't think you ever did."

"Yeah. You're right." I lie back on my bed. "What am I going to do?"

"Get back together with him."

"And then break up with him when I leave in the fall? No. I wouldn't do that to him. I hurt him once and it nearly killed me. I'm not going to do it again."

"Is he planning to stay there, or go back overseas for his volunteer work?"

"He's staying here. He's taking a summer class at the community college and he's going to take some more in the fall."

"What's he studying?"

"He's not sure yet. He's taking an accounting class so maybe he'll major in business."

"Sounds like he's changed from what you told me about him. You made it sound like he was just a hippie surfer who had no plans for his life."

"I shouldn't have said that. It's not true. That was just me trying to find excuses for why we shouldn't be together."

"Then stop making excuses and be together."

"It won't work. We want different things. If I want to make it to the top, I'll have to spend my life at work. Silas doesn't want that. He doesn't want to be with someone who's always at the office or traveling all the time. He wants to be with someone who's home every night for dinner and can go out to the movies with him. Someone who has time to lie under the stars."

"That sounds like a good life. You sure you don't want that?"

"Lilly, I know what I want to do. You know how committed I am to this."

"Yeah, but I don't know why. My dad was a CEO for years and it wasn't that great. He was never around for my brother and me. We never even saw him."

"But all his hard work paid off. Your dad is a huge success. People pay thousands of dollars just to hear him give a speech. And it's not like he didn't have a life. He got married, had kids. He always seems happy when I see him."

"Because he sold the company. But when he was the CEO, he wasn't happy. He never slept. He was always stressed. He had to work holidays and weekends and didn't get home until after I'd gone to bed. You know, maybe you should talk to him."

"I don't want to bother him. Besides, I'm kind of afraid to talk to him. He's very intimidating."

"If you want to be a CEO, you can't be intimidated by powerful people. Let me talk to him and see when he has time."

I agree to it, knowing it'll never happen. Pearce Kensington is a well-known billionaire. He won't take time out of his busy schedule to talk to his daughter's friend, who he barely knows.

"So tell me more about what happened last night," Lilly says.

"We went to dinner, then out for coffee, then he took me to the farm and we laid in the back of his pickup and gazed up at the stars. Then we started making out and ended up having sex."

"Have you talked to him since this happened?"

"No, because I don't know what to say to him. I don't know how to act. I keep telling him we can't be more than friends, so does that mean we're friends who have sex?"

"You're going to keep having sex with him?"

"I want to, but that would be wrong, wouldn't it?"

"It would if you're just leading him on, knowing this isn't going anywhere."

"He already knows that and it didn't stop him from doing it with me last night. And he's been flirting with me since he saw me at the dorm."

"Because he wants to date you. He wants you back in his life. So acting like his girlfriend all summer, knowing you're breaking up with him in the fall, isn't right."

"I know. It's just that I really want to be with him, and I'm not talking about sex. I mean that I want to spend time with him. I miss him. It feels like I haven't seen him in weeks but it's only been a day. I miss him after just one day. That's so pathetic."

"No, it's not. I miss Reed like that."

"How are you guys doing being apart?"

"It's hard. I really miss him, but we talk on the phone a lot. And it helps knowing he's spending time with his dad. Right now, he needs to be with his dad, not me."

That's one of the reasons I like Lilly so much. She cares about others more than herself. Her boyfriend, Reed, didn't really know his dad for most of his life, but now he's living with him for the summer. Lilly really wants Reed to form a relationship with his dad because his mom is a loser who doesn't treat him well. Some girls wouldn't care about that, but

Lilly does. So as much as she misses him, she encourages him to spend time with his father instead of her.

"Going back to you and Silas," she says. "I think you need to slow this down until you figure out what you want."

"I already know what I want."

"For a career, but not for your personal life. You've never even talked about that with me."

"That's not true. We've talked about it."

"But you never give me an answer. You always change the subject."

"Okay, fine. What do you want to know?"

"Do you want to get married someday?"

I hesitate, then say, "Part of me does, the other part doesn't."

"But the part that *does* want to get married wants it to be to Silas."

I get a lump in my throat and feel my eyes tearing up.

"Willow?"

"Yeah. I'm here." I sniffle.

"Are you crying?"

"No. It's just allergies." I take a breath.

"You don't have allergies. You're crying because you want to marry Silas someday. And if you don't marry him, you'll be alone because you can't imagine being with anyone else."

I nod, even though she can't see me, as tears run down my face.

"Am I right?" she asks.

"Yeah." I sniffle again and go over to get a tissue.

"Willow, why are you torturing yourself? This is crazy. Just be with him. He's the one, and you know it, so stop pushing him away."

"And give up on my goals? No. I'm not going to be one of those women who gives up everything for a guy."

"You don't have to give up everything. You just have to make some compromises. You both do."

"Then neither one of us will be happy."

"You need to stop making everything so black and white. There are ways for you to be together and still get what you both want career-wise."

"Like how?"

"I don't know. I just know it's possible. My brother, Garret, runs a company and is super successful but he still has time for his wife and kids. Some days, he sees the kids more than Jade does. My point is that if you really love Silas, which I know you do, then you'll find a way to make this work."

"It's more complicated than that."

"Because you're making it complicated when it doesn't need to be. We're hanging up and you're going to go talk to him."

"I'm not ready to."

"I'm hanging up now. Good luck!"

I'm left with silence. I set my phone down and bury my head in my pillow. This is so frustrating. How did everything become such a mess in just a matter of days? If Silas had just kept doing his volunteer work overseas I wouldn't even be having to deal with this. I'd still think about him but I'm used to that. I've been thinking about him for two years. But thinking about what we used to have is much different than having to think about the here and now and where we go in the future. My future is already planned and it doesn't include Silas.

Ugh...why did he have to come back?

Lilly's right. I need to talk to him. But not about us. Not yet. I need time to think, to really think about what I want in life, beyond just my career. After that, I'll talk to Silas. But until then, I want him back as my friend. I can't go any longer without seeing him. My heart hurts I miss him so much.

I shoot up from the bed, check myself in the mirror, adjust my ponytail, and leave my room, walking fast down the hall.

My mom passes me. "Honey, where are you going in such a hurry?"

"To see Silas."

I go out the front door and down the sidewalk to his house. I hope he's home.

Martin answers the door wearing his reading glasses, a book in his hand. He's always reading.

"Hi, Martin. Is Silas home?"

"Hello, Willow." He smiles, peering at me from above his reading glasses. "Silas is upstairs in his room."

"Okay, thanks." I walk past Martin and race up the stairs to Silas' room. I knock on his door. "Silas? It's me."

I hear him set something down, then wait as he walks to the door. He opens it and gives me that famous Silas smile. "Hey."

I put my arms around him and hug him, my head plastered against his chest as I give him a tight squeeze. He probably thinks I've lost my mind but it was my first instinct when I saw him.

"Willow, are you okay?"

"Yeah." I stop squeezing him but keep my arms around him. "I just needed to do this."

"Um, all right." He's hugging me back and it feels like heaven. A warm, sweet, heavenly place that I never want to leave. I inhale his scent, that perfect mix of Silas and the cologne he always wears. It's the cologne I picked out for him when we were dating.

"Do you want to sit down?" he asks.

I let him go. "I didn't come here to talk."

His eyebrows rise, suggestively.

"No!" I put my hand up. "I didn't mean I came here for *that*. I meant that I didn't come here to talk about last night or what it means. Because honestly, I don't know what it means, and until I do, I don't want to talk about it."

"I think we need to."

"I agree, but I'm not ready to. So for now, can we just go back to being friends?" I take his hand, glancing down at it. "I miss you, Silas. Just one day without you and I missed you. Really bad. I don't know what that means. I just know that I had to see you. That's why I'm here."

He lifts my chin up. "I'm glad you're here. I missed you too."

My eyes dart to the side and I see the accounting book on his bed. "I didn't know you were studying. I should leave."

"I'm done for the night. Why don't we watch TV?" He gets the remote and turns the TV on, then sits on his bed, leaning up against the headboard. I'm standing by the bed, staring at it. "What's wrong?"

"I don't know if we should be on a bed together."

He chuckles. "Am I that tempting?"

"Honestly? Yes. Especially after last night."

"Come on." He pats the area next to him. "I promise to keep my hands to myself." He smiles. "Or at least above your waist."

I climb over him and into his waiting arms. He hugs me. "I love—" He stops himself.

"It's fine. You can say it. We love each other as friends, right?"

He pulls back. "I don't know. Do you love me as a friend?"

"You know I do." I hug him again, then whisper, "More than that." I don't know if he heard me, but I hope he did because I'm still too much of a coward to come out and tell him how much I love him.

I snuggle under his arm, getting comfortable.

He hands me the remote. "I didn't watch TV when I was overseas so I don't know what any of the current shows are. You'll have to pick."

I flip through the channels, landing on a movie I've never seen. I watch a few minutes of it but it's boring so I turn my attention back to Silas. "So have you been studying all night?"

"No. I met Trent at the park for some basketball, then we went out for a burger. Don't tell my mom. She's been on my case about eating too much meat. She's trying to get me back on her vegan diet."

"I'm surprised Trent wasn't out with Haley."

"That's over. He broke up with her last night."

"They hadn't even dated two weeks."

109

"He was ready to move on. He's already out looking for someone new." He picks up the remote. "This movie sucks. There's gotta be something else to watch."

There's a knock on the door. "Silas?" It's his mom.

"Yeah, what do you need?"

She opens the door, looking surprised when she sees me. "Hi, Willow. I didn't know you were here."

"I got here a few minutes ago."

She smiles. "Well, I don't mean to bother you but, Silas, Trent's here to see you. He's waiting outside."

"Okay. Thanks for letting me know." Silas gets up and I follow him past his mom and into the hall. His mom has this sly smile on her face, like she assumes Silas and I are back together. I guess it does look that way, given that she caught us snuggling on his bed.

Silas and I go outside to the driveway. It's dark out, but the house lights are on. Trent isn't the only one there. Next to him are two blond girls in short, tight dresses. So one girl wasn't enough? Now he has two? Trent is such a manwhore.

"Willow," he says, looking shocked that I'm here. Why is everyone so surprised to see me tonight? "How's it going?"

"Fine. I see you brought some friends."

"Yeah. Tana and Tess. Silas and I met them at the park earlier."

Funny that Silas neglected to mention that. He's standing next to me, giving Trent an angry stare.

One of the girls goes up to Silas, standing very close and putting her hand on his chest. "We're heading to a club and I could really use a dance partner."

"You'll have to find someone else," I blurt out as I put my arm around Silas. "I'm Willow, Silas' girlfriend."

"Oh." She steps back, crumpling her face at me. I don't know what that means. Is she angry? Annoyed? Does she think I'm not hot enough to date him?

110

"I told you about Willow when we were at the park," Silas says as his arm wraps around my waist. "You must not have heard me."

"Come on, girls, let's go," Trent says. "I'm more than enough man for the two of you." He slings an arm around each of the girls, and as they're walking to his SUV, he looks back and mouths the word 'sorry' to us.

"What was that about?" I ask Silas once Trent's SUV is no longer in sight. "You mentioned the park but not the girls."

"There was nothing to say. They came up to us while we were on the court and Tana gave Trent her number."

"The other girl seemed pretty interested in you."

"Until you told her you're my girlfriend." His lips turn up and he folds his arms over his chest. "So *are* you? My girlfriend?"

"No, I just said that to get her away from you."

"So you refuse to date me, but I'm not allowed to date anyone else?"

"Yes," I say, fully aware of how bad that sounds.

"The whole summer?"

I cringe. "Forget I said that. I promised I'd never be that girl, so just forget I said that."

"What girl?"

"The girl who likes a guy but can't have him, but doesn't want anyone else having him either."

"You can have me." He spreads his arms out. "I'm right here. All yours."

"You know what I'm saying. I'm still not sure about this." I motion between him and me. "And until I am, it's not fair of me to try to forbid you from dating other people."

"So you're saying I should go out with Tess?"

"No." I cringe again, then take a calming breath. "What I mean is that, no, I do not want you going out with Tess. But that's for purely selfish reasons. If you'd like to go out with her, go ahead. I should probably get home anyway." I turn to leave.

"Hey." His catches my waist and draws me into him. "I don't want to go out with Tess. I don't even like Tess. I like the girl I'm looking at right now. The girl I've liked since meeting her in second grade. Now can we go inside and finish watching TV?"

"We weren't watching anything."

"Then we'll do something else."

"Like what?"

He smiles. "You didn't say no when I mentioned touching above the waist."

I laugh. "That will lead to touching *below* the waist."

"You have my word. I promise to control myself. Hands above the waist."

I smile. "It wasn't you I was worried about."

He tugs me closer and talks in my ear. "You're making this a very complicated friendship."

CHAPTER TWELVE

SILAS

"Seriously, what is wrong with you?" I say into the phone when Trent finally answers.

"What? What's wrong?" he yells back. I can barely hear him with the lawnmower noise in the background. I couldn't reach him last night so I called him on my break this morning. He's at the golf course.

"*What's wrong?*" I yell so he can hear. "You brought a girl to my house. Without even calling."

"Tess wouldn't shut up about you. She asked if we could stop by your house quick to see if you'd want to go out." A mower goes by him. "Just a minute. I have to move so I can hear." The mowing noise dies out and then he says, "Okay, go ahead."

I check to see that Carl isn't around. He's not, but I still lower my voice. "I just freaking told you I had sex with Willow. So why the hell would I be interested in going out with Tess?"

"You need to move on, man. Just because Willow had sex with you doesn't mean she wants you back. What did she say after I left last night? Was she pissed about Tess?"

"Yeah, she was pissed. She was also jealous."

"Which is why Willow told Tess she's your girlfriend. But after we left I bet Willow went back to saying you two are just friends."

I don't want to acknowledge that he's right so I don't.

"I'm right, aren't I? You see what I mean? She's using you, bro. For sex. Friendship. Running her errands. Driving her places. Who the hell knows? All I know is she's using you and it's wrong."

"She's not using me. She just needs time to think about our relationship."

"What's there to think about? She either wants to be with you or she doesn't. It's not that freaking hard."

"You know how Willow is. Everything in her life has to be neat and orderly and planned out. She can't handle change. Me showing up here threw her for a loop. She wasn't prepared for it. She needs time to figure it out."

"Well, while she's figuring it out, you need to be out with Tess, getting your needs met."

"I'm not going out with Tess. And my needs *are* being met."

"You and Willow had sex again?"

"We came pretty damn close, but we stopped before it got to that point."

After Trent left last night, Willow and I went up to my room to watch TV but we both knew we had no intention of doing that. As soon as we got there, we started kissing and touching, and right before I was about to break my no-touching-below-the-waist rule, she got out of my bed and said she needed to go home. So she did, and I took a long, very cold shower.

"So she teased you, then cut you off," Trent says. "That's fucking bullshit."

"We had an agreement. We said we wouldn't do it, so we didn't."

"Why not? What's the big deal? You guys have probably done it like a million times."

"When we were dating. But things are different now. I'm not going to sit here and explain it to you. This is between Willow and me."

114

"So you're just going to spend your whole summer waiting for Willow to make up her mind about you? And you're not even going to get sex? What the hell?"

"Right now I just want to spend time with her and we'll go from there. And I'm not interested in dating someone else, so stop bringing girls over to my house."

"She's gonna break your heart, bro."

"Then when she does you can get me drunk and fix me up with Tess. But until then, stay out of it. I have to get back to work."

"You didn't even ask me what happened last night."

"Fine. What happened last night?"

"I had sex with Tana."

"Big surprise."

"It sucked. The sex was mediocre at best and then she got all clingy when it was over. She wanted to spend the night but I told her I had to get up early for work. She's called me five times already this morning."

I laugh. "That's what you get for having sex with a girl just hours after meeting her."

"Shit, I just got a text from her. I might have to change my number. I gotta go. Talk to you later."

I get back to work, and at noon, as I'm washing my hands at the hose, Willow shows up with a big paper sack in her hand.

"Want some lunch?" she asks.

"Yeah, that'd be great. Thanks." I shake the water from my hands and follow her to my truck. "I should probably eat with the other guys sometime. They're going to think I'm avoiding them."

She hops up on the back of the truck and pulls me toward her. "But if we sit with them, I can't do this." She kisses me. A long, deep kiss that has me hoping her dad doesn't walk by.

I talk over her lips. "Why don't we do this later? When there aren't so many people around? Specifically your dad?"

"My dad doesn't care if we kiss."

"Still, let's save it for later, when we can do more than kiss."

115

"Okay." She smiles and kisses my cheek.

I sit next to her. "You're in a good mood today."

"Does that mean I'm usually not?" She laughs as she starts unpacking our lunch.

"No. I meant that you're usually more serious. Today you seem...not so serious."

"Because I'm not worrying about homework and tests. It's nice to finally be able to relax. And I like being home. College is great but I missed my parents." She hands me a sandwich.

"Did you miss anyone else?" I take a water bottle from the sack.

"I did, but I tried not to think about it. I didn't think I'd ever see you again." She glances back at the tables where the workers are having lunch, then turns my face to hers and kisses me, another hot and heavy kiss. Then she leans back and says, "Sorry. I couldn't stop myself. I've been dying to do that."

"You've been dying to kiss me?"

She bites her lip. "This is really embarrassing and you better not make fun of me. In fact, I shouldn't even be telling you this."

"Telling me what?"

She sighs. "I had this really hot dream about you last night. It was so intense. I thought it was real but then I woke up."

"What happened during this dream?" I casually ask, trying to hide the fact that I'm completely turned on by this. Willow never remembers her dreams so if she remembered this one, it had to be good.

She leans over to me, her eyes glancing behind us, making sure no one is there. "We had sex. Multiple times. Multiple ways. On multiple surfaces."

"Holy shit," I mutter, blood rushing to my crotch. "You sure you don't want to tell me this later?"

"You're lucky I'm telling you now!" she whispers. "This is embarrassing. I only told you so I could explain why I was kissing you."

116

"Isn't kissing me just making it worse? I mean, if you're needing to um...relieve yourself—"

"I already did that." She grabs her water bottle and takes a drink, leaving my mind full of images of her "relieving" herself. This is too much stimulation to be experiencing while at work. "Anyway, I just wanted to tell you that. So how's work going?" She bites into her sandwich.

"Forget work. I want to hear about this dream."

"Not now. I don't want my dad to hear. He's always sneaking up on me."

"So you'll tell me later?"

"Probably not. I told you, it's embarrassing."

"Sex doesn't embarrass you. It never has."

"It does when it's stuff I haven't done before. I don't even know where I came up with this stuff."

Now I'm even more curious. What the hell were we doing in her dream?

"We shouldn't talk about this." She points to my sandwich. "You better hurry and eat. Your lunch break is half over."

"What *is* this?" I ask as I unwrap my sandwich.

"Hummus and cucumber. We were low on groceries so I used what we had. With my mom working, she hasn't had time to go to the store. I'd go but I don't have a car. I'm just lucky your mom let me borrow hers again, but she needs it back in an hour."

"Why don't you take my truck? If you ever need it, it's yours. Take it for the whole day. I don't care."

"Then how would you get here?"

"You can drop me off."

"I guess that would work. Then I'd just pick you up at night."

The way she smiled when she said it, I think she's looking forward to this. She keeps finding ways to spend time with me. And now she's having sex dreams about us. I wonder where that will lead. Are we going to be friends with benefits? I

117

wouldn't say no to it but I'd rather have her agree to an actual relationship with me.

"Do you want to take it tomorrow?" I ask.

"Actually, I'm working here tomorrow so could you maybe pick me up?"

"I drive right by your house, Willow. Of course I'll pick you up. You don't want to ride with your dad?"

"No. He leaves too early. Plus I'd rather ride with you."

I smile at her comment. "Are you working a full day?"

"Yeah. I'm picking strawberries. That'll take all day and probably the next day as well."

"How about I bring lunch tomorrow?" I look down at my empty sandwich wrapper. "No offense but your lunches aren't very filling. I'm still starving."

"Sorry. I didn't have time to go to the store."

"It was good. It's just that I eat a lot, and hummus and cucumbers aren't enough." I kiss her. "But thanks for making it for me."

"Do you have something else to eat? What did you bring for lunch?"

"I didn't bring anything. I was going to go out, but then this hot girl stopped by and I couldn't leave."

She smiles as she puts our garbage in the sack. "I brought some kale chips. And my mom's black bean brownies." She holds up a brownie. It looks hard as a rock, burnt on the edges.

"I think I'll pass, but thanks." The wind gusts, blowing my hair on my face. I've always worn my hair long, around chin length, for no other reason than it's what I'm used to. My hippie mom didn't like short hair so she always had it cut this length when I was a kid and I never changed it. "I need to cut my hair."

"Then get a haircut." Willow bites into a kale chip and makes a face. "These are disgusting. I can't believe my mom likes these."

"I don't mean just a trim. I mean, I think I'm going to cut my hair off, short, like other guys."

"Really?" She frowns. "But I love your hair." She turns to face me and runs both her hands through my hair. It feels good. I always loved it when she'd do this when we were dating.

"So you don't think I should cut it?"

"It's *your* hair. You can do what you want. I'm just used to seeing you with it like this."

"If you like it that much, I'll leave it. I was just going to cut it so it wouldn't keep falling on my face when I'm trying to work. Sometimes I pull it back, but it doesn't stay."

She tilts her head, eyeing me. "Hmm. It would be interesting to see you with shorter hair. I love it long but maybe it's time for a change. Can I go with you?"

"Where?"

"To get your hair cut."

"Are you going to tell them what to do? Because I have no idea what to tell them. I've had this same haircut forever."

"I can help with that." She pulls my hair back. "You can't go too short. It'd be too much of a change. And I'd like to still be able to see your natural wave. This is going to be so much fun! Let's go tonight. I'm sure I could get an appointment somewhere."

"Tonight? That's kind of soon."

"Do you need more time to think about it? It is a big deal to change your hair. Sometimes it takes me months to decide what to do with mine."

I don't care about my hair. I only said that because I'd rather be alone with Willow tonight to see if she'd like to act out some of her dream. But that probably won't happen so I might as well cut my hair.

"Let's go tonight," I say.

"You sure?"

"Positive. Come over early. You can eat at my house. We've got some vegan chicken nuggets that aren't too bad if you cover them with barbecue sauce."

"We have those too. They're good." She jumps off the truck bed. "Just call me when you're ready and I'll head over."

I'd rather take her out for dinner but I have almost no cash and I can't keep asking my mom or Martin for it. They have no problem giving me money but I feel like a kid when I take it. I'd rather earn my own.

"You leaving?" I lift the truck gate up.

"Yeah. You need to get to work and I need to return the car to your mom."

"Thanks for lunch." I wrap my arms loosely around her waist.

"I know lunch wasn't very good but I wanted to see you." She's being very open about her feelings today. She was last night too.

"What are you doing this afternoon?"

"I was thinking of helping my mom with the farm stuff so she wouldn't have to do it tonight. She's really tired when she gets home from work."

"What farm stuff?" I ask, hoping I don't sound as anxious as I feel.

"Orders, payments, billings. That type of stuff. It would actually be good experience. I want to run a business and the farm is a business. Maybe I could be more involved with it this summer. Run the business side of the things. Help with the accounting."

"Willow, really? This is your summer break. You should be relaxing, having fun, not looking at spreadsheets."

"Spreadsheets! That's a great idea. My parents use this archaic system for tracking everything. Spreadsheets would be so much better. I'm going to go home right now and make some. I'll start with orders, then move on to payments. Within a few weeks, I could have everything organized into neat and orderly spreadsheets."

Shit. What the hell did I just do? I mention spreadsheets, thinking nothing of it, and now Willow's all fired up and ready to start digging through her parents' files. And when she sees the financial records and unpaid bills, she'll know what's going on. The girl lives to organize things so I don't know how I'm going to talk her out of this.

She's still talking, getting even more excited. "My parents can do searches, run variable analysis, or multiple variable analysis, and they can—"

"Willow, stop." I hold her arms. "Your parents will never do any of that. They don't want spreadsheets. They have a system that works for them and you shouldn't mess with it."

"But it's not a system. It's a disorganized mess. Just pieces of paper in folders. And the folders aren't even labeled!" She tosses her hands up. "Who doesn't label folders?"

Willow labels everything. When we were dating, I bought a variety pack of condoms just to mix things up and Willow divided the different kinds into plastic bags and labeled them. So yeah, she organizes and labels everything.

"I bought them a label maker for Christmas last year," she says, "and they didn't use it."

"Which just proves they'll never use your spreadsheets."

She sighs, her shoulders slumping. "That's probably true." She perks up again. "But I can still make them. I love making spreadsheets. I think it's fun."

"You do know how nerdy that sounds." I smile.

"It's not nerdy. It shows that I'm smart." She presses her palms against my chest and smiles up at me. "A smart, naughty school girl. I even like to dress like one."

"Yeah. I remember." I pull her against me as the image of her wearing that short plaid skirt fills my head. "You should wear that again."

"I will." She pushes me back. "But for now, I'm going to get started on those spreadsheets."

The naughty school girl image disappears as I remember what we were talking about.

"No. Willow, don't."

"Why not?" She picks up the paper sack that held our lunch.

"Because you'll hurt your parents' feelings. Doing this might make them feel like you don't think they're smart enough or capable enough of managing their business."

"They won't think that."

"They might. Why don't you talk to them before you do this? Don't just start going through their office. You wouldn't want them going through your room without asking, would you?"

"No. I don't even like them going in there."

"And your parents wouldn't like you going through their files."

"I guess you're right. I'll talk to them before I do it." She reaches up and gives me a peck on the cheek. "I'll see you tonight."

When she's gone, I walk over to the trailer to find Carl. He needs to tell Willow the truth before she finds it out herself.

Before I reach the trailer, my phone rings. It's Dan, the doctor I became friends with when I was overseas. He's forty, divorced with no kids, and worth several million thanks to a large inheritance and good investments. I left him a message a week ago and never heard back.

"Dan, hey, how's it going?" I sit down on one of the picnic tables since the workers are now back in the fields.

"It's going well. I've got a couple more weeks here and then I'm heading home."

"How's your leg?"

"Much better. I finally got rid of the cane."

Dan's leg was injured when a snake bit him. It was a poisonous snake that almost killed him. We were working in a remote village in India and one morning we went to get water. Dan set the bucket down near some tall grass and when he went to pick it up, a snake bit him on the leg. I heard him yell and when I got to him, the snake was slithering away and Dan was writhing on the ground in pain. Then he passed out and I didn't know what to do. I knew the snake was poisonous but I didn't know how to treat a snake bite.

Our base camp had a medical clinic but it was a half mile away. I knew Dan needed medical treatment right away so I picked him up and carried him all the way back. The doctor said I got him there just in time. He would've died if he'd had to wait any longer for medical care. He was in the hospital for a week and then had to use a cane to walk.

To thank me for what I did, Dan gave me his pickup truck. When I got back to California, his sister, who's housesitting for him while he's away, had the truck ready and waiting for me, including the paperwork.

So that's how I got the truck. But I didn't tell Willow or my mom that because they don't need to know. They'd freak out if they knew about all the dangers I faced when I was volunteering. One time I was even shot at by a group of protestors who didn't like the organization I worked for. They were shooting at my entire group, not just me, but still, it's something my mom doesn't need to know. Or Willow.

"When I didn't hear from you I was starting to get worried," I say to Dan. "I almost called your sister."

"No need to worry. I'm fine. I just wasn't able to get into town to make a call until today."

"Thanks for the truck. It's been great. I still can't believe you gave it to me."

"You saved my life. The truck is the least I could do. If you ever need anything, just let me know."

"Well, actually, did you get my message?"

"About investing in the organic farm?"

"Yeah. What do you think?"

"I'd have to learn more about it. I have an investment firm that manages my portfolio. They do all the research, then provide me with their recommendations. When I get back I'll have them look into it."

"I'm kind of on a deadline here. The farm could really use the money."

"So you're saying the farm is in trouble? So this is more of a loan than an investment."

I hesitate. "Yes, but if we can turn it around, it could become profitable."

"I'm sorry, Silas, but I'm not a big risk taker. I'm very conservative in my investments. And I'm not in the business of giving out loans. I'd like to help but I already support a large number of charitable causes."

"Yeah. I understand."

"So did you decide to take a class this summer?"

"Yes. I'm taking an accounting class and I've decided to take classes in the fall."

"Silas, that's great. I'm proud of you. Hey, if you need help paying for college, that's something I would be willing to do. I'm a big supporter of young people pursuing the education they need to get a good career. I know you said your parents were helping you out, but if you need help beyond that, just give me a call."

"Thanks. I'm at work so I should probably go. But it was good talking to you. Give me a call when you're back in the States."

"I will. Goodbye, Silas."

Shit. There goes my one and only chance to get money for the farm.

"Hey, Silas." Carl walks over to me. "You okay? You don't look so good."

I notice I'm bent over so I sit up straight. "I'm fine. Just sitting down for a minute."

"You've been putting in a lot of hours. Why don't you go home? Get some rest."

"No, I'm good." I put my phone away. "I need to talk to you about Willow. She was here for lunch and she mentioned taking over the business side of the farm now that Candace has that other job. She was going to start going through your office at home this afternoon but I think I talked her out of it."

"Everything is locked up. She can't get to the files."

"Does she have the passwords for your accounts?"

"No. And we change them all the time."

124

"Still, she's going to ask you if she can help so what are you going to tell her?"

He sighs, rubbing his jaw. "I'll have to make up an excuse. Candace doesn't want to tell Willow for at least another month. We received some new restaurant orders last week and the farmers' markets are always busier in the summer, so she's hoping that will give us enough cash to make our payments on time."

"I should let you know that I just talked to Dan, that guy I worked with in India. He's from Napa but does volunteer work overseas. I told you about him last week. Anyway, I was hoping he'd be willing to offer up some financial support to the farm, but I just talked to him and it sounds like it's not gonna happen."

Carl puts his hand on my shoulder. "Silas, don't worry about this. I know we're like family and I know you love my daughter, but you're already doing too much. This isn't your problem to fix." He stands up. "I need to get back to the field. Oh, and I ordered those flower seeds. They should be here by Friday."

"I'll get them planted this weekend."

"Take the weekend off. Do something fun." He walks off before I can talk him into letting me work this weekend.

He keeps telling me to stop working so much but I feel like I have to. I know this farm isn't my responsibility but I don't want to see it fail and the land be sold to someone else. Willow and I used to play here when we were kids. We'd pick strawberries and eat them right in the field and get berry stains all over our clothes. We had races down the rows between the plants. And when we got older, we'd sit out here and watch the sun set. Or gaze at the stars.

This is more than just a farm. It's part of our life. Our memories. And I'm not ready for it to go away.

CHAPTER THIRTEEN

WILLOW

I ring the bell at Silas' house but the door's unlocked so I just go in. Growing up, I never rang the bell or knocked. I'd just walk in as though I lived here, because I practically did. I was always hanging out here with Silas.

"Diane? It's Willow. I brought your car back." I follow the sound of scissors dropping and find her in the spare bedroom where she makes her jewelry.

Her jewelry supplies are scattered all over the house and the garage. She even has stuff stashed in the bathroom. It drives me crazy. I just want to organize it all in neat little boxes with labels, then make a detailed inventory of each and every item. Once I even offered to do that for her and she quickly turned me down. She loves the chaos. She says it fuels her creativity.

Diane is sitting on the floor, her supplies spread out all over the place. Her wiry black hair is knotted behind her head and she's wearing wide-legged bright blue pants made out of some silky fabric and an oversized yellow t-shirt with a scooped neckline. She and Martin have plenty of money but she loves shopping at second-hand stores so that's where she gets all her clothes.

"How was lunch?" she asks as she uses mini pliers to secure beads onto a chain.

"Good, but your son said I didn't give him enough food."

She laughs. "That boy's stomach is a bottomless pit. And being outside working all day gives him an even bigger appetite."

I plop down on the worn recliner in the corner of the room. It was one of Martin's contributions when he moved in with Diane years ago.

"I feel bad. I made Silas a cucumber and hummus sandwich and now he's probably starving. But it's all we had and I didn't have time to go to the store."

"Go now. You can take my car."

"I thought you needed it to go to an appointment."

"It was cancelled, so the car's yours."

"Thanks, but I can't today. The money jar is empty."

My parents have a money jar where they keep cash for groceries, gas, and whatever else we need. They like paying with cash. They have a credit card but never use it. It's only for emergencies.

"Let me give you some money," Diane says. "You can take my car and run to the store."

"Don't worry about it," I tell her. "I'll ask my dad for money and go tomorrow."

Diane has this sad look on her face. Why does she look so sad?

"Diane, are you okay?"

She snaps out of it and smiles. "Yes. Sorry. My mind drifted off for a moment." She holds up a blue beaded necklace on a gold chain. "What do you think?"

I don't want to tell her this, but the necklace is kind of ugly. It looks like something an old lady would wear, which makes sense. Diane has a lot of old lady customers.

"You don't like it," she says, setting it down.

"It's not really my style, but I think older women would like it."

"I think so too. That's why I made it. Next week, I'm setting up a booth at a vendor fair hosted by the senior center."

"My mom should sell her lotions there."

My mom makes homemade soaps and lotions but she doesn't sell them. She just makes them and gives them away as gifts. She also makes an all-natural healing salve that is amazing. It reduces swelling and speeds healing of cuts, bruises, bug bites. I keep telling her to sell it but she doesn't think anyone would buy it.

"There's still space left for more vendors," Diane says. "But I doubt your mom could get off work."

"I could do it. What day is it?"

"Next Wednesday afternoon. But does your mom have enough to sell?"

"She has a whole box full of stuff. She could probably make more this weekend. And I could sell her granola. People love that."

"If you really want to do this, I'll call the coordinator and get you set up, but you should ask your mom first."

"I will. I'll ask her when she gets home." I pick up a box of beads from the floor. They're all different colors. I would've separated them by color, but Diane likes them all mixed together. I scoop up a handful and let them fall through my fingers.

"Still wearing Silas' bracelet?" She points to my wrist.

"Yeah." I hold it up. "I love this bracelet. I wear it almost every day."

"You know, when Silas was overseas and would call me, he'd always ask how you were doing. Every single time."

I nod, feeling ashamed for not answering his calls.

"I understand why you didn't talk to him," she says, stringing neon green beads on a silver chain.

"You do?"

"Sometimes it's easier to forget than remember. You and I are forgetters. Silas is a rememberer. Martin is too."

"What does that mean?"

"We like to forget the things that hurt us."

"Silas didn't hurt me," I say quietly, scooping up more beads. "I hurt him."

"But it hurt you to no longer be with him. So you tried to forget him and all the memories you two had together. That makes you a forgetter. Silas would rather remember. As much as it hurts him, he remembers every moment you spent together."

"How do you know that?"

"Because he's my son." She smiles. "I know my son. I'm always amazed that he'll remember the most obscure things about when you two were kids. Like just the other day, he was telling me he has an accounting test on Saturday, and that led him to remember a story about when you were eight and were upset that the school didn't give out grades."

She's referring to the private school I used to go to with Silas. Our hippie teacher thought grades weren't necessary, saying everyone learns at their own pace and excels at different things, so assigning grades would only discourage a child's ability to grow into the person they're meant to be. I couldn't take not knowing how I did on a test. I knew kids in public school who got grades and I wanted them too.

"I wanted a report card," I say.

"Yes." She laughs. "So Silas said he made one for you. He said you kept threatening to leave and go to public school but he didn't want you to go, so he made you a report card, hoping it would make you stay."

"Yeah, I remember that. He gave me all A's except in Art, which he gave me a B in. I was so mad."

"He said that was because you had an assignment in which were you were supposed to rip up magazine pages and make a picture using the scraps, but you refused to do it that way."

I laugh. "I'm surprised he remembered that. *I* barely remember it. What did he say I did wrong?"

"He said you approached the project too logically. Instead of ripping the pieces, you cut them into orderly squares with scissors, then put them back in place, like you were putting together a puzzle."

"Did I get in trouble for it?"

"No. There were no rules at that school. Your teacher said you were just expressing your personality. You like logic and for things to make sense. There's nothing wrong with that. But Silas had to give you a hard time for not following instructions, which explains the B you got in Art." She holds up the green necklace she just finished. "What do you think of this?"

"I like it better than the other one. I'd probably wear that."

She sets it down and starts on a bracelet. "Silas was in the garage the other day, using my metal stamper."

"He's making more charms?"

"I think he was making just one, for a certain someone." She grins, her eyes on the beads she's holding as she tries to decide which ones to use.

"He said he's making me a bracelet."

She nods and picks out two yellow beads and sets them next to her. "He still has the ring he made you."

She's talking about my engagement ring. I gave it back to him when we broke up.

"I loved that ring," I say softly to myself, picturing it in my head. He used his mom's equipment to make a setting for the stone. Instead of a diamond, he took a stone we found on the beach and shaped it into an oval and polished it. That ring was so beautiful that I cried when I saw it and couldn't stop. And the fact that he made it himself made me cry even more. It was a million times better than any diamond ring he could've bought from a store.

After we broke up, Silas insisted I keep the ring, but I wouldn't do it. Keeping it would make me remember, and as Diane said, I'm a forgetter. Remembering is too hard, too hurtful, too sad.

"He wore it on a chain around his neck the whole time he was away."

"Because he's a rememberer," I say under my breath, but Diane heard me.

"Yes. And it reminded him of you."

"Diane, why are you telling me this?"

She holds a bead in her hand and looks up at me. "Sometimes it's good to remember. Forgetting is often easier in the short term, but in the long term it can lead to regrets. And a life of regrets is worse than the heartache of remembering."

I'm not sure if I should ask this, but I've always talked openly with Diane and I know she'll give me an honest answer. "Diane?"

"Yes, dear." Her head is down as she goes back to picking out beads.

"Do you want Silas and I to get back together?"

"That's not for me to decide."

"But do you want that? Do you want that for Silas?"

"I want him to find love, and he's found that with you. But if you don't reciprocate the feelings, then no. He's put his heart out there and I'm proud of him for that but I don't want to see him get hurt again. Well, I know he'll get hurt again. That's part of life. But it hurts even more when it's your first love. I don't want to see him go through that again."

I thought for sure she wanted us back together. But now I'm thinking she doesn't. That she doesn't trust me with his heart. And the truth is, I'm not sure I do either.

"I'm not blaming you, Willow. What happened between you and Silas isn't anyone's fault. You were both so young. You still are. You're both still trying to figure out who you are and what you want out of life. There's nothing wrong with that. But having already been through this, I just hope you both have learned from it and don't end up repeating the past." Her cell phone rings and she has to search under her boxes of beads to find it. "Hello?...Hi, honey...She's here right now...Yes, I'll tell her...Bye." She sets her phone down.

"Was that Silas?"

"Yes. He said he tried to reach you but your phone was off."

I check it. "The battery's dead."

"He just wanted you to know he's staying at work until six tonight. He mentioned something about a haircut?"

131

"Yeah, he wants to get his hair cut and I'm going with him." I glance at her phone. "Was that a photo of Silas on your phone?"

"Yes. It's a picture of him with some of the kids he met when he was building a school in the Philippines." She hands me the phone. The photo shows Silas crouching down with kids all around him. They look like kindergarteners and they're all trying to hug him at once. "That's a cute photo."

"You can look at the other ones. He sent me pictures from all the different places he went."

I go to the photos and swipe through them. There are several pictures of people hugging Silas, not just kids, but also adults, like they're grateful for all he's done to make their lives better. Like he's a hero. Because he is. Silas is a hero to those people. He took time out of his life to help them and he didn't even get paid.

Looking through these photos makes me see Silas in a whole new way. I always knew he was generous and selfless. He was always that way with me and with his friends. But seeing him be that way with total strangers halfway across the world is amazing. And inspiring. It makes me feel like I should be doing more to help others. I've spent the whole last year focused on me and what I want to accomplish. I guess that's what most people do, but Silas took a different path. A more difficult path. He spent two years helping strangers instead of worrying about himself. I have so much respect for him. And I'm so proud of him.

"Willow, can you hand me those wire cutters?" Diane is pointing next to my feet.

"Yeah. Here." I get up and bring them to her, along with her phone. "I should go. It was nice talking to you."

"You too. If I don't see you later, have fun tonight."

I leave and go back to my house. When I get there, there's a car I don't recognize in the driveway.

A woman gets out of the car when she sees me. "Do you live here?"

"Yeah, why?"

"I was hoping I could see the house."

I'm confused. What is she talking about?

"You want to see my house?"

"Yes. I was hoping to see the inside. Do you have time right now?"

"I don't understand. Why do you want to see the inside of my house?"

"Isn't it for sale?"

"No. You have the wrong house."

She searches her purse. "I had the address written down somewhere. I thought for sure this was it."

"No, it's not for sale."

"Well, I'm sorry to have bothered you. Have a nice day." She gets in her car as I go inside the house.

When that lady said my house was for sale I got a little panicked. I've lived in this house my entire life. I don't want my parents to even think about selling it. I want them to live here until they're old and gray, and then maybe I'll buy it, just so nobody else can live in it.

At seven-thirty, Silas and I arrive at the hair salon. It has an industrial look inside, with exposed brick and metal piping. Silas usually gets his hair cut at a barber shop near his house, which is fine for a trim, but since he's getting a lot cut off I suggested he go someplace better.

A girl with long black hair and a piercing in her nose sees us walk in and immediately smiles at Silas. This is a common reaction wherever we go. Girls are always smiling at Silas in a flirtatious way. Back in high school, this would sometimes happen when we went out, but it happens way more often now, probably because he's even hotter than he used to be. I glance at him in his low-hung jeans and gray t-shirt that fits close to his chest, showing off his lean torso. The soft fabric clings to his shoulders which lead down to his muscular arms. I'm still amazed at how much his body has changed in two years.

"Can I help you?" the girl with the piercing asks. She leans over the counter, giving us a good view of her breasts, which are pushed up and out, framed by the plunging neckline of her tight black shirt.

I instinctively wrap my arm around Silas' as we walk up to the desk. "He has an appointment at seven-thirty."

Silas looks down at my arm in his and notices how close I'm standing. A slight grin appears on his face before he turns back to the girl.

"Silas Sparks," he says.

She glances at the computer screen that's off to the side. "Looks like you're with me."

What? I made an appointment with Alex. I assumed Alex was a guy, but I guess that name works for both guys and girls.

I'm instantly jealous. Why am I jealous? She's just doing his hair. But her breasts will be in his face as she washes it and cuts it and—

"Right this way." She motions Silas to follow her.

"Can I come with?" I ask.

She looks annoyed so Silas says, "She's helping me. I wasn't sure how to cut it."

Alex smiles at him. "I can help you with that."

"I need to come with him," I blurt out. "I'm very particular about his hair."

"Are you his sister?" she asks in a tone that implies I could never be his girlfriend. I find it insulting and am starting to wonder if we should find a different stylist.

"I'm his girlfriend," I say, holding his hand.

Silas squeezes my hand. His mouth is turned up slightly like he's trying not to laugh. He finds my jealousy amusing. I find it irritating and yet I can't seem to control it.

"Follow me." Her tone is more business-like now that she thinks I'm his girlfriend. She turns and walks quickly past the row of other stylists to the shampoo area at the very back of the building.

"Have a seat," she says to Silas. He sits down, leaning back into the sink. She shampoos his hair, and just as I predicted, her breasts are right over his face. The shampooing seems to take longer than it should as she slowly massages his head in long, drawn-out strokes. I'm about ready to tell her to hurry this along but then she turns on the sprayer and finishes up.

She takes him to her station and I sit in the chair beside him.

"So what are you thinking?" she asks, looking at him in the mirror, running her hands through his hair.

"I want it short," he says, "but not too short. Willow, describe what we were talking about earlier."

"He wants most of the length cut off," I say, "but leave it a little longer on top, shorter on the sides. He doesn't want to have to style it. He needs something easy. More of a wash and wear look."

Alex picks up some strands of his hair, holding them out. "With your hair texture and the way I'm going to cut it, you shouldn't have to style it. Just let it air dry and it'll be good."

She gets to work. It's not even my hair, but I feel nervous seeing big chunks of hair falling to the ground. The haircut takes about a half hour and when she's done, I admit, she did a really good job. It's much shorter, but not too short. God, he looks hot. No wonder girls are always flirting with him.

"What do you think?" Alex hands Silas a mirror so he can see the back.

He takes a quick glance at it, then hands her the mirror. "Looks good. What do you think, Willow?"

"I love it. It looks great."

We go to the front to pay and Alex hands him her card. "You want to make an appointment for next time? Maybe in three weeks?"

I'm thinking he'll say no because this place charges twice as much as his barber does.

"Sure. Put me down for the same time, if that works."

She checks the computer. "Yeah, that'll work. I've got you down. See you then." She smiles, only at him, ignoring me.

When we get outside, he rakes his hands through his hair. "It's going to take a while to get used to this."

"You don't like it?"

"I do. It's just different. Do you like it? Be honest." He stops and faces me so I can see it.

"I really like it. I liked it the old way too, but I think it was time for a change. You can always grow it back if you decide you like it long." I tousle the hair on the top of his head. "I like how she gave it some movement and texture. She did a good job."

"Yeah. I liked her."

"Liked her as a hairdresser? Or more than that?"

He chuckles. "Willow. Don't ask me that. I told you I don't like talking about other girls with you."

"Why not? We're friends."

He leans down and lowers his voice. "Friends who fuck."

"That was one time."

"So it's not happening again?"

I glance to the side. "I don't know. Probably not." Who am I kidding? I know it'll happen again. It shouldn't, but I'm sure it will. We can't seem to control ourselves around each other. I look back at Silas. "So are you going to ask her out?"

"I just met her. I haven't thought about it."

This is so infuriating. Why did I ever tell him to date other girls? Because I'm not dating him, that's why. He's not mine.

"What if she calls and asks *you* out?"

"She's not going to do that. She thinks I have a girlfriend."

"Oh, yeah. I forgot about that."

"Why were you pretending to be my girlfriend?" A smug grin appears. "This is the second time this has happened."

"I just..." This is embarrassing. I'm usually not this outwardly jealous. I at least try to hide it, which is why I say, "I didn't think she was right for you."

"Why not?" He starts walking down the street.

"She had a nose ring." I catch up to him. "You don't date girls with nose rings."

"I never have, but that doesn't mean I never will. I liked the nose ring."

"You did?"

"I don't like it on every girl, but it looked good on Alex."

Now he's using her name, like they're good friends, soon to be more than that. Damn. Why did I pick that salon?

"What I like even better is a navel ring." He grins. "Those are sexy."

I hold his arm, stopping him. "I want one."

He laughs. "Yeah, you're funny."

"Why is that funny? I'm serious."

It's true. I've always wanted a navel ring but never told anyone that.

"Willow, you're not that type of girl."

"What type of girl?"

"The type who gets her navel pierced, or any part of your body pierced, except for your ears."

"You're wrong. I've always wanted my navel pierced. I was just too afraid to do it. It seems like it would hurt. But I'll do it if you go with me. There's a place just down the street that does them. That tattoo place next to the dry cleaners."

"Let's get something to eat." He takes my hand and continues walking. "Dinner wasn't enough. I'm still hungry."

"Silas, stop." I yank my hand back. "I'm not kidding. I want a navel ring."

He looks at me like he still doesn't believe me. "You've never once said you wanted one. And now you suddenly do?"

"I've wanted one for years. I didn't tell anyone because I didn't think I'd ever get one."

"So why now?"

"Because you're here to keep me from being afraid. You'll go in there with me, right? Maybe let me squeeze your hand when they put the piercing in?"

"Willow, are you seriously going to do this?"

"Yes," I say emphatically.

"You won't get hired as a CEO if you have a navel ring."

I roll my eyes. "An employer is never going to see it. "I'm not going to wear a half-shirt to work."

"Don't you want to think about this some more?"

"I've already thought about it. I'm ready to do this."

He sighs. "Okay. Let's do it."

I smile and grab his hand and pull him reluctantly down the street. This is so unlike me to do this, especially on such short notice. But I love that I'm doing it. I feel this sense of exhilaration. Freedom from my usual cautious self. From the person I normally am.

And yet, oddly enough, doing this feels more like the real me than the me I'm used to living with every day.

CHAPTER FOURTEEN

SILAS

I can't believe Willow wants to do this. A navel ring? Really? This is so unlike her, although I always knew she had this side of her. The carefree, uninhibited side. The side that lives in the here and now instead of in the distant future. I wish she'd let that side of her come out more often. She's happy when she's like this. She's generally a happy person, but she's even happier when she lets loose and does something she normally wouldn't do.

We go in the tattoo place and are greeted by a tall, wide guy who's probably about 22. His blond hair is spiked up on top and shaved on the sides and he's a wearing a black t-shirt and jeans. Tattoos cover his thick neck and both of his arms.

"Can I help you?" he asks, directing the question only at me.

I guess I look more like the tattoo type than Willow does, in her black shorts and fitted white t-shirt. She tends to dress in conservative colors and styles. She likes a sophisticated look, a complete contrast to her mom's style, which is a mismatched hodgepodge of colorful clothes that drape over her body instead of the tailored fit that Willow prefers.

Willow's clothes match her serious personality. But then sometimes she'll wear something totally different that takes me by surprise, like when she bought those red cowboy boots years ago. Or when she wears cutoff jean shorts. When she does that, it's like that other side of her is peeking through again.

"I'd like a navel piercing," Willow says to the guy.

"That's it? Just a navel piercing?"

She thinks for a moment, then says, "Yes."

"Let me get the form." He goes behind the desk and brings back a clipboard with a piece of paper on it.

She takes it and we sit down on the chairs that line the back wall. As she's filling out whatever form he gave her, I say, "Why did you hesitate when he asked you if that was all? Were you going to change your mind? Because if you don't want to do this—"

"I want to do it. When he asked, I was just thinking if I wanted anything else done. Like another piercing. Or a tattoo." She continues filling out the form.

"A tattoo?" I pick her hand up from the clipboard. "Who *are* you, and what the hell did you do with Willow?"

She smiles and takes her hand back and signs her name. Then she hops up from her chair and hands the clipboard to the guy.

"Follow me." He motions her to a hallway.

I catch up to them in the hall. "I'm coming with."

"I'm afraid it'll hurt," Willow says to the guy. "So I brought a friend with to hold my hand."

So now I'm just a friend? An hour ago I was her boyfriend. Clearly that was just to keep Alex away from me. Willow was so jealous, especially when Alex kept putting her breasts in front of my face. She couldn't exactly help it. The height of the chair put her breasts at eye level. She had nice breasts.

"I'll need you to unbutton your shorts," the guy says, and my attention swings back to Willow, who is now lying down on a table in this tiny room the guy led us to. Willow has her shirt pulled up but still covering her bra, and the guy is wiping the skin around her belly button with a cotton ball that's soaked with some kind of antibacterial solution. He's wearing gloves but I still don't like seeing his hands on her.

Willow unbuttons her shorts and my blood starts pumping harder. Now *I'm* the jealous one. Actually, I'm more angry than jealous. I don't like this guy seeing her exposed like this.

140

"You need to unzip them and fold them down a little," he tells her.

I grit my teeth, trying to keep calm, but I'm about ready to bolt up from the stool I'm sitting on and cover her up. Instead, I hold her hand and move closer to her, close enough to signal to the guy that Willow and I are more than friends.

Willow's nervous. She's breathing fast and her hand is ice cold. The guy turns to get something from the table.

"You okay?" I ask her.

She nods. "Yeah."

I lean down and whisper, "We can leave if you're not ready to do this."

"I'm fine." She fakes a smile. "Just a little worried about the pain."

I kiss her to take her mind off it, and also to remind tattoo guy that she's off limits. As I back away, he's sitting across from me on the stool, waiting.

"Which one do you want?" he asks Willow. He's holding a plastic tray displaying an assortment of navel rings.

"Hmm. I'm not sure. Silas, you pick."

I look them over. Some of them look cheap or trashy, but there's a sparkling fake diamond one that's both classy and simple. It'd be perfect for Willow.

"Let's go with that one." I point to it.

"That one costs an additional five dollars," the guy says. "The other ones are free with the piercing."

"That's fine. I'll pay for it."

"Silas, you're not—"

"Willow." I smile at her. "That's the one I like. It's going to look great on you."

She bites her lip, in a sexy, suggestive way. I get the feeling she wants to show off this piercing to me later, without any clothes on. And damn, that's a sight I would like to see. I'm getting aroused just imagining it. I never thought she'd get a navel ring, but now that she is, I can't wait to see it. It's going to

141

be sexy as hell, that shimmering stud decorating her flat tan stomach.

The guy has the piercing tool ready to go. Willow squeezes my hand and closes her eyes. The piercing takes just seconds, then he maneuvers the stud in place and it's done. Her skin is a little pink where it went in, but the sparkling stud already looks really good.

"Is it in?" Willow asks, her eyes still closed.

"Yes," I tell her as I rub her hand. "You're all done."

The guy tells her how to take care of it, then hands her an instruction sheet to take home and we go out front to pay.

When we're back outside she says, "You didn't have to pay for that."

"It was worth it. I have a feeling I'll be getting more enjoyment out of it than you will."

She flashes that sexy smile again. "And why is that?"

I shrug a shoulder. "I just do." I grab her hand and walk to my truck. "Does it hurt?"

"Not at all. It stung when he did it, but I don't feel anything now."

She's swinging our arms, grinning like she's both happy and proud of herself for doing that.

"Look at you, all badass with your navel pierced."

She laughs. "I'm not a badass."

"You went into a tattoo place and got a piercing. Without even planning it. That's badass. And I went and cut my hair short. Guess I'm the conservative one now and you're the wild one."

"I'm not wild."

We're at the truck and I open her door for her. "Can I see it?"

There's no one around so she lifts her shirt up to just under her bra. I softly run my finger around her belly button.

Her breath catches and her stomach muscles tense.

"Does that hurt?" I ask.

"No," she breathes out.

I knew it didn't. I could tell by her reaction that she was aroused, not in pain. She reacted that way because I touched her in a very sensitive area and it turned her on. I love turning her on. Now I'll always have an excuse to touch her there or look at her there. I think it's safe to say I'll be getting enjoyment out of this. That was money well spent.

We stop for a slice of pizza, then go back to my house. My mom comes up to us as we walk in. She's staring at my hair.

"Who is this strange man?" she jokes.

"I know. It's a lot shorter."

"I like it. It looks good on you."

"And Willow got her navel pierced."

She hits my arm. "Silas! You weren't supposed to tell her! Now she's going to tell my parents."

"Your parents won't care."

"He's right," my mom says to Willow. "That's not something they'd be upset about. Oh, I talked to your mother. She was excited about having a booth at the vendor fair next week but she can't get off work. You'll have to set it up and manage it yourself."

"That's fine. Sign me up. Can we ride together?"

"We might need to borrow Silas' truck. I don't think everything will fit in my car."

"It's all yours," I say walking around her to the kitchen to get some water.

I like that my mom and Willow get along so well. And it's good my mom set her up with this opportunity to sell stuff. Willow's family could use any amount of cash they could get right now. That's why Willow's mom agreed to do this. Normally, she doesn't sell her soaps and lotions. She likes to stick to selling food.

Willow finds me in the kitchen. "Silas, it's getting late. I'm going home."

"I'll walk you back."

We go outside and she walks backward down the sidewalk, smiling at me. "Can you believe I got my navel pierced?"

143

"It was a little surprising."

"A *little?* I never do stuff like that."

"No, but I think you want to." I grab her around the waist and tug her against me. "You have a wild side that you need to let come out more."

She laughs and looks up at me. "I don't think so."

I set my eyes on hers. "You also have a sexy cowgirl side. A sexy school girl side. And now a badass side. You need to let those sides come out and play."

"I did." She bites her lip.

"Not just now and then. I want to see those sides of you more often." I tilt my head and put my mouth over hers, gently sucking her lip from her teeth. She exhales sharply and I kiss her, hard, while pulling her against me. Then I soften the kiss, and she parts her lips, and I slide my tongue over hers.

There's no space between our bodies and I feel her chest moving in and out as she breathes. She grips my shirt and kisses me back, her tongue tangling with mine. I move my hand to behind her neck, my fingers threading through her hair.

I'm so turned on right now. That navel piercing started it and it's been building all night.

She breaks from my lips, breathless, and whispers, "God, I want you so bad."

Shit. As if it wasn't hard enough. Now it's starting to ache. If I'd known she was going to say that, I would've taken her somewhere instead of coming home.

"Let's go," I say, still kissing her.

"Where?"

"To the farm. The sleeping bag's still in my truck."

I take her hand and we start walking back to my house.

"Willow?" It's her mom, yelling from the driveway. "Honey, are you going to be home soon?"

Willow turns back. "I'm not sure. Why?"

"Diane told me about the booth. I thought we could start planning it. But if you're leaving, we could work on it tomorrow."

Willow turns to me. "I should probably go. I haven't had much time with her since I've been back."

"Yeah, go ahead."

She yells back to her mom, "I'll be home in a minute."

"No rush." Candace goes back in the house.

"Sorry," Willow says. "I really wanted to."

I smile. "Raincheck?"

"Yeah." She reaches up and kisses me. "Goodnight."

I hug her. "See ya tomorrow. And since you're working in the fields, I'll expect to see the sexy farm girl side of you."

She laughs as she walks to the door. I wait for her to get safely inside, then walk back to my house, and once again, take a long, very cold shower.

The next morning, I stop by Willow's house to take her to work. She comes out the door wearing a white tank top and denim overall shorts.

"What do you think?" she asks as she hops in the truck. "Do I look like a farm girl?"

"A *sexy* farm girl." I back out of the driveway.

"This isn't sexy." She pulls her hair up in a ponytail, securing it with a band.

"It's sexy." I smile at her. "Makes me think of having sex in the back of a pickup."

She laughs. "Yeah. I wonder what that's like."

"Maybe we should try it and see." I raise my brows. "Like tonight?"

She shakes her head. "I can't tonight. I'm helping my mom make lotions. She's really excited about the vendor fair, which is weird because she's never wanted to sell this stuff before."

"Can't you work on that this weekend?"

"My parents won't be here. They're going to see one of my dad's friends from college. He lives in San Jose. They're staying overnight on Saturday. They should be back by Sunday afternoon."

So she'll have the house to herself. We can finally get some privacy.

My phone rings and I pick it up. It's Trent.

"Hey, you at work?" I push the button to put it on hands-free mode.

"Yeah." His voice fills the car. "How was—"

"Willow's here," I interrupt before he says something he shouldn't. Every time we talk he asks if I've had sex with her again and I don't want her hearing that.

"Hi, Trent," she says. "How's the golf course job?"

"Good. Hey, I don't have much time to talk. I was just wondering what you guys are doing this weekend."

I glance at Willow. "Why do you ask?"

"I'm having a party over at the house. It's a cookout around the pool. It'll start around six-thirty and end whenever people go home."

"It sounds fun," Willow says. "Am I invited or just Silas?"

I give her a look, wondering why she asked.

"Of course you're invited," he says. "So can you guys make it?"

"Yeah, we'll be there," I tell him. "Do you want us to bring anything?"

"Only if you plan to eat that vegan shit. I'm cooking burgers and steaks, not tofu."

"Willow and I are good with burgers. We'll see you Saturday." I end the call.

"Now we have something to do this weekend," Willow says.

I was hoping to spend Saturday night alone with her, but I'm sure we'll only spend a couple hours at the party. Then we can go home and have alone time.

"Why did you ask if you were invited?" I say.

"Because Trent doesn't like me."

"He *likes* you."

"No, he doesn't. He keeps setting you up with other girls, twice that I know of. Maybe more than that. He doesn't want me with you."

"It's not his decision."

"So you agree he doesn't want me to be with you?"

I sigh. "He just doesn't want a repeat of the past. But I told him to mind his own business."

"He thinks I'll hurt you again." She looks out the side window.

"Willow." I put my hand on her knee. "The past is the past. It just wasn't the right time for us back then."

I want her to say that *now* is the right time, but she doesn't. I knew she wouldn't, but I had to give her a chance to.

When we arrive at the farm, the other guys are already in the fields. Usually I would be too, but I didn't want to make Willow get here that early. She has no idea how many hours I normally work.

"Why is my mom still here?" she asks, noticing their car. "She should be on her way to the office by now."

"Maybe she's going in late today."

"Yeah, maybe." Willow gets out of the truck and starts walking to the trailer. I'm worried about what she'll find in there. Her parents might have gotten here early so they could meet privately without her overhearing.

"Willow, wait up." I catch her hand, stopping her. I need an excuse to keep her outside. I spot the sunscreen bottle sitting on the picnic table. "Could you put sunscreen on me? I forgot to get my neck, and it might burn now that my hair's not covering it."

We go over to one of the picnic tables and I sit down so she can reach. She squirts some lotion in her hand and rubs it on the back of my neck.

When she's done, she hands me the bottle. "Could you put some on mine too?"

"Sure." I rub it on her neck, extra slow, trying to kill time.

"That should be good." She pops up from the bench. "Thanks."

I motion to the fields. "We need to get out there before it gets too hot."

"I'm just going to say hi to my mom quick. She and my dad left before I got up so I didn't see her."

Before I can stop her, she goes in the trailer. I follow her in there.

"What are you guys doing?" she asks when she sees paperwork scattered all over the table her parents are sitting at.

"Willow." Carl stands up, sporting a big wide smile. "You're early."

"It's almost eight. I'm not that early."

Candace gathers the papers and stuffs them in a folder. "Is it that late? I need to get to work."

"What's all that paperwork for?" Willow asks.

"Your father and I were just looking at the schedules for the farmers' markets this summer." Candace stuffs the folder in the giant bag she calls a purse and walks over to Willow, kissing her cheek. "Bye, honey."

"Why don't you give that to me?" She points to the folder. "I'll make a calendar of all the farmers' markets for the summer and a spreadsheet that will track sales."

"We don't need that," Carl says to Willow. "But thank you for offering." He goes over to Candace and gives her a kiss. "Bye, honey. See you tonight."

"Carl can ride home with us if you need to work late," I say to Candace.

"I won't be late tonight. Willow and I are making lotions." She smiles. "You could come help if you want."

"Okay," I say, willing to do most anything to help them make money.

Willow laughs. "Silas, she was joking."

"I don't mind helping. It's just mixing stuff up, right?"

"Yeah, smelly girly stuff."

I grin. "I love smelly girly stuff."

"Especially when it's on a pretty girl," Carl says, giving Willow a wink.

Candace heads to the door. "Great! I'll see you both tonight. Oh, and Silas, come over early. You can have dinner with us."

When she's gone, Carl says, "I'll order a pizza."

I smile. "Thanks."

He knows how bad his wife's cooking is and yet he still eats whatever she makes. Now *that's* love. But at least he doesn't make Willow and me eat it.

"Well, we better get to work," Carl says. He takes his hat from the hook and goes outside.

That was a close call. If Willow had overheard her parents talking, their secret would be out.

I'm so sick of this secret. They just need to tell her. They can't keep hiding it from her. I can't either. It's getting harder and harder to not tell her the truth.

CHAPTER FIFTEEN

WILLOW

"I'll be shocked if Silas shows up," I say to my mom. She got home a few minutes ago and we're gathering the supplies we need for the soaps. We decided to make soaps tonight and lotions tomorrow.

"I'm sure he'll show up." She smiles at me. "Any excuse to see you."

"That's not why he's doing it."

"Willow, stop denying how much that boy likes you." She nudges me as she goes by. "And how much you like him."

I don't bother denying it. She can read me like a book.

"Are you two going out this weekend?"

"Yeah. To a party at Trent's house. I might need a few dollars for the weekend. Just for food and stuff. I noticed the cash jar was empty."

"I'll give you some money before we leave."

"The jar's been empty all week. Any reason why?"

"Your father had to buy some tools for the farm and he didn't want to charge it. And I had to buy the supplies for the soaps and lotions."

She takes out a box that contains the scraps of paper that her homemade soap recipes are scribbled on. She spreads them out on the kitchen table.

"Mom, let me type those in the computer and print them out. You're going to lose those scraps."

"I don't mind the scraps." She hands me one. "Do you want to make the peppermint?"

"Sure." I take a seat at the table. "What's Silas going to make?"

"You pick." She slides the paper scraps over to me.

"Oh, I forgot to tell you. Some lady came by here the other day wanting to look at the house."

My mom drops the dish towel she was holding. "What lady?"

"I don't know. Just some lady. She was in the driveway when I was coming back from Silas' house. She asked if she could come inside. She thought the house was for sale. I told her she had the wrong address." I start sorting through the soap recipes. "I panicked when she said it. I thought maybe you put it up for sale and didn't tell me. But I know you and dad would never sell it. You guys love this house. So do I. In fact, I was just thinking that I kind of miss your crazy rainbow-colored walls. Remember when I colored on them when I was really little? You and dad didn't even get mad. You told me to keep going. I drew a picture of a giraffe and his turtle friend, George." I laugh. "I don't know why I gave the turtle a name but not the giraffe."

She doesn't respond. I look up and see her covering her mouth, tears going down her cheeks.

I jump up and hug her. "Mom, what's wrong?"

"Nothing, honey. It's just hearing you talk about that made me miss those times. And you're right. I do love this house. I love all the memories it has."

My dad walks in. "Is everything okay in here?"

My mom wipes her face and smiles. "Yes. We're just getting everything set up."

I sit at the table again. "I told Mom you guys better never sell this house. I couldn't handle someone else living here."

My mom hurries down the hall. Where is she going so fast? She's acting strange tonight.

"What's wrong with Mom?" I ask my dad.

151

He shrugs. "Nothing. She seems fine to me."

Men. They're so clueless. They never notice anything. She's clearly upset about something. Maybe her new job is causing her stress. She should quit. It's not worth being that stressed.

What am I saying? That's going to *me* someday. Working all the time. Not sleeping. Stressed. I've told myself I'm okay with that but sometimes I'm not sure that I am, especially at times like this, when I'm here at home, relaxed and hanging out with my family. And Silas. I smile because he just walked in.

"Hey." He smiles. "Everything ready?"

He's wearing jeans and a light blue t-shirt that looks really soft. It makes me want to snuggle up to him and rub my hands over his chest.

I snap out of it when I feel his hands on my shoulders. He's now standing behind me and I tilt my head back to see him. "I told my mom you wouldn't show up."

"As usual, you were wrong."

My dad chuckles. "Those are fighting words, Silas. Willow doesn't like being wrong."

"Yeah." I reach back and whack his arm. "And I bet I *wasn't* wrong. You're probably just here for dinner and then you'll leave."

"Wrong again. I'm staying here until we're done." He rubs my shoulders. "How much of this lotion stuff are we making?"

"We're not doing lotions. We decided to make soaps tonight." I close my eyes as he massages my shoulders. "That feels awesome. My shoulders are killing me from all that strawberry picking."

"You could take tomorrow off," my dad says as he takes stuff out of the fridge.

"That's okay. I'll be fine by tomorrow."

I like being at the farm. Today was a lot of work and I'm exhausted, but it felt good to help out. And from the strawberry fields I had a great view of Silas, his biceps flexing as he dug holes and pulled weeds. Late afternoon he took his shirt off and after that I didn't get much work done. I pretty much just ate strawberries and watched his muscles flex, the sweat glistening off them. It's kind of pathetic, I know, but it's not every day you get a view like that.

"I'm going to go make the pizzas," my dad says as he carries the ingredients outside.

"Your dad's making dinner?" Silas asks.

"Yeah. He's grilling pizzas. My mom doesn't have time to make dinner. She's too busy getting ready for our soap-making marathon. You sure you want to do this? Because you really don't have to."

"I want to. I've always had this burning desire to make my own soap."

I laugh. "You'll have to take a bar home with you. Test it out."

He leans down by my ear. "Why don't we test it out *together?* This weekend?"

My heart races and I shiver, his breath tickling my ear. "Stop it," I whisper, smiling.

"Yes or no?"

I close my eyes to get my composure back, but instead I see images of Silas and me in the shower. We've showered together exactly three times and I remember every single detail. The way his hands felt sliding down my skin. His wet lips kissing me. The hot steam surrounding our naked bodies.

"Yes," I blurt out.

"Really?" He sounds shocked as he takes the seat next to mine.

I shake my head. "No. Sorry. I didn't mean that."

"Too late." He's grinning. "You already agreed to it."

"I didn't—"

"Did your dad get dinner going?" My mom walks in.

"Yeah. He's outside at the grill."

"I think we'll eat out on the patio since we have all our supplies spread out on the table." She smiles at Silas. "You showed up. Willow was sure that you wouldn't."

"She was—"

"Wrong," I say, interrupting Silas as I roll my eyes. "I got it. You don't need to say it again."

Silas laughs.

"Well, thank you for helping out," my mom says. "Did Willow assign you a soap to make?"

"No, but we were just talking about it." He gives me a sideways glance.

"Willow's favorite is the peppermint, so she's going to make that one."

"Peppermint, huh?" Silas looks at me. "I'd like to try that one."

"You should," my mom says, having no idea what Silas is implying. "Take one and try it out."

"I think I will." He nudges my foot under the table because I'm ignoring him, my eyes on the recipes.

"We should make extra lavender ones," I say to my mom. "People love lavender."

"I agree." She picks up one of the recipes. "Maybe Silas could make the honey oatmeal one. It's a more masculine soap. No flowery smell."

He takes it from her. "I can do that. Honey oatmeal? Sounds like something you could eat."

"The oats are an exfoliant and the honey makes your skin soft," I explain. "I just used it last night in the shower. Made my skin really soft."

I know that'll get Silas going, which he deserves after making sexual innuendos with my mom around.

"I'm going to go check on your dad." My mom goes outside.

I feel Silas staring at me. "If you keep this up, we're going to be trying that soap out *tonight*."

"I didn't do anything." I pick up a sprig of rosemary. "People like it when you add herbs and flowers to the soap. Gives it more of a handmade feel."

He places his hand on my thigh and leans over to my ear. "You love teasing me, don't you?"

"Sorry. I shouldn't do that."

154

"Don't stop," he whispers. "I like it when you get me all worked up. Makes it that much better when we actually do it." He gently squeezes my thigh, then sits back.

I'm trying to breathe normally, but it's hard when my heart's going this fast.

Silas gets up. "I'm going to see if your dad needs any help."

My mom comes back in as Silas goes outside.

"Pizzas are almost ready," she says. "You want to help me with the drinks?"

As I get up to help her, I glance out at the patio and see Silas and my dad talking next to the grill. For a moment, I imagine Silas and me in the future, married, and coming over here to have dinner with my parents. Maybe we'd even have a kid or two.

"What are you smiling at?" my mom asks, handing me two glasses of water.

"Oh, um, nothing."

"You seemed deep in thought." She smiles. "Was it about Silas?"

"No. Something else. I'll take these outside."

As I'm walking to the door I hear her behind me. "Whatever it was, you sure seemed happy about it."

She's right. That image of Silas and me in the future made me happy, and obviously made me smile, which I didn't even realize I was doing until my mom said that.

Why am I even letting myself imagine Silas and me together? I know what my future holds and it's not marrying Silas, having kids, and coming to my parents' house for dinner. In my real future I'll probably be single with no kids, eating dinner at my desk every night. God, that sounds horrible when I think about it, but I have to make sacrifices if I want to succeed.

We have dinner outside and the pizzas are great. My dad should cook more often. He's better at it than my mom.

After dinner, my dad goes into his home office to do whatever it is he does in there, while Silas, my mom, and I make soaps. Silas keeps coming up with new variations and not following the recipes. My mom doesn't care. She's all about being creative and trying new things. She just tells him to write down what ingredients he used so she can put it on the label. Actually, *I'm* making the labels. I've already got a template set up on the computer.

By eleven o'clock we have more than enough soap to sell. I'm sure we'll have some left over, which we can sell at the farmers' market.

"It's getting late," my mom says. "I need to get to bed." She says goodnight and she and my dad go to their room.

I walk Silas to the door. "Thanks for helping us."

"No problem. I can't wait to make lotions next."

I laugh. "You're not doing that. We worked you hard enough with the soaps. You need a night off."

"I don't have anything else to do. And besides, your mom really liked the new soaps I came up with. I have even more ideas for lotions."

"Are you going to test those out too?"

He smiles. "This weekend."

"Silas, that's not going to—"

He kisses me mid-sentence. "See you tomorrow." And then he leaves.

The next day he's there at seven to pick me up. We wanted to get to the farm early because it might rain later. The day goes by fast, mostly because I'm staring at Silas for most of it. It's amazing how entertaining it is to watch a hot man do physical labor.

That night we make the lotions, putting them all in cute little jars. My crafty side is really coming out. I didn't know I had a crafty side. I guess Silas is right. I have all these sides of me I didn't know existed.

On Friday, I pick berries in the morning, then after lunch Silas drops me off at home and I get to work finishing up the soaps and lotions. In addition to the labels, I make signs with the prices listed out. My mom and I went over the prices last night. I had to talk her into charging more because what she was going to charge was way too low.

My phone rings as I'm walking to the printer. "Hello?"

"Willow, it's Taylor." Taylor is one of my friends from college. She's from a family of golfers and is on the college golf team. This summer, she's back home in Phoenix, living with her parents and brother, who's a pro golfer. Living in their guest house is Luke, her brother's friend, who's also a pro golfer and the guy Taylor's in love with. Or maybe it's not love, but she has a huge crush on him.

"Taylor! I'm so glad you called. How's your summer going?"

"Great." She sighs. "But complicated."

"Because of Luke?"

"Yes. I knew this would happen. I knew having him live here would be next to impossible."

"Have you two talked?"

"We did more than talk."

"You had sex with him?"

"No, but we kissed and—never mind. It doesn't matter. I can't date Luke."

"Why not?"

"Willow, we've been over this a million times. Luke is friends with my brother and my brother would kill him for dating me."

"Who cares what your brother thinks? Tell him to stay out of it."

"It's not just him. My parents made it clear to Luke that he needed to stay away from me. It's a condition of him living here."

"Why?"

"Because they're doing him a favor letting him stay here and they think it's disrespectful for him to start something with their daughter while he's living under their roof."

"It's not disrespectful if you and Luke both want to be together. It'd be different if he was hitting on you and you had no interest in him."

157

"My parents don't see it that way. They don't want Luke getting involved with me."

"Do they think anything's going on with you two?"

"No, and it needs to stay that way."

"I think you should date him." I plop down in the desk chair and spin around on the casters.

"Willow! You're supposed to talk me out of this!"

"It doesn't have to be anything serious. Just date him for the summer."

"Just like you're dating Silas for the summer?"

I stop spinning. "I'm not dating Silas."

"That's not what I heard. Lilly said you've spent all your time with him since you got back."

"When did you talk to Lilly?"

"Yesterday. I had to tell her about Luke."

"You called Lilly before me?"

"You never have your phone on."

"It's on but the battery keeps dying. I think I need a new phone."

"So tell me what's up with Silas."

"Nothing's up. We're just friends."

"That's not what it sounded like," she says in sly tone.

"We only did it one time."

"You had sex with Silas?" she yells.

"Lilly didn't tell you that?"

"No. She just said you've been hanging out with him, not having sex with him."

"Well, I did."

"So you're dating him," she says like it's a fact.

"We're just friends."

"Who have sex. So friends with benefits."

I cringe because I hate that term, but unfortunately it's true. "I guess that's what we are. I'm not really sure."

"Are you going to do it with him again?"

"Apparently I can't control myself around him, so yeah, I'm sure it'll happen."

She laughs. "You spent all last year saying you were over him and now look at you. Back with Silas after a couple weeks."

"More like a day. But like I said, we're not really dating."

"Willow, sorry, but I have to go. I forgot I have an appointment with my golf coach. I was supposed to be there ten minutes ago. My dad's gonna kill me. This coach costs a fortune and you have to pay even if you don't show up."

"Okay, we'll talk later. Bye!"

I probably won't talk to Taylor again for a month. She told Lilly and me she'd try to stay in touch this summer but I think she's going to be too busy with all her workouts and time on the golf course. And if she starts secretly dating Luke, she'll be even busier.

Just as I'm about to set the phone down, it rings again. I feel a rush of excitement when I see it's Silas calling. How does he cause this reaction from a simple phone call?

"Hey. Are you on break?" I ask.

"Yeah. How's the label making going?"

"Slow. I keep changing the design."

"Why? What's wrong with it?"

"It's too plain. It looks homemade, not professional."

"They're homemade products, so why can't the label look homemade?"

"I want it to look homemade, but not *too* homemade. You know what I mean?"

"Not really."

"The ones I have now are colorful and cute but they're missing something." I pick up one of the labels I printed out. "Right now I have the type of soap it is and the farm's name and web address. That's it."

"Maybe you need a logo. That always makes things look professional."

"Yes, that's it!" I jump up, tossing the label aside. "The farm needs a logo. Not just for the labels, but in general. We always just print the name in this ugly font. An actual logo would be so much better. Silas you're a genius!"

"Um, okay. Thanks."

"But it'll cost thousands to get one designed. My parents won't go for that."

"Just do it yourself."

"I'm not good at art. But you are. Can you help me design something?"

"Sure, but I can't tonight. I have to study for that test tomorrow."

"Maybe we could do it Sunday." A surge of excitement hits me as I imagine what else we could do in addition to the logo. We could make the farm into a brand, give it a new image—a younger, fresher image. Something that would make customers seek us out. "Silas, you have no idea how much you have my brain going right now."

"Just your brain?" he asks in a flirty tone.

I laugh. "For now, yes. I'm sure you'll get other parts of me going when I see you. Are you coming over for dinner?"

"I can't. I promised Trent I'd go over and help him get stuff for the party tomorrow. We're going to his parents' house and loading up my truck with extra chairs and coolers."

"Then I guess I'll see you tomorrow."

"Yeah. I need to get back to work. Bye."

I thought he'd want to stop over tonight after he helps Trent, but maybe he's tired. He must be exhausted after working at the farm all week. I've never seen someone work so hard. I have to bring him lunch just so he'll take a break.

I'm bummed I won't see him tonight. And a little sad. If I feel this way after one night without him, how am I going to feel when I go back to school in the fall?

I'm not going to think about that. September is a long ways away.

CHAPTER SIXTEEN

SILAS

I decided to take a night off from Willow. One, because I have to help Trent. Two, because I want to see if she misses me when I'm not around. And three, because I'm getting too attached to her.

It's only been a couple weeks and I'm already even more in love with her than I was two years ago. If this continues, Trent's prediction will come true. Willow will destroy me. Again.

She destroyed me when she broke up with me after our brief engagement, but I was younger then and able to get over it, telling myself we were too young to be that serious. But this time? It'll take a lot longer to get over her, maybe because everything seems more real now that we're older. My future seems less like a dream and more like reality.

We're both still young, but we've matured a lot the past couple years. Willow has always been mature for her age, but I wasn't until I went overseas. Living on my own, being in different parts of the world, and seeing people in extreme poverty, matured me to the point that I now feel much older than 20. So now, more than ever, I could see myself marrying Willow. But that's not what she wants, or if it is, she won't let herself believe it.

So where does that leave me? What do I do? Slow things down with her? Tell her we can only be friends? Do I date other girls and give up on Willow?

161

The truth is I don't want to do any of those things. What I want is to keep this going. To keep spending time with her. To keep flirting with her. Taking her out. Kissing her. Pretending like there's no end to this, even though I know there is.

I wish Willow could see what a great thing she and I have together. We're best friends. We make each other laugh. We understand each other. We can read each other and know when something's wrong. We know how to cheer each other up. And we have a chemistry that I know we'll never have with anyone else.

Yet Willow refuses to see all that. Her focus is all on school and her future career. I admire her ambition but there's more to life than that.

"You want to hang out after we unload?" Trent asks as we put the last two coolers in the back of my truck.

We already loaded the folding chairs and two long foldout tables. His mom gave us plastic tablecloths, which Trent told her he'd never use, but she insisted we take them. She also gave us three large plastic containers of homemade cookies and brownies. His mom is really nice but she treats us like we're kids. She even gave us a giant container of powdered lemonade.

This is not a cookies and lemonade type of party. It's more like burgers, beer, and hard liquor. I'm sure Trent's high school football friends will be there, along with as many hot girls as he can convince to come over.

"I need to study later, but yeah, I can hang out for a while." I go around and get in the truck.

"What do you want to eat?" Trent asks as we're driving away from his parents' house. "It's on me since I made you do this."

"Let's go to the barbecue place."

"Sounds good, but we're taking it home. I'm not eating there." He says that because the place is a dive, but they have the best barbecue in town.

"If you're buying, I'm getting ribs."

"I just got paid so let's get the works. Ribs, cornbread, beans. I got beer at the house."

"You don't have a girl lined up for tonight?"

"I need a break. I'll hook up with someone tomorrow at the party."

"What happened to Tana?"

"I told her I was engaged."

I laugh. "And she believed you?"

"Yeah, she was pissed. But at least she won't be calling me anymore. Her friend called me last night."

"Now Tess wants to go out with you? Didn't Tana tell her about your supposed engagement?"

"She wasn't calling about me. She was calling about *you*. She asked for your number."

"You didn't give it to her, did you?"

"No. But she knows where you live. She might stop by."

"Why didn't you remind her that I have a girlfriend?"

"Because you don't," he mumbles as I pull into the barbecue place.

I ignore his comment. I don't want to fight with him tonight.

We order our food and take it home and eat out by the pool.

"I'm stuffed," I say after finishing off a rack of ribs, three pieces of cornbread, and two of his mom's brownies.

"That place is a shithole but they have the best ribs in town." He gets up and dips his napkin in the pool to wet it, then comes back and sits down and wipes the sauce off his fingers. "So why aren't you out with Willow tonight?"

"Because I had to help your sorry ass get ready for a party, which we all know you're only having to meet girls."

"Girls like a pool." He motions to it. "I have a pool. Why not use it to my advantage? And it's not like you're not benefitting from this. You get to see girls in bikinis all night."

"I only want to see Willow in a bikini and I doubt she'll wear one tomorrow."

"Dammit, Silas." He throws his napkin down and shakes his head.

163

"What?" I gulp down the rest of my soda.

"You gotta end this obsession with Willow. She's not interested in you. It's time to move on."

"She's interested enough to have sex with me."

"One time. And that doesn't mean anything. She doesn't want a relationship with you. Love. Marriage. Whatever it is you're hoping for. She's not the one."

"And this is coming from someone who's never been in a relationship." I lean back in the chair, stretching my legs out. "Yeah, I don't think I'll be taking your advice, Trent."

"So you're just going to let her keep using you all summer as her little boy toy?"

He's been lecturing me about this all week and now he's just pissing me off. "That's not what she's doing, so back off."

"I'm trying to be a friend."

"Friends support each other."

"Not when your friend's doing something stupid."

I bolt up in my chair, glaring at him. "And you never do stupid shit?"

"Not the kind that ruins my life."

"Willow is not ruining my life."

"Not yet, but she will when the summer ends."

I slam my soda can on the table. "Why don't you just mind your own fucking business? I'm sick of you saying bad shit about her. And if you're not going to be nice to her tomorrow, I'm not coming to your party."

"I AM nice to her."

"It's not coming off as nice. She thinks you hate her. That's why she didn't think she was invited to the party."

"Listen, Silas." He faces me, his arms on the table. "I have no problem with Willow as a person, but I don't like her jerking you around."

"She's not—"

"Let me finish."

I sigh. "You got two seconds and then I'm done listening to this."

164

"The thing with Willow is that I don't think she's intentionally trying to hurt you. I think she's just confused about what she wants, but while she's trying to figure that out, she strings you along, making you think you two have a future together."

He's not telling me anything I don't already know. I know Willow is confused. She says she wants a certain type of life, but deep down, I know she's not sure if that's really what she wants. Which is why I'm trying to convince her to think about other alternatives. Do those alternatives include me? Yes, but my main concern is that she's happy. Even if she chooses not to be with me, I still want her to be happy.

"Are you done now?" I ask.

"Yeah." He gets up. "Let's go unload the truck."

After we do that, I go home and study for my test. Willow calls at ten.

"Did you get everything for the party?" she asks.

"Yeah, he's all set. It sounds like there's going to be a lot of people there. You need to bring a suit so we can go swimming."

"I don't think I want to swim."

"It's part of the dress code. Trent wants all girls to show up in a bikini."

She laughs. "Yeah, that sounds like Trent. That's probably the only reason he's having the party. I'll bring a suit, but I don't know if I'll wear it."

"So what'd you do tonight?"

"I went to a movie with my parents. It wasn't that great." She pauses. "Can I come over?"

"I really need to study."

"Oh." She sounds disappointed. "Okay. Then I'll talk to you tomorrow."

"Yeah. Goodnight." I really want to see her, but I think we need time apart. I need Willow to see what it's like to not have me around so she can decide if that's really what she wants.

The next morning I go to class. It's taught on Saturday mornings because most of the people taking it are a lot older than me and have full-time jobs during the week.

After class I stop by the farmers' market to see if my mom needs any help, but she and Martin are handling the crowds fine without me. I stop over at Carl and Candace's booth, which is just across from my mom's. Candace is there and says Willow is home making signs for the vendor fair. She's really getting into this fair. I hope she sells a lot, given how much work she's put into it.

I go home, grab some lunch, then head to the beach. It's been forever since I surfed, and surfing will keep my mind off Willow. It's crazy how much I miss her but we need our space. We can't spend every second together.

At five I head over to her house. She called at three to say her parents had left, but I was still at the beach and had to go home and clean up.

"Finally!" she says as she hugs me at the door.

She's wearing a short black dress with a halter neckline that leaves all kinds of skin exposed for me to kiss; shoulders, neck, cleavage.

"What do you mean?" I ask as we go inside.

"You're finally letting me see you. It's like you've been hiding out for a day." She drags me to the couch. I sit down and she sits right next to me, our bodies touching.

"You can't go a day without seeing me?"

"I can. I just don't want to."

If she really feels that way, then why doesn't she want to be with me? Beyond just this summer?

"Trent called and asked if we could head over there early and help set up the food, but we don't have to."

"I don't mind. Let's go." She jumps up, holding her hand out to me.

I take her hand and pull her onto my lap. "Don't you want to say hello first?"

"Hello." She smiles, then leans over and kisses me.

I kiss her back. "You look really sexy in this dress."

"Thanks. I wore it just for you."

"Seems like something a girlfriend would do."

She doesn't respond as she scoots over on my lap.

I slide my hand up her leg and kiss her bare shoulder. She smells sweet and flowery. "Did you use one of our soaps?"

"Yeah. The almond lavender."

"You were supposed to wait and try it out with me."

"We'll try a different kind." She kisses me, slowly, her tongue going in my mouth. Then she whispers over my lips, "Let's go, so we can hurry up and get back." She gives me one last kiss, then gets up.

Between her kisses and her hint that we'll be doing a lot more than that later, Willow is acting like we're dating, and yet she refuses to admit it. It's starting to bother me. Maybe it's because of that talk I had with Trent. As much as I try to ignore what he said, his words keep replaying in my head, telling me Willow is just using me. Part of me knows he's right and that I'm stupid to think this will go anywhere. Despite that, I'm not ready to give up on her. But I do need her to stop denying the fact that we're more than friends.

When we get to Trent's place, I park along the street but remain in the truck.

"Willow." I hold her arm as she goes to open her door. "I need to say something before we go in."

"Go ahead." She turns to me, giving me her full attention.

"Tonight at the party, I don't want you telling people I'm your boyfriend. Unless that's really what I am."

She pauses, seeming surprised at my comment. "I um...wasn't going to tell people that. I know we're just friends."

"And yet every time a girl comes up to me, you tell her I'm yours. That I'm your boyfriend. But I'm *not*. We're not dating. Because you don't want that. Isn't that right?" I look in her eyes as I say it. I need her to answer me and be honest with both me and herself about what this is between us.

Playing the role of her boyfriend was fine at first, but I'm not doing it anymore. If she wants me to be her boyfriend in front of other people, then we need to actually be dating. And if that's not what she wants, then she needs to stop telling people we're a couple, because all that does is get my hopes up, only to be crushed later by her saying we're just friends.

"Silas, I don't want to have this conversation right now."

"Then when do you want to have it?" I keep my eyes on her, my face serious so she knows I'm not kidding around.

"I don't know." She faces forward. "I don't know why we even *need* to have it. Everything is going so well between us. Why ruin it by adding labels?"

"Willow, you're the one who keeps labeling me as your boyfriend, but only when you're using it to keep girls away from me. You, yourself, admitted that wasn't fair. You can't say you don't want to date me and then get mad when other girls show interest in me."

"So you want to date other people," she says quietly, glancing down.

"No." I reach over and hold her hand. "I only want to date you. But you won't let me."

"Silas, we spend all our time together. If you want to call that dating, then go ahead."

"I need *you* to call it that. I need to know this is more than just two friends hooking up."

She doesn't respond.

"Willow." I rub her hand and wait until she looks at me. "I love you. And I've made it clear that I want us to get back together."

She nods, and her gaze lowers.

I tilt her chin up, forcing her eyes back to mine. "I know you never thought I'd be back in your life so I realize you need time to think about this. But I can't wait all summer. And as you're thinking about what it is you want, I don't want you telling other people we're dating and then telling me we're not."

She swallows and shuts her eyes, then opens them again. "I can't commit to you, Silas. I just can't. Not right now." She pulls her hand from mine. "If you decide to date other people, I understand."

"That's not what I—"

"So does this mean we're back to just being friends?" She folds her arms over her chest, closing me off, trying to pretend this doesn't bother her when I know it does. I can see the sadness on her face.

"Willow, I'm not the one deciding this. You know I want a relationship with you. I want to be more than friends."

"We *are* more than friends. What we're planning to do later tonight proves that we're more than friends."

"It makes us friends who have sex. That's not a relationship."

"Then I guess we should just be friends and nothing else. Nothing physical. No more kissing. Flirting. Hand-holding." Her voice cracks.

I sigh, beyond frustrated with her. She's so stubborn. So black and white. Hot and cold. I know she wants this. She wants us back together as much as I do, but she won't let it happen. She won't even try. I don't understand it. I'm not asking her to marry me. Just date me. That's it.

But she won't do it. Maybe Trent is right. Maybe a future with Willow just isn't possible.

CHAPTER SEVENTEEN

WILLOW

Someone knocks on my window. I turn and see Trent's big head, smiling at me like he's already had a few drinks.

"You guys coming in or you gonna sit out here all night?" he asks through the glass.

I open my door. "We're coming."

He helps me out of the truck, his eyes sweeping over my body. "Holy shit, Willow, you look hot. You wanna be my date tonight?"

"Trent," Silas says in a warning tone as he meets up with us on the sidewalk.

"Yeah, I forgot," he says, walking beside me as we head to the house. "You have a boyfriend. What's his name again?"

"Shut up, Trent," Silas says, glaring at him.

I keep quiet. After that conversation we just had, I'm not addressing any questions about Silas and me. If people ask about us at the party, I'll change the subject. And I'll keep my distance from him. I'll have to control my natural inclination to hold his hand, kiss him, flirt with him. Those are all things a girlfriend would do and I made it clear just now that I am not his girlfriend. He gave me a chance to tell him how I felt about him, and about us, and I didn't. I just sat there and said nothing.

Now tonight, I'll have to watch as other girls go up and talk to him and flirt with him. I'll have to be okay with that, even though I'm not.

170

"Willow, I put you in charge of drinks," Trent says as we go in the house. He leads us to the kitchen, which is filled with grocery sacks.

"Good thing we came," Silas says. "Nothing's ready."

"I know." Trent hands him some sacks. "Start unloading. I don't know where the bowls are so you can just set the chips out in the bag."

"You can't do that," I say, taking the bags from Silas. "This is a party. It has to look nice. Do you have a table set up for the food?"

"Yeah." Trent nods toward the patio. "It's out by the pool."

"Do you have a tablecloth?"

Trent and Silas both laugh, then Trent says, "My mom would love you."

"Why? I don't get it."

"Never mind. Here." He hands me a plastic bag and inside it are two plastic tablecloths; a red one and a navy one.

"These are exactly what we need." I take them outside and put them on the two long tables that are set up by the pool. When I come back inside, I start searching for bowls. Silas and Trent are standing there watching me.

"Aren't you guys going to do something?"

"You seem to have this figured out," Trent says. "We don't want to get in the way."

I grab a stack of plastic serving bowls from under the counter. "You're just saying that so you don't have to help."

"Just tell us what to do and we'll get it done," Silas says.

I scan the kitchen, quickly figuring out what to do first. "Okay, you guys gather all the paper products and bring them outside. Then get the coolers set up. People will want drinks when they arrive. Then they'll want snack foods so those will go out next."

The guys get to work while I fill the bowls with chips. This is a good distraction. I need to be kept busy right now so I'm not thinking about Silas and what he said in the truck. Because when I think about it, it hurts. It hurts to not be able to tell him what he wants to hear. It hurts to want to be with him, but know that I can't. It hurts to think of him meeting someone else tonight, or sometime in the future. Because Silas is mine. I know I can't claim him like that, but my heart already has. He's my first love, and even if we're not together, a part of me will always love him.

"Hey." Silas walks back into the kitchen. "We got the paper stuff set up. Trent's out in the garage, filling the coolers with ice. What do you need me to do?" He smiles, which doesn't make sense. He should be mad at me for not saying something during that conversation. He was open and honest and I just shut down.

I'm holding a stack of plastic cups, but I set them down and hug him, squeezing him really tight.

He hugs me back. "Willow? Are you okay?"

"Yeah." I step back. "Sorry. I'm not sure why I did that."

He laughs a little. "It's okay."

"I guess I just wanted to give you one last hug since I know I shouldn't be touching you at the party."

"Willow, of course you can touch me. What are you talking about?"

"You were right, Silas. I can't keep pretending you're my boyfriend. It's not fair to you."

"Then don't pretend." He circles his arms around my waist and pulls me toward him. "Let's just do this. Let's get back together."

"It won't work."

"Tell me why."

I don't know how to answer him, so I don't. I just look into his eyes as if they have the answers. Then, without thinking, I reach up to kiss him, but stop when I hear Trent behind me.

"You guys see a bottle opener in here?" He walks past us, acting like he didn't catch us about to kiss. "I used it the other day and now I can't find it."

I step away from Silas. "I'll find it and bring it out."

"Silas, I need some help getting the pool cover off."

172

"Yeah, okay." He follows Trent outside.

I look out the window and see Trent talking with his hands in the air like he's yelling at Silas. He's probably angry I'm here. He's acting nice to me, but I know he doesn't want Silas getting involved with me again.

We get everything set up and an hour later people start arriving. At first it's just a few guys from my high school, mostly football players who were in Trent's class. They all brought girls with them; hot girls with big breasts and long legs, wearing short little dresses to cover up their bikinis, which they show off when they get to the pool. I notice Silas checking them out. He's a guy. Of course he's going to look. Even *I'm* looking because these girls have great bodies, and they're tall so I'm jealous of their height.

People continue to arrive over the next hour, so many that the back yard is getting crowded and the pool is filling up. I see some more people from my high school but none who were in my class. Since being home, I haven't even tried calling any of my high school friends. I've been too busy hanging out with Silas.

Speaking of Silas, he's looking extremely hot tonight with his new haircut, deep tan, and a layer of stubble across his face. He's wearing a black t-shirt and jeans and a thick black leather band around his wrist. The leather band is one he made himself. He used to make ones just like it to sell at his mom's jewelry booth. They'd always sell out within an hour. Girls bought them for their boyfriends or guys bought them because they knew girls liked them.

Silas is standing by the pool, talking to people, a bottle of soda in his hand. He won't drink alcohol tonight, knowing he'll be driving later. I, on the other hand, could use a drink. I've been in the kitchen the past hour, bringing burgers and steaks out to Trent, who's been manning the grill. But he appears to be done grilling because he's now downing a beer with a blonde on each arm.

I grab a cup and fill it with the rest of the margarita from the blender. Leah, one of Trent's friends, keeps coming in and making them. She's made all different flavors but this one is strawberry. I take a big gulp. It's really good. And strong.

"Do you like it?" Leah comes bouncing in. She's one of those people who bounces instead of walks. She's high energy and moves really fast. She's about five feet tall with long, silky black hair. She's really tan, which looks good with her orange bikini.

"I love it. It's probably the best margarita I've ever had. I hope you don't mind that I took some."

"Not at all." She goes around me to the blender. "I'll make some more. Do you want strawberry again?"

"Yeah, that sounds good." I lift my cup. "What do you put in these? They taste better than the typical margarita."

"I add a few mint leaves. It adds a fresh flavor and cuts the sugar so it's not so sweet." She opens the fridge and grabs a sprig of mint. "I'm a bartender in San Francisco. Margaritas are my specialty."

"Do you go to school there? In San Francisco?"

"No. I just bartend." She tosses some strawberries in the blender and adds the mint. "I like the job and I make a lot of money. It's an upscale bar. A lot of business people go there to unwind after a stressful day." She pours a generous amount of tequila over the berries. "We have the same people show up there almost every night."

Will that be me someday? Going to the bar every night because I'm so stressed from work?

"How do you know Trent?" I ask.

"I met him at a party." She drops a handful of ice cubes in the blender. "Just a minute." She whirs the blender until the mixture is smooth, then opens the lid and dips her finger in.

"Hey, Willow, did you—" Trent stops mid-sentence, his eyes on Leah. I turn and see her licking the margarita off her finger, oblivious to Trent.

"Did you need something?" I ask him.

He didn't hear me, his attention completely focused on Leah, who finally notices him and says, "What do you need?"

He snaps out of his trance. "I, uh..." He glances to the side. "I can't remember." He shakes his head. "Never mind."

"You want one of your beers?" Leah asks. She brought him a six pack of a locally-made beer that he likes.

"Sure." He walks toward her, and as she turns to open the fridge I see his eyes drop to her ass. She has a round ass that fills out her orange bikini.

"See something you like there, big boy?" Leah laughs at him as she hands him his beer.

"What?" His eyes rise to her face and for the first time ever, Trent seems flustered.

"It's okay." She walks around him and back to the blender. "Go ahead and stare. I do look damn hot today." She winks at me like she's kidding but she *does* look hot. So hot that Trent can't keep his eyes off her. And he's definitely flustered. He's usually so bold and confident that it's the girl who ends up flustered. But Leah is completely calm, smiling like she's enjoying the effect she has on him.

Trent walks up behind her. "You, um, coming back outside?"

"In a minute." She adds a couple more strawberries to the blender. "Why do you ask?"

"I just—"

She interrupts him with the whir of the blender, and when it stops she turns around as if waiting for him to finish what he was saying. But now he's too distracted by her breasts, which I think might be fake because they're huge for someone her size.

"They look good, don't they?" She smiles up at him. "Sweet. Juicy. Makes you want take a bite out of one."

His eyes are now on hers and I notice his Adam's apple move as he swallows.

Leah reaches behind her and picks up a strawberry. "Here. Have one." She holds it at his lips and he parts them, letting her put the strawberry in his mouth. I feel like I'm watching a porn movie, except it's comical because Leah is totally playing him. And Trent is taking the bait.

She leaves the strawberry in his mouth and returns to the blender, lifting the lid off. "I think it's done."

Trent's left standing behind her, chewing the strawberry, stem and all.

"So Trent, did you remember what you came in here for?" I ask, smiling.

He glances at me. "Um, no."

"Then you should probably get back to the party," I say.

Leah ignores him as he walks back outside. I think Trent has finally met his match. And she's not even blond.

"Have you guys ever gone out?" I ask Leah once Trent's outside.

She laughs. "No."

"Why is that funny? You don't like him?"

"I like him. I'm just not looking for a relationship."

"Trent's not either."

She shrugs. "Then maybe we'll hook up sometime. He *is* cute. And he's tall. I like tall guys."

Trent's only six feet but Leah's a foot shorter than him so he must seem like a giant to her.

"So how do you know Trent?" she asks.

"We went to the same high school and he's friends with my boy—I mean, my friend, Silas."

She smiles, noticing my slip-up. "You're no longer with him?"

"No," I say, feeling sad just saying it.

"Is he here?"

"Yeah."

"That's tough, especially when you still love him."

Is it that obvious I love him? So obvious that even a total stranger notices?

"Ready for a refill?" She's holding the pitcher and reaching for my glass. I hand it to her and she fills it up, then gives it back to me. "Did he cheat on you? Is that why you broke up?"

"No. I'm the one who broke up with him." I take a drink and notice this batch is even stronger than the last one.

She pours a glass for herself. "If you love him, why'd you break up with him?" She hops up on the counter, her legs dangling as she swirls her finger in her drink.

"Because I just didn't see a future with us. Silas and I want different things in life."

"He doesn't want to get married? Have kids? I had a girlfriend who dumped her boyfriend because he didn't want that. It was too much commitment for him."

"It's not that. Silas wants all that."

"And you don't?"

"I do. But I also want a good career. I want to run a large company someday, which means I'll have to work a lot of hours and travel a lot. I probably won't even have time for a family."

"No offense but that sounds horrible. Spending the rest of your life in an office? Or on a plane?" She licks the margarita off her finger. "I mean, it's good there's people who want to do that. It's just not for me. That would suck the energy right out of me. I like working at a bar because it's such a high energy environment. I love it. It doesn't even seem like a job."

"Do you think you'll want to do that forever?"

She shrugs. "Who knows? I'm not one of those people who plans out my future. I believe in doing what feels right in the moment. If someday I'm not happy at my job, I'll quit and find another."

She's just like Silas. This is the type of girl he should be with. The fun, laid-back, live-in-the-moment type of girl. She probably doesn't even organize her closet or her sock and underwear drawers. I organize everything, to the point it probably drove Silas crazy when we were dating, although he never said it did.

"You want some more?" She holds the pitcher over my half-empty glass.

"No thanks."

She turns to face the patio, still seated on the counter. "So which one is he?"

I search for him but can't see him with all the people in the way. "I can't find him. He was standing by the pool but he must've moved. He has dark hair, tall, muscular, wearing a black t-shirt and jeans."

She whips back to me. "Holy shit, that was your boyfriend? I saw that guy earlier and almost begged him to go out with me, but he was talking to some other girl."

"He was?"

"I can't believe you broke up with that guy. He is HOT."

"And sweet. Thoughtful. An amazing kisser." I go to take a drink but she grabs my cup. "What are you doing?"

She sets my cup down and hops off the counter. "Get out there."

"Why?"

"Go get your man before someone else does."

"He's not my man. Silas and I broke up."

She rolls her eyes. "You're one of those girls who can't see what's right in front of her, which is why you need someone like me talking some sense into you."

"You don't understand. It's complicated."

She stands right in front of me, a little too close, but I think she's drunk. "Does he love you?"

"Yes."

"And you love him?"

"Yes."

"Then it's not complicated." She faces me toward the patio. "Go tell him you want him back."

"I can't." I turn back toward the kitchen.

She sighs and hands me my drink back. "Then I guess you'll just be sitting in here all night, drinking your sorrows away." She fills up my glass. "If you want more, come and get me." She walks to the patio door. "Looks like Silas already found someone."

She leaves and I race to the patio door and see Silas with a girl. She's average height, has dark hair that's shorter than mine, and a curvy figure. She's wearing a white, barely-there bikini and standing really close to Silas.

I almost bolt out the door to get her away from him, but then remember that I promised I wouldn't do that. Dammit, this is really hard. I turn away from the door and down my margarita. I should probably ease up on the drinks. It doesn't take much to get me drunk and I've been so busy helping with the party I haven't eaten anything.

A few minutes later, Silas walks in from the patio. "Why aren't you outside?"

"I was helping keep the food table filled." I open the fridge. "I should probably put more meat on the grill."

He comes over and closes the fridge. "You're done in here. You've helped out enough. It's time to have fun. Come on. Let's go outside."

"I'm okay in here. It's kind of hot out."

"Then take off your dress."

He says it casually, and I'm looking at him like he's lost his mind.

"Just wear your suit." He points to the bikini strings around my neck.

"Oh, yeah. I forgot I was wearing this." I feel my face heating up.

He smiles. "You just thought I was asking you to strip?"

I go around him. "I need to eat something. Did you eat yet?"

"No. I was waiting for you. I thought you were outside but I couldn't find you."

We make our way to the food table. People are drinking more than they're eating so there's a lot of food left. We each take a burger and some chips and grab a soda. I'm feeling the alcohol now and it's making me lightheaded.

"Willow, over here." Silas is sitting down on one of the lounge chairs by the pool. All the other chairs are taken so we have to share. I sit on the opposite side and hear Silas behind me, "You don't want to sit next to me?"

"I don't want people getting the wrong idea."

He sets his plate down and leans over to me, lowering his voice. "Stop worrying about other people. What I said earlier didn't have anything to do with other people. It was about us. And I don't want it ruining our night. I'm sorry I even said it. It was the wrong time to bring it up. Now can we go back to acting normal?"

I don't know what 'normal' is anymore. Our 'normal' just hours ago was friends who kiss and flirt and make plans to have sex later. But now, I don't know what we are, and that's my fault because I won't give him an answer.

Silas picks up his plate and starts eating. "Willow," he says under his breath.

"What?"

"Get your ass over here."

I laugh at the way he says it, all annoyed with me.

"Hold this." I hand him my plate and swing my legs over the lounge chair so that we're sitting on the same side. "The chair's going to tip over with all our weight on this side."

"Stop complaining." He hands me my plate.

"I wasn't complaining." I laugh and I can't stop.

Silas takes my plate back before I drop it. "Are you drunk?"

"I might have had a teeny tiny sip of a margarita."

"And by 'teeny tiny sip' you mean one big cup?"

"Maybe two?" I take the burger from the plate he's holding and bite into it. "Mmm, that's really good."

He gives me the plate again. "Eat some more of it. You need to sober up."

"Why? I'm more fun when I'm drunk." I stuff a few chips in my mouth.

"You're always fun. When you're drunk you get flirty and that's not a good thing when you're surrounded by drunk guys looking for action."

"I'm not drunk." I take a bite of my burger and ketchup drips out.

He laughs. "You're a mess." He puts his thumb on the side of my mouth, wiping away the ketchup. I swipe my tongue over his thumb, licking it off. He holds his thumb there and our eyes meet and I lick his thumb again, slower this time. And suddenly, it's just him and me sharing a moment. A steamy hot, I-want-to-rip-off-your-clothes-and-do-you-right-here moment.

Someone jumps in the pool and splashes us. Silas and I both move back and the moment is gone.

We go back to eating our food. His phone dings and he checks it, then looks up and waves at someone. I glance over to see who it is and find it's the girl he was talking to earlier. The one in the white bikini.

"Who's that?" I ask before I can stop myself.

"Anya," he says, picking up his soda and taking a drink.

"Like the singer?"

"No, that's Enya. This is Anya."

"That's an odd name."

He smiles. "Willow? Silas? She could say the same thing about us."

"Our names aren't that odd. Anya is odd."

"I like it. I've always liked it."

Always? So he's heard that name before?

"Did she text you just now?" I ask.

"Yeah. We're meeting for coffee on Monday."

"In the morning?"

"No. We're going at night."

"Oh." This is really hard. I need to act happy for him. Be a friend. He found a pretty girl to date and I'm sure she's very nice. So why do I hate her? I force out a smile. "Well, that's a good first date. Coffee. Gives you time to get to know each other."

"It's not a first date." He sets his plate aside and wipes his hands on his napkin. "I dated Anya back in high school before you and I were going out."

181

Freshman year, when I switched to public school, I assumed Silas and I would grow apart, and we did. We dated other people, but agreed not to talk about it. Then right before my sophomore year, we finally admitted how we felt about each other, and soon after that, we started dating. Silas was a junior at the time and I knew he'd been out with girls and likely slept with at least one of them, but I never asked him about it.

Silas stands up. "I'll throw your plate out if you're done."

"Thanks." I hand it to him.

So Silas is dating Anya. I feel sick. I thought I could handle seeing Silas with someone else, but I can't. It hurts way too much. I don't want the person I love dating someone else.

"Do you want to get dessert?" he asks.

"No. I need to go inside for a minute."

Forget dessert. I need to finish my margarita.

CHAPTER EIGHTEEN

SILAS

Now I'm regretting having that conversation with Willow back in my truck. We needed to have it, but I should've done it later, not right before the party. She's been acting strange ever since, hiding away in the kitchen like she's afraid to be seen with me.

I was just trying to get her to be honest with herself and admit her feelings for me instead of pretending they don't exist, but instead she took my comments to mean that I want to date other people. That's not at all what I meant, but when I told her that, she didn't believe me. She acted hurt that I even brought it up. But I couldn't keep having her pretend I'm her boyfriend only when it's convenient for her. I need her to commit to it. Otherwise, she'll never take our relationship seriously and I won't even have a chance of getting her back.

When Willow said she doesn't like labels, it's not because she thinks they're meaningless. It's just the opposite. To her, labels are a commitment. If she calls me her boyfriend, she'll be more committed to our relationship than if she just calls me her friend. In fact, I'm the only guy she's ever called her boyfriend. Willow's dated other guys, but according to her friends, she's never given any of those guys the 'boyfriend' label.

Five minutes have passed and Willow still hasn't returned to the patio. I go in the kitchen and find her standing by the counter, downing a margarita. Willow gets drunk on a few beers. She said she's already had two margaritas so she shouldn't be drinking any more.

"Willow, why don't you slow down there?" I take the cup from her. "Is this your third one?"

"I'm not sure." She leans against the counter. "I've lost count." She reaches over to the blender, picking up the empty pitcher. "Could you go find Leah? She'll make us some more."

I take the pitcher from her. "I think you're done. Why don't you have some water?"

She grabs the front of my shirt and stumbles forward, falling on me. "Would you go find Leah? Please?"

"Willow, you're drunk. You need to lay off the margaritas."

"Leah's the one with short dark hair and the orange bikini. She's really nice and she wants to go out with you." Willow lays her head on my chest. "Are you gonna go out with her?"

"No, I'm not going out with her. I don't even know her. Let's go home. You need to sleep this off."

She pushes away from me. "Not yet. We haven't even gone swimming." She slips the straps off her dress.

"Willow, what are you doing?"

"Going swimming." She shimmies out of her dress.

"We're not going—" I stop when I see her in her bikini. Where the hell did she get that body? She's always had a good body, but two years ago she didn't look like this.

When we had sex in my truck that night, it was so dark I couldn't see her. I had my hands all over her body and I could tell she'd filled out in certain places, mainly her breasts, but seeing her now...holy shit, she's hot.

"Aren't you going to change?" she asks.

"No. Because we're not going swimming. We're going home." I don't want any other guy seeing her like this. Her breasts are spilling out of her bikini top and the bottoms barely cover her ass. And then she has that navel ring.

I feel a twitch in my jeans as blood rushes to my crotch.

"I'm going swimming." She turns and walks off.

"No. Willow!" I race up behind her and pick her up, turning her the other direction. "We're going home." I set her down.

"But I want to swim. I'm hot."

"Yeah, you're definitely hot," I mumble, picking her dress up off the floor. "Put this on."

She's rising up and down on her toes. She's at the hyper phase of her drunkenness. She always starts out hyper then gets really relaxed and eventually falls asleep. I've only seen her drunk a few times, but it followed this same pattern each time.

"See ya later!" She runs off before I can catch her.

I follow her outside and see all the guys' heads turn to check her out. Even some of the girls are checking her out.

"Willow." One of Trent's football buddies goes up to her, eyeing her breasts. "You look hot."

"Back off," I say, standing behind her.

He looks at me. "You two are together?"

"They're not together," Trent says, standing next to the guy.

I glare at Trent. "Willow and I are going home."

"You go," Willow says to me. "I'm gonna stay here a little longer."

"Willow." I lean down and lower my voice. "You're drunk. You need to go home."

"I'll make sure she gets home," Trent's football friend says, a grin on his face that says he plans to have sex with her.

"Yeah. Not gonna happen." I put my arm around her waist and pull her in front of me in a protective hold.

"If you're not dating her, maybe you should keep your hands off her," the guy says, glancing at Willow's chest again.

"Trent," I say, urging him to get his friend under control.

"Brian." Trent nudges his friend. "Let's go get a beer."

He ignores Trent and says to Willow, "You want to hang out tonight?" He smiles at her. "Like we used to?"

Used to? Did she go out with this guy back in high school? Did she sleep with him? I don't even want to know.

"No, thanks." She pulls her hair up in a ponytail, then lets it fall back around her shoulders.

"Come on," he says. "You don't want to be with this guy, do you?"

"This is Silas." She tilts her head back and smiles at me. A drunk, lazy smile. "I love Silas."

My heart jerks hearing her say it. I wish she meant it but I know she's only saying it because she's drunk.

"Besides," she says, focusing back on Brian as she rests her body against mine. "You have a small dick and you were done in a minute."

I almost burst out laughing, but I don't because she just confirmed they had sex, which makes me want to kill him.

"What the fuck?" Brian backs away. "You're a bitch!"

She laughs. "And you have a small dick."

"Willow, let's go," I say by her ear.

"Bitch," Brian says, walking away.

She turns around and looks up at me, that drunk smile still on her face. "I love you, Silas."

"Yeah, okay. Let's get out of here." I take her hand and start walking.

"But we didn't go swimming."

"We'll swim some other time." I lead her into the house and grab her dress. "Put this on."

"Just leave it. I don't want it on." She holds onto my shirt. I think she's getting even drunker. She's having a hard time standing up.

I grab a water from the fridge and take the cap off. "Drink this."

She takes a sip, then gives it back to me.

"Willow, just take it. You can drink it on the way home."

Instead of taking it, she wraps her arm around my waist and leans her head on my shoulder. "Silas?"

"Yeah." I glance down and see her eyes are closed.

"I miss you."

"I'm right here."

"I miss you when you're not here. I've missed you for two years."

I stand there a moment, wondering if that's the liquor talking or if it's really her. But I don't know why she'd make that up, so maybe it's what she's really thinking. Maybe she *has* missed me. God knows I've missed her.

I kiss her head. "I missed you too."

Her chin drops forward on her chest like she's going to fall asleep. I get a better hold on her and walk her outside to the truck. I lift her up into the seat and buckle her in.

As I close her door, my phone dings. It's Trent, texting me.

Did you leave?

I'm in the truck. Heading out.

With Willow?

Yeah.

Drop her off and come back.

She's drunk. I'm staying with her.

Let her parents deal with her.

They're not home.

Let her go, Silas. She's not worth it.

Fuck off.

I'm pissed at him. I'm sick of him getting on my case about Willow. He thinks he's being a friend, keeping me from getting hurt, but I don't need him to protect me. I'm fully aware that Willow could break my heart, but I'm willing to risk it. This summer is my last chance to get her back and I'm not going to pass that up. And if doesn't work out, then it's over. I won't try again.

We arrive at Willow's house and I help her inside. I have to keep holding her up, which means my hands are all over her nearly naked body. I'm going to need an ice cold shower after this. I've been having a lot of those since she got back to town.

"Silas, don't go," she says as I lay her down on her bed.

"I'll just be in the living room, watching TV."

"I want you right here." She pats the spot next to her.

Is she testing my self control? If so, I feel like I'm about to fail.

I lie next to her on my back.

"You can't have your jeans on," she says. "I want to get under the covers."

I sigh and take off my shoes, then my jeans.

"And your shirt."

"Willow."

"Please?"

I sigh again and yank my shirt off, leaving me in just my boxers. She pulls back the covers and we get into bed.

She slings her arm and leg over me and puts her face in the crook of my neck. She smells like strawberries from the margarita, with hints of lavender from the soap she used. The soap reminds me of the shower we'd planned to take, but I force that thought out of my head because I can't have any more blood flowing down there. It's already throbbing.

"Silas?" Willow lifts her head up and I get caught up in how beautiful she is. That long dark hair, those deep brown eyes, those perfectly shaped lips. "I meant what I said." She looks me in the eye. "I love you. I always have and I've never stopped."

"Why don't we talk later?"

She nods, then puts her head on my shoulder. "I missed you when you were away. I told myself I didn't love you so I wouldn't miss you so much. But I still did. I missed you. And I never stopped loving you, no matter how hard I tried."

I hear her sniffling. I reach down and brush my fingers over her cheek and feel the wetness from her tears. I wish this wasn't just drunk rambling. I wish she really meant what she said.

A few minutes later, she falls asleep and I do too. When I wake up, the room is still dark, except for the moonlight filtering through the thin drapes covering the windows.

Willow is no longer laying on me, but I feel her beside me, sitting up in bed.

"What are you doing?" I sit up next to her.

"Drinking some water." She's holding the bottle I gave her earlier. I'd left it on the nightstand in case she needed it.

"Do you feel okay?"

"Yeah. I just needed to sleep it off."

"Do you want me to get you anything?"

"No. I'm good." She seems fully alert now, no longer sleepy or drunk.

I check my phone and see that it's two in the morning. We left the party so early that we probably went to bed around nine. I'm not sure because I didn't check the time.

"Here." Willow hands me the empty water bottle and I set it on the nightstand.

She lies down on the bed.

"Do you want me to go?" I ask.

"No." She tugs on my hand. "Come here. I want to talk to you."

I lie down, facing her. "What do you want to talk about?"

"I need your advice and I need you to be honest with me. Can you do that?"

"Yeah. Go ahead."

She lets out a heavy sigh. "There's this guy...a guy I really like."

She's telling me about some other guy? I don't want to hear this, but I let her continue.

"Actually, I don't just like him. I love him."

So she doesn't love me. Her earlier confession was just drunk rambling. She loves some other guy. Probably some guy she met at college.

"What about him?" I ask, trying to hide my annoyance.

"The thing is...I had my future decided. Everything was all laid out in an orderly plan. I even typed up all the steps and attached them to a timeline and printed it out. I can show it to you later. Anyway, I never included marriage in my plan because the guy I would want to marry wouldn't be happy in this plan. And I want more than anything for him to be happy, so I had to let him go. But now he's back and I don't know what to do."

Wait—she's talking about me! Not some other guy.

"Willow, what are you saying?"

189

"I'm asking you what to do. I love this guy so much that it hurts to be away from him for even a day, so how do I go day after day for the rest of my life without him?"

"You don't." I hold her hand. "You let him back into your life and you never let him go."

"But I want him to be happy. I want us both to."

"Then you talk about it and find a solution that works for both of you."

"What if we can't?"

"If you want something bad enough, you'll find a way to make it happen."

"It's not that simple."

"It IS that simple, once you decide what you really want and what's important to you. Is this guy really that important to you?"

She nods. "Yes. When I made that plan for my future, there was always something missing. I knew it was him. I just didn't want to admit it because I didn't think I could have him. I thought I'd lost him."

"You haven't lost him." I lean in and kiss her. "He's right here."

She hugs me. "I love you, Silas. I love you so much."

I hug her back, squeezing her tight. "I love you too."

Is this really happening? Or am I dreaming this? It's the middle of the night so it could be a dream, but it feels real. Did she really just say all that? The words I've been waiting to hear for two years?

"I want us to get back together," she says.

"I do too."

"And you won't date anyone else?"

I pull back. "Is that why you're doing this? Just so I won't go out with someone else?"

"No. I want us to get back together because I love you and miss you. And because I want to be able to hold your hand and kiss you and call you my boyfriend. Seeing you do those things with someone else hurts too much."

"I don't want to do those things with anyone else. Just you."

"But you have a date on Monday."

"It's not a date. It's a business meeting. I'm meeting with Anya to talk about having her design a new website for my mom's jewelry. My mom's been looking for a web designer and Anya showed me some of the websites she's built and they were really good, so we're meeting to discuss pricing and timing and then she's going to do a prototype."

"Oh. When I saw you with her I thought—"

"Yeah, I might've let you think that but I shouldn't have. Sorry. I should've explained."

"You didn't have to. You didn't owe me an explanation. I'd made it clear we weren't dating."

"So what changed your mind?"

"That talk we had before the party. I didn't want to hear you say all that, but I needed to hear it. That's one of the things I love most about you. You're always honest with me, even when you know I don't want to hear whatever it is you're going to say."

And now I'm lying to her. I've never lied to her until this issue with the farm. I promised her parents I'd keep quiet, but I hate it. I understand that they don't want Willow to worry, but it feels wrong not to tell her what's going on.

"You were right, Silas. It wasn't fair of me to tell other girls you're my boyfriend just to keep them away from you, and then tell you we're just friends. That was just me wanting to be with you but not wanting to commit to you. I was afraid to make that decision."

"Why?"

"Because I don't want to hurt you again."

"Willow, what happened back then was nobody's fault. We were too young. You weren't ready to be engaged."

"It doesn't matter. I still hurt you by pushing you away and not talking to you for two years. I panicked and did everything wrong."

"It's history. It doesn't matter now."

"But it *does* matter. Because we still have the problem of you and me wanting different things in life."

"Stop worrying so much about the future. You still have three years of college left. We have plenty of time to figure this out. The important thing is that we both agree we want to be together. Everything else we'll figure out as we go."

"I can't do that. I have a plan and I—"

I kiss her until I feel her body relax, then I smile over her lips and say, "I'm going to take that plan of yours and burn it."

"You are not! I worked on that for months."

"I'm sure you have back-ups. A few printed copies. One on your hard drive, and probably two flash drives."

"Three. In different locations, just to be safe."

I kiss her. "You're crazy."

"You're disorganized."

I kiss her again. "You're obsessive."

"You're too laid back."

"You're a pain in the ass." I kiss her, longer this time. "And yet I love you."

CHAPTER NINETEEN

WILLOW

Telling Silas how I feel is both the best and worst thing I've ever done. It's the best because I can finally stop hiding the fact that I love him and want to be with him. But it's the worst because I'm afraid of how this will end.

I'll worry about that later, because right now, Silas' lips on mine are the only thing I can think about, along with his hands, which are slowly moving over my skin. I've always loved the way he touches me. Other guys go straight to the action zones, but Silas gives special attention to all the sensitive areas that most guys forget about or completely ignore, like the area just under the ear, the inside of the wrist, the inner thigh. He takes his time, never rushing.

"Can we just do this all night?" I whisper, tilting my head back as he kisses my neck.

"All night. All day." He trails kisses along my collarbone. "Let's just stay here all summer."

I run my hands over his tight abs. "I'm so turned on right now."

"Oh, yeah?" I hear the smile in his tone.

"You may have to go faster tonight."

"Fast now? Slow later?"

"Yes. Fast now, slow later. Just hurry up."

He puts his mouth by my ear. "You're so impatient."

A shiver skitters down my spine as he breathes over my ear, his finger drawing a line down the center of my core.

"Your impatience makes this even more fun."

"Silas," I beg.

He reaches behind my neck and unties my bikini. It falls forward, exposing my breasts, which he quickly devours with his mouth, first one, then the other. He undoes the strings behind my back and tosses my top aside. Then he kisses his way down my belly to my navel ring, circling his tongue around it as his hand moves up and down my inner thigh.

I'm moaning, gripping his hair, the sheet, anything I can get my hands on. The tension coiling inside me is killing me but I refuse to beg again for relief. Instead I get even. I slide my hand down to his boxers and touch him, in the way I know he likes.

"Shit," he groans, squeezing his eyes shut.

I smile. "Want to speed things along now?"

"You win." He rips free the ties on my bikini bottom and yanks it off. His body covers mine and he sinks into me, slowly, inch by inch.

"Oh, God," I breathe out, grasping his back as sensations ignite like fireworks inside me, reaching all the way down to my toes.

His hips move at a languid pace, positioned to hit all my sensitive spots, the ones he knows will get me there every time. He kisses me, his tongue tangling with mine in a slow sensual dance that matches the rhythm of his grinding hips.

He keeps going, until finally I'm relieved of the tension as it unwinds its hold on me in wave after wave of pleasure. I hear Silas groan, his body tensing up then shuddering with its release.

That was freaking amazing. Even if I didn't love Silas, the sex alone would be enough reason to spend the rest of my life with him. I'm joking, of course, but I bet other girls would be with him just for that. I'm lucky that I get both; a guy I love who's also great in bed.

He remains over me, catching his breath.

"That was awesome." I smile.

He smiles back. "Yeah, it was."

194

"Aren't you glad we hurried up and got straight to the action?"

"Yeah." He kisses me. "But next time, I'm slowing it down. I've got to teach you how to be patient."

"I know how to speed you up."

"I'll tie your hands up so you can't."

"That sounds fun."

He watches me a moment to see if I'm kidding. I'm not. I'd try most anything with Silas. I trust him completely, more than anyone else.

"You're trouble," he says, kissing a ticklish spot on my neck.

"Stop!" I yell, laughing.

He shifts onto his back and I sit up and straddle him. He reaches up and strokes my hair, then runs the back of his hand along my cheek. "I love you."

I smile. "I love you too."

"Come here."

I lower my body over his chest, and he wraps his arms over me and kisses my head.

"Silas?"

"Yeah." He strokes my hair.

"Please don't leave again."

"Willow, you're the one who's leaving, not me."

"I'm just going to college. I'm talking about you, going overseas again. Even if this...if this doesn't work out...don't go over there again. It's too far away and it's too dangerous. I worried about you constantly when you were there."

"You did?"

"I didn't know where you were and I kept having dreams of you getting hurt and nobody ever knowing what happened and...just please don't go there again."

"I won't. I'm staying here with you."

"But what about in the fall? What are we going to do when I go back to school?"

He kisses my head again. "Let's not think about that right now. We can talk about it later."

Silas doesn't worry about the future, but I do, and uncertainty about the future is one of my greatest fears. I'm not even sure why. It's not like my parents are that way. They don't plan for anything, not even the future of their business. And it seems to work for them. The farm is doing well and they always seem to have plenty of money, even enough to send me to a very expensive college.

I push off his chest. "I'm starving. Let's get something to eat."

"Like go out? There's nothing open at two in the morning."

"Then we'll eat here."

"What are we going to eat? Kale chips and yogurt?"

I laugh. "We might have some other stuff. Let's go check." I get out of bed and grab his t-shirt and slip it on. I love wearing his t-shirts. They're really soft and they smell like him.

"I'm keeping this," I tell him as he puts his jeans on.

"You're going to start doing that again?" He says that because I used to always steal his t-shirts. "I don't have that many shirts, Willow."

"Then you'll just have to walk around shirtless." I plaster my hands against his muscular chest and smile at him. "I wouldn't mind that."

He chuckles. "I wouldn't mind if *you* walked around shirtless too."

"Nice try, but I'm keeping it on." I take his hand. "Come on. Let's find some food."

We go in the kitchen and I search the cupboards while Silas looks in the fridge.

"Soy milk, soy yogurt, tofu and some kind of unidentifiable leftover," he says, holding up a glass jar. My parents won't use plastic containers so everything goes in canning jars.

"That's it?" I ask.

"Pretty much. Did you find anything?"

I hold up a bag of kale chips. "Your favorite."

"Yeah, you can have those. What else is there?"

"Just a couple boxes of cereal, some bread, and a jar of almond butter." I shut the cupboard door. "My parents need to go shopping. It's been like this since I got back. We never have any food. With my mom's new job, she hasn't had time to go to the store. I told her I'd go, but we never have any money in the cash jar." I go over and check it. "There's still no money in here. Isn't that weird?"

"Your dad probably just forgot to fill it." Silas rushes out the words.

"Why are you talking so fast?"

"I'm not." He points to the kitchen island. "Check the drawer. Sometimes your mom puts granola bars in there."

I open the drawer but it's empty. I go over and stand in front of Silas. "You don't think my parents are having money problems, do you?"

"How would I know?" He opens the fridge again.

"I thought you just looked in there."

"I did, but maybe I missed something."

"So I guess we're not going to eat." I lean back against the counter. "Maybe you could sneak in your house and steal some junk food from your stash."

"My mom's a light sleeper. She'd hear me come in and think I'm a burglar and probably knock me in the head with a baseball bat."

"So she knows you're staying here tonight?"

"I texted her right after you feel asleep."

"Did you tell her we're back together?"

"No. Because when I texted her, I didn't know we were."

"Do you think she'll be happy?"

He places his hands on the counter on each side of me, blocking me in. "You know she will. She loves you." He smiles. "She'll probably make you another sweater."

I laugh. "Oh, God, I hope not. If she does, I'm going to tell her to make you a matching one."

"I don't wear sweaters. She knows that."

"Apparently you don't wear t-shirts either." I run my fingers down his chest.

He leans in and presses his lips to mine. "Not when my girlfriend steals them."

"I like it when you call me your girlfriend."

"You also like it when I do this." His hand slides up my inner thigh, landing between my legs.

"Silas," I whisper, my eyes shutting as I sink back against the counter.

His mouth covers mine for a slow, deep kiss. My hands go to his jeans and I undo his belt and yank at his zipper.

"I think it's time to try out that soap," he says.

I grin. "I think you're right."

He scoops me up and throws me over his shoulder, all caveman-like, and it makes me laugh. We go back in my room and straight to the shower, totally forgetting about the soap. The soap was just an excuse anyway. Not that we needed one. At this point, we'll do it anywhere, anytime. It's been two years and we're starved for each other, our bodies craving it, wanting it, desperate for it.

"Holy shit," Silas says, breathing hard after the best shower sex we've ever had.

"I know, right?" I tip my head back against the tile, trying to catch my breath.

"We're definitely doing that again."

"We can't do it when my parents are home."

"Then we need to get them out of the house because that was..." He takes a deep breath.

"Are you speechless?" I laugh.

"I guess I am." He kisses me.

"I'm still starving."

He thinks for a moment. "You know what?"

"What?"

"I think I have a stash of food in my truck. Like some candy bars and chips. I might even have some soda."

"Why is it in your truck?"

He grins. "Because there's this girl who comes to the farm and brings me lunch but I'm always still hungry so I have to bring extra food."

"Why don't you just tell this girl to stop bringing you lunch?"

"Because her bringing me lunch is the best part of my day. I look forward to it all morning."

"You do?"

"Yeah, but she doesn't have to bring me lunch. Just her stopping by would make my day. I just like seeing her."

"You're going to be seeing her a lot more because it's berry season and I heard she's the only one who will pick the berries."

"Then work just got a hell of a lot better." He shuts the water off. "Let's go."

"Where are we going?"

He hands me a towel. "We're driving out to the farm and we're going to eat candy bars and look at the stars."

"And then what?"

He kisses me. "Then we're going to set off some fireworks."

"We're not going to sleep tonight, are we?"

"Did you want to?"

"No. I had that nap earlier. I'm not even tired."

It's after three in the morning when we get to the farm. I brought some blankets because it's chilly at night. I also brought some pillows because laying your head on a truck bed isn't very comfortable. It has a liner but it still hurts your head to lie directly on it.

Silas sits down on my makeshift bed, holding two grocery sacks. "This is way better than last time."

"You didn't like last time?"

He drops the grocery sacks and lies over me. "I loved last time. I just worried about you not being comfortable."

"I wasn't at first, but then I forgot all about it." I lift his shirt up. For some reason he put it on again. I changed into shorts and the sleeveless plaid shirt he thinks makes me look like a cowgirl.

He yanks his shirt off and my hands immediately go to his chest. I love touching him, knowing he's all mine.

He kisses me, pulling my lower lip between his and gently tugging, then releasing it and slipping his tongue in my mouth. He undoes the top button of my shirt, then the next one. His lips move to my now exposed chest as he finishes undoing the last few buttons. His warm hand slides under the fabric and he grips my waist as his mouth lowers to my stomach, his tongue swirling around my navel ring, igniting a swell of sensations just below it.

I grip his hair, arching up.

"You like that?" he asks.

"Yes." I breathe out the word.

His mouth returns to mine as he unbuttons my shorts. I feel his lips smile against mine as his hand slides under my panties. "You're ready to go again."

"It's your fault."

He laughs a little. "You said you were starving. Maybe we should eat first."

"I'd rather have *you* first."

"I was hoping you'd say that." He quickly undoes his jeans while I rip off my shirt and bra. We just did this at my house and yet here we are, in a frantic rush to get naked so we can do it again.

The sex is fast. Hard and fast and...

"Oh, god, yes!" I yell as the pleasure explodes through every inch of my body. Silas is gripping my hips, pounding into me and then I hear his sexy groan as he gets his release.

His hips still and he kisses my neck, then my mouth. He breathes heavy over my lips. "I love you."

"I love you too." I kiss him, then rest my head back on the pillow, feeling lost in a blissful state of happiness. I wish I could just stay here forever. Here with Silas. Under the stars. Happy.

Why did I ever let him go? Why did I think I could live without him? I made a plan for my life, and it sounds good on paper, but truthfully, this is the life I want.

200

CHAPTER TWENTY

SILAS

If Willow and I keep this up, she's going to be sore later. But I don't think she cares. Right now, we can't get enough of each other. We're officially together again and now it's time to reunite. In the bed. The shower. My truck.

Sex with Willow is addictive. There's something about us. The way we fit together. The way we connect. The way we practically read each others' mind. It all comes together for mind-blowing sex that makes you want to do it again and again.

I want this night to go on forever. Just the two of us with nobody around. No talk of the future. No worrying about her parents and the farm.

When Willow asked me if I thought her parents were having money problems I almost told her the truth. I can't do this anymore. I can't keep this secret. It's not fair to her. If it were my parents and she knew they were in trouble and didn't tell me, I'd be pissed.

But I can't tell her. Not yet. I need to at least talk to her parents first and let them know I'm done lying to her. This has gone on long enough. They can't keep this from her all summer.

"Want some?" Willow holds up her candy bar. We're lying under the blankets on the pile of sleeping bags she laid out on the bed of the truck. I've got her wrapped in my arms, exactly where I want her, skin to skin, our warm, naked bodies intertwined.

I take a bite. "I think I got some caramel on me. Can you help me out?"

She reaches up and kisses it off. "You want some more?"

"Yeah, I'll take some more." My hands are on her hips and I lift her closer to me and kiss her, tasting her warm chocolatey mouth.

"That's not what I meant," she says, smiling. "I was going to—"

I taste her again, not letting her finish. We did it less than an hour ago but I'm ready for another round. But we should probably wait so I force myself away from her lips.

Willow looks at me. "Why'd you stop?"

"I thought you'd want a break, but if you don't then..." I kiss her again.

She pushes me back and climbs over me, straddling me. "You're probably right. We should take a break." She takes me in her hand, positioning me.

I smile at her. "This doesn't seem like a break."

"I changed my mind." She lowers herself onto me and we do it again.

And then we take a break. Willow returns to her place under my arm and we gaze up at the sky.

"I love being here," she says.

"I've always loved it here."

"It's so quiet. So dark. The stars look so much brighter out here. Remember when we'd lay in your back yard and look at the stars? You'd always make them into animals or people or scenes. I never knew what you were talking about."

"My mind naturally sees shapes and patterns and turns them into things. I get that from my mom. She's the same way."

"I love that about you. The way you're so creative and can imagine all these different things that other people can't see. I can't do that. If I don't have a clear picture of something, it doesn't make sense to me."

"Like your future."

"What?"

"Your future. If you don't have a clear picture of what it's going to be, you can't make sense of it. And you're someone who has to make sense of things. You're very logical. I'm not."

She pauses. "I never thought about it that way. I mean, relating it to how I see things, like the stars or abstract art."

"Yeah, you hate abstract art. When we went to that modern art exhibit with your parents, you couldn't get out of there fast enough."

"Because I couldn't understand how people could consider that art."

"It is. You just can't see it."

"I can see paint splattered on canvas. But what's that supposed to be? It doesn't make any sense."

"It doesn't have to. Art is whatever you make it. There's no right or wrong answer. You just look at it and let your mind explore what it could be."

"I can't do that. I look at it and it just looks like paint splatters."

"You just need to practice." I point at the sky. "What do see in the stars right above us?"

She takes a moment, then says, "I see four really bright stars and seven tiny ones."

"You're using logic again. Counting instead of seeing."

"What do you see?"

I pause, letting my mind play with the bright dots until an image is formed. I chuckle. "That's funny."

"What? What do you see?"

"Us." I point to it. "The four big stars look like the truck bed and the four smaller stars lined up look like me, because I'm taller, and the three smaller ones are you. See how close together they are?" I motion to us. "It's you and me lying next to each other in the truck."

She nudges my side. "You're crazy."

"Willow, I'm serious. Don't count them. Just look at them and think about what I said."

I wait as she gazes up at the sky. After a while, I say, "I guess you can't see it."

"No, wait. I'm actually starting to see it. And you're right. It does look like us. Except where's the rest of the truck?"

"It doesn't have to be a complete picture." I kiss her cheek. "You need to keep that logical side of yours turned off."

"That's impossible."

"At least you could see something up there. That's a start."

She flips on her side to face me. "You should be an artist."

"Why an artist?"

"Because you're creative and you can make things. Look how fast your jewelry sells out."

"I don't want to spend my life making bracelets and charms."

"But you also paint. And sculpt."

"I used to, but I don't anymore. That was just a hobby."

"Why are you studying business?"

"Because business is something you can use for a lot of different jobs."

"But you hate it."

"I don't hate it. I just don't like accounting. But it doesn't matter because I'm not planning on being an accountant."

"What are you going to be?"

"I don't know yet." I lean over and give her a kiss. "Unlike some people, I haven't planned out my whole life. I'm only 20. I have no idea what I'll be doing years from now."

"And that doesn't bother you?"

"Not at all. It would bother me to have a plan."

"But a plan gives you direction. If you don't have direction, you're just floundering, wondering what to do next."

"I'm not floundering. I'm finding myself. Discovering what I like and what I don't like. If you're locked into a plan, you'll never give herself the option to find out what you really want in life. You're trapped, going down a road that may not be right for you. And if you veer off the plan, you risk feeling like a failure."

I'm saying all this for Willow's benefit because I know this path she's headed down isn't right for her, and from some of the things she's said, I think she's starting to realize that. She just refuses to accept it. Once she sets her mind on something, she's so determined to see it through to completion that she has a hard time stepping back and figuring out if she really wants to keep doing it.

Willow's quiet, lost in her thoughts, so I leave her alone and gaze up at the sky. Now the stars look like a house with people around it. The four big stars form the house and the smaller stars look like a family; parents and a couple kids. I wonder why I'm seeing that. Is it because I'm thinking about marrying Willow? Having kids with her? I've never even thought about kids. That's so far into the future that my mind doesn't even go there. I close my eyes and open them and see the truck again, with Willow and me inside it.

"I still think you should be an artist," she says, flipping on her back to look up at the sky. "Maybe a graphic designer."

"Huh. That's not a bad idea, actually. Maybe I'll forget business and go into graphic design."

"Really? I changed your mind just like that?"

"Maybe. I'm definitely going to look into it." I look at her. "You see what happens when you're not stuck following a plan? You can change your mind whenever you want. Try different things. If you don't like something, you can do something else."

"I wish I could do that."

"You *can* do that. You can do whatever you want."

She turns on her side and snuggles up against me. "I need a quick nap."

"We've barely slept. We should take more than a quick nap."

"Goodnight." She kisses me, then lays her head on my chest and we fall asleep.

I wake up to drops of rain falling on my face. I open my eyes and see dark clouds above us.

"Willow, get up." I kiss her head, which is in the crook of my arm.

She rubs her eyes. "Silas, you're spitting when you talk."

"I'm not spitting. It's raindrops. We need to get in the truck. It's going to start pouring any minute."

She looks up. "Those clouds are really dark."

"Yeah, let's go." I kick the blankets off us.

"Wait." She grabs my arm.

"What?"

"Let's do it."

"Do what?"

"Let's have sex."

"In the rain?"

She smiles really wide. "I've always wanted to do it in the rain. Is that crazy?"

"Who the hell cares? Crazy is good."

The rain's getting heavier but it's a warm, steady rain.

Willow sits up on her knees and stretches her arms out, letting the rain wash over her bare skin. I can't take my eyes off her. This might be the sexiest thing I've ever seen. Water droplets trickle down her breasts, her head tipped back toward the sky, her lips soaking wet.

I grip her wet hair, pull her toward me, and smash my mouth against hers. She shoves the blankets aside and lowers herself onto my lap, grinding into me. The rain is pelting us, soaking us, and it's sexy as hell. Willow's arms loop around my neck and I feel her hips rise slightly, then lower again as she sinks down on me.

My arms are wrapped around her as she moves, her hips gyrating. I never thought of doing it in the rain but this was an awesome idea. And I love that Willow suggested it. It shows she can be spontaneous and free-willed and go with whatever life gives her, in this case a total downpour. If she could just let that part of her come out more often, I think there would be a real chance for us.

Willow is gasping for breath, her thighs pressed against my sides, riding me, fast and furious, until she's yelling my name, grasping my shoulders, her body trembling as she comes. She collapses onto my chest, completely out of breath. I flip her over and finish myself off with a few final thrusts. I remain over her, protecting her from the rain but it's no use. We're both completely soaked.

Willow starts laughing.

"What's so funny?" I ask, kissing her forehead.

"Nothing. I'm just happy. That was best thing I've ever done, but I can't believe I did it."

"Why not?"

"Because it's crazy."

"You need to be more crazy. Crazy is so much better than not-crazy."

She laughs again. "Maybe you're right. Maybe I need to be more crazy."

"If you hang out with me, I'm sure that'll happen. I seem to have that affect on you. First the navel ring and now sex in the rain."

"The navel ring was because I was jealous of your hairdresser and her erotic shampooing."

"Willow, there was nothing erotic about her doing my hair."

"She had her breasts in your face the entire time."

"And yet the only breasts I was thinking about were yours. So is that really why you got the navel ring? Because you were jealous?"

"No. I've actually always wanted one. Your hairdresser just prompted me to do it. So yeah, it's all your fault. You make me do crazy things." She leans up and kisses me, then shivers as a gust of wind blows.

"Let's get in the truck. I have a beach towel in there. You can dry off."

"What am I going to wear?" She looks at our pile of wet clothes.

"Either wet clothes or the towel. Your choice."

"I'll take the towel."

"The truck's open so go ahead. Do you need help getting down?"

"Nope. I got it." She hops over the side of the truck. Just a few weeks ago she couldn't even step up into the front seat.

I put my soggy jeans on and slip on my shoes and meet her in the truck.

"Look at us." She's still laughing. I love seeing her laugh. And seeing her happy.

"You look a lot better than I do." I start the truck and turn the heater on.

"I think you're sexy all wet like that." She bites her lip.

"Seriously, Willow? We've done it like ten times."

She forces her smile into a straight face. "You're right. We need to stop."

I lean across the seat and kiss her. "I'm kidding. You know I'd do it again but I need to get you home. I don't want you getting sick."

"You can't get sick from rain, can you? I thought that was a myth."

"I don't know, but I'm not taking any chances. And I need to feed you. We'll dry off and then I'll take you for breakfast. What time is it?"

She checks her phone. "Ten-thirty."

"Really? It's so dark out I thought it was earlier than that."

"I hope my parents aren't home."

"What time were they supposed to be there?"

"Not until noon. We should be good."

When we get to her house, their car isn't in the driveway so they must still be gone. They rarely park in the garage.

We go in her house, my shoes sloshing around and my wet jeans feeling like lead weights. Willow's still wrapped in only a beach towel, her bare feet leaving footprints on the tile.

"Willow, is that you?" Her mom appears, followed by her dad.

Shit. So I guess they parked in the garage this time.

CHAPTER TWENTY-ONE

WILLOW

How am I going to explain this to my parents? They don't even know Silas and I are back together.

"Why are you guys back so early?" I ask, ignoring the fact that I'm standing here soaking wet, wearing nothing but a beach towel.

"We wanted to get some work done on the farm," my mom says. "We didn't realize it was going to rain but it looks like it's clearing up."

"We were just there," Silas says. "At the farm."

What is he doing? He can't tell them what we did. Even though we're adults and my parents wouldn't care, I still don't want them knowing I spent all night having sex in the back of a truck on the farm.

Did I really do that? It's so unlike me. And yet it was the best night of my life.

"Why were you at the farm?" my dad asks.

"Willow and I were going to pick berries but then it started to rain. We were in the fields and couldn't get back to the truck in time and ended up getting soaked."

"Luckily he had a towel in his truck," I say.

My parents eye us suspiciously.

"Willow, why don't you go get dressed?" my mom says.

"I will."

"I'll head back to my house," Silas says. "Just call me, Willow, if you want to meet up later."

"We have to work on that logo, remember?"

"Yeah, that's right. Text me when you're ready."

"Okay, bye."

"Bye." He gives me a quick kiss goodbye. "Shit," he whispers as he backs away.

I freeze and glance up at my parents. They're both staring at us, their lips turning up.

"Is there something you'd like to tell us?" my mom asks, putting her hands on her hips.

"Um, yeah." I glance at Silas. "Silas and I are dating again. We got back together last night." I quickly put my hand up, my other hand holding onto my towel. "I mean, not like we literally got together, but we had a long talk and..." My voice trails off. It's no use trying to hide it. They know what Silas and I were doing last night.

Silas backs away toward the door. "I need to change clothes so I'll see you guys later."

"I'm sure you will," my dad says, a smug grin on his face.

As soon as Silas is gone, my mom turns to my dad and says, "Well, you win."

"I told you." He puts his arm around her. "But I thought it would take longer. What's it been? A couple weeks?"

"That sounds about right." My mom smiles at me.

"What are you guys talking about?"

"You and Silas. Your father and I had a bet going to see if you two would get back together this summer."

"I bet that you would," my dad says, "but your mother didn't believe me. She said you were too stubborn to get back with Silas." He kisses my mom. "But even stubborn people can't fight the heart. It knows what it wants."

My mom smiles and kisses him back and then he kisses her again and it's like they forgot I was here.

I wave my hand in front of them. "Okay, do that some other time. So did you really have a bet going?"

"Yes," my dad says. "And since I won, your mother is taking me to the concert I wanted to go to."

"Folk singers," she says, rolling her eyes. "My least favorite type of music."

"What if *you'd* won the bet?" I ask her.

"Your father would've had to clean the garage."

Our garage is a disorganized mess. I can't even go in there. It's too much chaos.

"Silas' parents also had a bet going," my dad says. "But I'm not sure what they bet."

"Diane has to take Martin to a steakhouse," my mom says.

My dad laughs. "Diane will love that."

"What are you saying?" I ask. "Martin won? He thought Silas and I would get back together but Diane didn't?"

My mom motions to my towel. "Honey, go put some clothes on. You must be freezing."

"Why did Diane bet against us?"

"Because you're stubborn," my dad says as he walks to the living room. "Just like your old man."

"But you just said stubborn people cave when they're in love, so why did Diane—" I stop, noticing the big smile on my mom's face as I replay what I just said.

"You're in love with Silas?" my mom asks.

"And you're admitting it?" my dad yells from the living room. "It's about time."

My mom hugs me. "Honey, I'm so happy for you!"

This is embarrassing, and yet part of me wanted to tell them. Part of me wants to shout to the world that I love Silas.

"I need to shower," I say.

"Go ahead." She lets me go, still smiling.

I go down the hall to my room and realize I'm smiling too. It feels good to be back with Silas. I never thought it'd happen but it did, and maybe there's a reason for that. Maybe we're meant to be together despite whatever the future holds.

I take a quick shower, then call Silas.

"Did you know our parents placed bets on us?" I ask.

"What are you talking about?"

"Our parents bet whether we'd get back together and only my dad and Martin thought we would."

"That doesn't surprise me."

"It doesn't surprise you that our moms didn't think we'd get back together?"

"They know how stubborn you are."

"Why does everyone keep saying that? I am *not* stubborn."

He laughs. "Yeah, okay."

"Fine. Whatever. But our moms still shouldn't have bet against us."

"So what did Martin win?"

"Your mom has to take him to a steakhouse."

"Now it makes sense. I heard him making the reservation and thought it was some kind of joke. But I guess they're really going." I hear water running in the background.

"What are you doing?"

"Shaving."

"Why are you shaving?"

"I'm trying to look presentable for your parents. Now that they know I'm dating their daughter, they'll be keeping a closer eye on me."

"Silas, they've known you forever. You don't have to try to impress them."

"I still needed to shave." I hear the water shut off. "So what time should I come over?"

"Just come over now. You can have lunch with us."

"Why don't you guys come over here? My mom's making her vegetable lasagna."

"But she didn't invite us."

"She won't care. Just head down here. It should be ready soon."

"You have to ask her. We're not just coming over."

"Hold on." I hear him walk to the door and yell something to his mom. "Okay, we're good. She said to come on over. She said she wants to hang out with her future in-laws."

I laugh. "I don't know why she thinks they're her future in-laws when she bet against us."

"Just get over here. See ya soon."

I finish getting ready, then go find my parents. They're in their home office with a stack of papers in front of them.

"Hey, Diane invited us over for lunch."

"That was nice of her." My mom reaches over and closes the drawer on the file cabinet.

"Why do you guys keep locking that? I was trying to get in there last week and I couldn't find the key."

"Willow, I told you I don't want you making those spreadsheets." My dad stuffs some papers in a folder and hands it to my mom. "We don't need them."

"I don't have time now anyway. I've decided to focus on our marketing instead. Silas is going to make us a new logo. The old one is too dated, and truthfully, it's not even a logo. It's just our name in an ugly font."

My parents look at each other, not saying anything.

"Is something wrong?" I ask.

"No." My mom smiles. "So when will the logo be done?"

"I was hoping to have it done for the vendor fair this week but I don't think it'll be ready by then. I'll talk to Silas about it after lunch. We should head down there."

"You two go ahead," my dad says. "I'll be there in a few minutes." He waits for us to leave, and when I turn back I see him locking up the file cabinet again.

We have lunch at Silas' house like one big happy family. Our families have been friends forever. My parents are over here all the time, but this is the first time since I've been back that we've all been here together. As usual, Diane and my mom take off after lunch to go talk and make jewelry in Diane's craft room. And Martin and my dad go outside and have a beer. Martin brews his own beer and he's always using my dad as his taste tester.

Silas and I go to the kitchen table and get to work on a logo. He already has a million ideas, so now we just have to figure out which ones we like best and then he'll draw them out. He's good at drawing. And painting. Sculpting. Making jewelry. He really needs to be a graphic designer. Just watching him now, seeing how much he's getting into this logo design, it's clear this is a career he needs to look into. I wish I had that same passion for my future career. I keep thinking I will once I get a job.

I stay at Silas' house for the afternoon and my parents do too. We're there so long that Diane invites us to stay for dinner. Afterward, Silas and I show my parents some of Silas' rough sketches for logos. They're really impressed with his work. They like all his designs but they pick their two favorites for Silas to keep working on. Hopefully one of them will be our new logo.

The next day, I go to the farm to pick strawberries. They're ripening all at once so I'll be coming here every day, except for the day I'm at the vendor fair. I've decided I'm going to bring strawberries to the booth. It doesn't go with the lotion and soap theme, but who doesn't love fresh strawberries? I'm sure someone will buy them.

"I just had a great idea," I say to Silas as we're having lunch at one of the picnic tables.

"Let me guess." He leans over and kisses me. "You want to skip lunch and sneak off to my truck for a quickie?"

I laugh. "No. My idea is to match the soaps and lotions with what we grow on the farm. Like cucumber lotion or strawberry or mint."

"Can you put those things in a lotion without it going bad?"

"I'm not sure. I'd have to research it. Maybe it's not a lotion. Maybe it's a facial mask and you sell it in a single-size portion you use right away so it doesn't go bad. Dried herbs won't go bad so you could definitely make products with those, like mint or rosemary, which we already grow. We could plant a bigger variety of herbs to use in our soaps. The point is that we're connecting the farm to other products besides food. Adding beauty products creates a whole new source of income."

"Maybe you could use flowers too. I've got that whole section of the farm planted with flowers."

"Or," I set my sandwich down, "we could dry the flowers, glue them on card stock and make greeting cards. We'd leave them blank so people could write their own message." My head is spinning as ideas keep sparking in my head. "We need to start making this stuff and selling it at the farmers' market."

Silas is smiling at me because I've entered my super excited mode, in which I get an idea and get overly enthusiastic about it and want to try it right away. This doesn't happen very often, but it's happened enough that Silas knows the signs.

"Are you going to race home right now and get to work?" His arm goes around my waist and he slides me over on the bench until I'm right next to him.

"No. I need to pick more berries. But tonight I'm going to start making a list of ideas."

"You don't want to hang out with me tonight?" He gives me a kiss, and then another.

"We'll still hang out. Let's come back here later tonight. We'll bring some snacks and make the list together, then when it's dark we'll..." I kiss him in a way that implies what we'll be doing later. He kisses me back, pulling me closer.

"Hey, you two." I hear my dad's voice behind me and back away from Silas. "No kissing at work."

"Sorry about that," Silas says, grabbing a candy bar from his lunch sack.

"Yeah, sorry, Dad." I pick up my sandwich.

He chuckles. "If it were your mother and me, we'd go sneak back behind the shed to kiss."

Silas snickers under his breath.

"Dad, I was just telling Silas we should sell beauty products that would be themed to match what we grow, like a cucumber lotion or mint soap."

My dad looks at Silas. Silas gives him a sideways glance and does a quick head shake.

"What's going on with you two?" I ask Silas.

"Nothing." He continues eating his lunch.

"Anyway," I continue, "there would be a small initial investment at first, but I'll run some numbers before we do this so we can see how long it'll take to get a return on investment."

"Willow, why don't we hold off on that," my dad says. "We have a lot going on right now. This is our busiest time of the year."

"Which is why the timing is perfect. We need to be selling these products now, when people are already lining up to buy stuff from us."

"Let me think about it before you do anything."

"Okay, but I don't know what there is to think about. I'm home all summer so I could make everything. You wouldn't have to pay labor costs. You'd just pay for the ingredients, containers, and labels."

"I'll let you two finish your lunch." He fakes a stern Dad face. "And remember, no more kissing."

"Got it," I say in a serious tone. When he's gone, I say to Silas, "If he only knew what we've done on this farm."

"He didn't ban sex. Just kissing."

"Yeah, I think the no sex rule is a given."

He nudges me and lowers his voice. "Hurry up and finish your lunch so we can go behind the shed."

I laugh. "My dad was just kidding. We don't have to go hide behind the shed to kiss."

"I don't think he was kidding. He probably doesn't want us making out in front of the other workers."

I look over at the men sitting at the other tables, eating their lunches. They could've been watching us but I doubt it. Most of them are too busy checking their phones.

"But if you don't want to kiss me," Silas says, "we could just sit here until our break is over."

"I'm done," I say, setting my sandwich aside. "Let's go."

"You're not going to finish that?" He points to my half-eaten sandwich.

"No. I'm full."

He snatches it up and eats it in one big bite.

"I don't know how you eat so much."

He finishes chewing, then leans over to me and says in sexy voice, "I'm a big boy."

He *is* a big boy, in all the right places, and he's making me want to do more than just kiss. But that'll have to wait until later.

CHAPTER TWENTY-TWO

WILLOW

After dinner, Silas and I return to the farm and I make my list of ideas while Silas sits next to me, patiently waiting for me to finish but also offering up a few of his own ideas. By the time we're done, we can't keep our hands off each other. Clothes get ripped off, strewn all over the truck, and we do it. Twice. And then we go home.

That pattern repeats for the rest of the week. I'm sure our parents know what we're doing every night but they don't say anything. We usually get back so late that they're asleep by the time we get home.

It's now Saturday and I'm exhausted. Between working at the farm and getting everything ready for that vendor fair, it's been a tiring week. The fair was on Wednesday and I sold a little over half of my inventory, which I didn't think was great, but Diane only sold a third of what she brought and most of the other vendors sold even less than that. So I guess in comparison, my booth was a success. My mom brought the remaining products to the farmers' market today. If it sells out, I'm going to make more for next week.

It's after ten when I finally roll out of bed. I throw a sweatshirt over my tank and make my way to the kitchen. I take a box of cereal from the cupboard and the soy milk from the fridge. The doorbell rings as I'm pouring my cereal.

It can't be Silas. He's at class, and even if he wasn't, he'd just come in. He wouldn't ring the bell.

I open the door and see Trent there in a faded red polo shirt and khaki shorts, a baseball cap covering his short dark hair.

"Hey," he says. "Can I come in?"

"Yeah." I step aside. "What are you doing here?"

"I wanted to talk to you for a minute."

He walks in and I close the door. "About what?"

"Can we sit down?"

"Sure. Go wait in the living room. I'll put some shorts on." I'm in my skimpy pajama shorts so I go to my room and throw on my cut-off denim shorts. I don't bother putting on a bra because my oversized sweatshirt covers me up.

I return to the living room and plop down on the couch. "So what do you want to talk about?"

"Silas." Trent's tone is serious. His expression is too. He's never serious.

"What about him?" I curl my feet under me on the couch.

"You need to stop dating him."

I raise my brows. "That's why you came over here? To tell me not to date him?" I sigh. "I don't know why you hate me so much, Trent, but this needs to end. I'm dating Silas, and we don't need your approval or your blessing. So just leave."

"I don't hate you. I just don't want you dating Silas."

"Why? Because you have someone better for him?"

"Anyone would be better than..." His voice trails off.

"Than ME? Is that what you said? Anyone would be better than me?" I huff. "What the hell is that supposed to mean?"

"It means you're leading him on. Getting his hopes up. You're going to destroy him and you don't even seem to care."

A dull pain rattles my chest because part of me feels like he's right. Hurting Silas is a lingering fear I've had ever since he came back into my life and I can't seem to make it go away.

"I'm not going to hurt him," I say.

"Oh, really? So what happens at the end of August? What happens when you go back to school? Are you going to ignore him? Stop talking to him like you did last time?"

"No. And this is none of your business so you need to leave. I'm not listening to this."

"I'm not leaving until I've said what I need to say."

"Then hurry up and say it and get out."

"I was the one Silas talked to after you broke off the engagement. And I talked to him after he left. I actually answered his calls the past two years, unlike you." He glares at me and that dull ache in my chest becomes a sharp pain.

"Yeah, I should've talked to him. I told him I was sorry for that."

"Sorry's not good enough. You owed him an explanation, telling him why you wouldn't even give your relationship a chance. Why you were in love with him one day and hated him the next."

"I didn't hate him. Stop making assumptions. You don't know what went on."

"Silas told me everything, so actually I *do* know. He said he went over there that day to take you to dinner. You were going to plan your backpacking trip. He had maps of Europe and the two of you were going to plot it out that night. It was his dream to backpack through Europe with you and it was finally happening."

I swallow past the lump in my throat.

"He was so freaking excited," Trent says. "I even made fun of him for it. But he didn't care. At that point he was so damn happy that you agreed to marry him that nothing could bring him off that high. At least I didn't think anything could. Until *you* did. When you told him it was over and gave him the ring back, he hit rock bottom. I'd never seen him that bad. We went out to a park and he burned the maps and almost tossed out the ring. I took it from him and told him I'd give it back when he calmed down. I knew he'd want it later. I mean, shit, he spent months making the damn thing."

Tears are now spilling down my cheeks and I don't wipe them away because I don't want Trent to notice. But he's looking right at me so I know he sees them.

"Why are you telling me this?" I ask. "I don't need to hear this. It's the past."

"And the past has a way of repeating itself."

"It won't. I promise."

He rolls his eyes. "Your promises are worthless. You promised Silas you'd marry him, then a week later, you broke up with him."

"I wasn't ready. I was only 17."

"Then you shouldn't have said yes. You shouldn't have got his hopes up."

"You're right. I shouldn't have agreed to marry him, but I can't go back and change it."

"But you CAN change what's going on now. You need to end this before you destroy him again."

"I'm not going to hurt him."

"That's bullshit and you're lying to yourself if you can't admit that."

"It's different this time. We're older and we've had two years to think about this."

"You spent the last two years contemplating a future with Silas?" He lets out a harsh laugh. "Yeah, right. Were you thinking about him when you were fucking half the football team?"

"What?" I jump up from the couch. "I never did that!"

"That's not what I heard."

"From who? Is Brian going around telling people that?"

"Brian said you slept with him then moved on to some other guys on the team."

"I was with Brian. That's it. No one else on the team. And I was only with Brian one time."

"You were with other guys at our high school."

"Yeah, and you were with just about every girl, but it's different for me? Because I'm a girl? And what about Silas? Do you really think he wasn't with anyone else the past two years?"

Trent doesn't answer.

"So you know he was with other girls and yet I'm the villain here? Do I need to remind you that I wasn't dating Silas during that time? He was halfway around the world. I didn't think I'd ever see him again!"

"Exactly. So for you to say you've been thinking about this for two years is a lie. That's all you do, Willow, is lie. You lie to Silas, you lie to me, you lie to yourself."

"I'm not lying! I've thought about Silas every single day since we broke up. Was I thinking about our future together? No, because I didn't think I'd see him again. But I still thought about him! I haven't even had a boyfriend the past two years because I expected every guy I dated to live up to Silas and none of them could." I pause to take a calming breath because I'm about to explode. "You need to stay out of this, Trent. Right now, you're the one hurting Silas by telling me to break up with him. He's happy and so am I."

"For now. But what happens at the end of summer?"

"I'll go back to college and Silas and I will continue dating. I'll come home on the weekends and see him, or he can come see me."

"Camsburg is over three hours away. You're really going to come home every weekend? And then what? What happens after you graduate? You told Silas he didn't fit in your plan. So did your plan change?"

"I'm not talking to you about this. This is between Silas and me."

"Silas is too blind to see what you're doing to him. If I don't intervene, he'll fuck up his life again and you'll go on as if nothing happened."

"What do you mean when you say he fucked up his life? After we broke up, he went backpacking in Europe. That's what he wanted to do."

"Yeah, but after that, he was going to come back here and work all summer to earn money for school and to save up for an apartment. In the fall he was supposed to start college. He'd already registered."

"Wait...what?" I sit down again, that lump in my throat getting bigger. "Why didn't he tell me that?"

"He was going to. The night you broke up with him. It was supposed to be a surprise. He was going to go over the trip stuff with you and then he was going to tell you the other stuff." Trent takes his baseball cap off and runs his hand through his hair as he sighs. "He did it all for you, Willow. He wanted you to have a good life and to always have whatever you needed. He didn't want you two having to struggle after you got married. He wanted to show you that he was responsible and would take care of you. But all his plans fell apart when you told him it was over. He cancelled his registration for fall classes and took off for Europe and didn't come back until now."

I drop my head and rub my eyes, thinking about what Trent said. Going to college? Working all summer? That wasn't the Silas I knew back then. He was a free spirit. Sometimes he took odd jobs for extra money, or made jewelry for his mom to sell, but he never had a regular steady job. He didn't want one, at least that's what he told me. He also told me he had no interest in ever going to college. But now that I think about it, he hadn't said those things in the months leading up to his proposal. So maybe that whole time, all those months, he was planning for our future and I didn't even know it.

"He's starting to get back on track now," Trent says. "He's taking classes in the fall and he's starting to think about his career. And I don't want you coming in and ruining it like you did last time. It's not fair to him, Willow. You can't just use him for the summer, then toss him aside."

"I'm not doing that," I whisper. But am I? I love Silas and I want to be with him, but if I don't see a future with us, then what am I doing? Just using him? "I want a future with him," I think to myself, then realize I said it out loud.

"Do you want it enough to change the future you've already laid out for yourself? Because I know you, Willow, and I know how freaking rigid you are. You decide to do something and you do it. You don't let anything stand in the way. Not even Silas."

"That's not true. I just need time to think and make some decisions."

"You need to make your decision *now*. If you're breaking up with Silas, you can't wait until August or sometime next fall. You can't keep stringing him along."

"I'm not breaking up with him. I love him."

"You said you loved him before, and you still broke up with him."

He's right. So what am I doing? Am I just repeating the past? Is this going to end the same way it did last time? Back then, I panicked, thinking we'd never get what we wanted in life if we stayed together. We wanted such different things back then, but now? I feel like things have changed. We're more grown up. But what if the summer ends and I panic again? I can't do that to Silas. Like Trent said, I need to make a decision. Either I stay with Silas with the idea that we're going to have a future together, or I let him go.

Trent gets up from his chair. "Just end this. Let him move on with his life. You've done enough damage."

His words and his tone set me off and I shoot up from the couch. "You don't know anything about Silas and me. Maybe you did in the past but you don't now. So stay the hell out of our relationship. Stop badmouthing me to Silas and stop trying to set him up with other girls. Silas and I are together. Deal with it." I point to the door. "Now get out of my house."

"I'm not giving up on this, Willow. I'm not letting Silas fuck up his life because of you. I sat back and watched it happen before, but I'm not doing it again. And I'm not letting you use him all summer, then dump his ass in the fall. He doesn't deserve to be treated that way, especially after all the shit he's doing for your family." He storms off toward the door.

I run after him. "Trent, wait. What are you talking about? What's he doing for my family?"

"Shit." Trent sighs and closes his eyes.

"What? What does that mean?"

He opens his eyes. "I wasn't supposed to tell you this but what the hell? Maybe knowing this will get you to finally let Silas go."

"Knowing what? What did Silas do?"

"He's working for your dad all summer for free."

"What? No. That's not right. My dad pays him. He's not working for free."

"Willow, I'm not making this up. He's not getting paid. Before you got back from college, Silas was working sixteen hour days, seven days a week. All for free. He got back to town early May and was signed up to take three classes this summer. But he dropped two so he could help your dad."

"I don't understand. Why would Silas drop his classes to work on the farm for free? And why wouldn't my dad pay him?"

Trent sighs again and looks me in the eye. "Because they're losing the farm. If your parents can't find a way to pay off their debt, they're going to have to sell the farm."

"What debt? They don't have debt."

"I don't know all the details. I only know that Silas is doing anything and everything to keep your parents from having to sell it. That's why he dropped his classes and why he's working for free."

"And why we hardly have any guys working for us," I say quietly to myself.

It's all making sense. Why we have so few workers. Why our fridge is empty. Why the cash jar hasn't been filled. Why my mom got a job.

"I have to go," Trent says, opening the door.

"Why did they hide this from me?" I'm staring at the floor in a daze, trying to make sense of this. When I look up, Trent is gone and I'm left alone, with nothing but questions and no answers.

CHAPTER TWENTY-THREE

SILAS

"Willow," I call out as I go in her house. "Are you in your room? I have a surprise for you."

I'm in a really good mood today. Actually, I've been in a good mood ever since Willow got back from college, and my mood got even better when we got back together.

My surprise is that her favorite local band is playing tonight and I got tickets on my way over here.

"Willow?" I go to her room but she's not there. I know she's home. I told her I'd come here right after class. We have two hours before her parents get back from the farmers' market. While I was in class, Willow kept texting me with what she'd like me to do to her in those two hours. I swear she only did it to embarrass me. I had a hard-on practically the whole damn class. I didn't even look at the last few texts she left me. If I had, I wouldn't have been able to walk out at the end of class.

"Willow, where are you?" I check the kitchen and then the living room. "I got your texts." I smile. "I didn't know you had such a dirty mind."

It's true. Willow used to be kind of shy when it came to sex, which made sense because she was younger then and inexperienced. She was only 16 and a virgin when we first did it. But even after we'd been doing it for months, she never took the lead, never wanted to try anything new, never talked dirty. And I was okay with that. I never pushed her to do anything she wasn't comfortable doing and I never would.

But now, being with her again, it's totally different. She isn't afraid to take charge or tell me what she wants, which is damn sexy, to the point that just thinking about those texts has got me hard again.

"Come on, Willow. No more teasing." I walk down the hall. "Where are you?"

I've searched every room but the office. The door is closed so I open it and see her sitting on the floor. The file cabinet is open and papers are scattered all around her. Her eyes are red and puffy and she's staring straight ahead, a dazed look on her face.

"Willow?" I slowly approach her, and as I do, I notice a piece of paper on the floor next to her leg. It's a bill stamped with the word 'overdue' in bright red ink.

She knows. Shit.

"Willow," I say quietly, kneeling down in front of her.

"You knew," she whispers, her eyes looking past me.

"Yes, but I was going to—"

"You knew and you didn't tell me." Her voice is shaky and a tear slips down her already wet cheek.

"Just let me explain." I reach for her but she shoves me away.

"Get out!" she screams. "Get out of my house!" She starts kicking at me, pushing me back.

"Stop." I grab her legs, holding them down. "We need to talk about this."

"You had weeks to talk about this! And instead you lied to me!" She struggles to get her legs free and starts hitting me. "Get out!"

"I'm not leaving."

"I don't want to see you." She stops fighting me and looks down. "I need to be alone."

"What you need is a friend." I let go of her legs and sit cross-legged in front of her. "Willow, say something."

"You're not my friend." She hiccups the words as she breaks down into a full-out cry. "A friend would've told me what's going on. But instead, you hid it from me. Acted like everything was great." She takes a breath. "Is that why you wanted to get back together with me? Because you felt sorry for me?"

"No! You know that's not the reason."

"Then is it because you knew I wouldn't be going back to school in the fall? You knew I'd be staying here so you thought you'd—"

"Willow, stop making up shit." I grab her hand and hold onto it as she tries to pull away. "First of all, you're going back to school in the fall. That hasn't changed."

She picks up one of the bills and shoves it in my face. "Do you see this? It's a bill for $3,000! It's overdue and racking up late fees. And it's just one of I don't know how many. There's no money for college, Silas! My parents don't even have money for food." Her head drops and she starts crying again.

"You're still going to college." I rub her hand. "They haven't touched that account."

Her head lifts. "But they need the money."

"Yes, but they want you to go to school."

"Who cares about school?" Her sadness is suddenly replaced by anger. "They need to pay off their bills! What the hell is wrong with them?" She tries to rip her hand from mine but I grip it tighter.

"It's important to them that you finish college. They don't want you to get off track."

She's quiet, and I see the guilt on her face. She thinks this is her fault. She has a timeline for her life, a list of what she needs to accomplish along with dates for when those things must be done. Her parents know this, and they know how much it means to her to achieve her goals. They agree with me that the path Willow is going down won't make her happy, but they also know they can't talk her out of it, so they've always been supportive of her and never tried to hold her back.

"I'm not letting them do this," she says. "I'm going through each one of those bills and paying them off. I don't care if it drains my college account. It has to be done."

"That's not your decision, Willow. This is your parents' decision. It's their farm. Their house." Shit. Why did I say that?

"The house?" Her face crumples and the tears fall again. "We're losing the house?" When I don't answer, she says, "That's why my parents redecorated, isn't it? That's why they painted all the walls. Got rid of the clutter. They were getting ready to put the house up for sale. That's why that lady came by to see the house. Has someone already bought it?"

"No. It's not even up for sale yet so I don't know why that lady came over. Maybe she heard it might be going up for sale. Maybe your mom told her."

"We can't lose the house," she whispers, sniffling.

I sit next to her and force her into my arms. "They may not have to sell it."

She rests her head against my shoulder. "Do you know that for sure? Or are you just saying that?"

"Nothing's for sure. But at this point, they're not ready to sell."

Given how angry she is at me, I'm surprised she's not shoving me away. Instead, her body relaxes against mine as I continue to hold her.

"They're losing the farm, aren't they?"

I sigh. "You should really be asking your parents this. I don't know all the details."

"They'll just lie to me. They'll make it sound like it's not as bad as it really is. I need you to tell me the truth, Silas. Please."

I sigh again. "The truth is...yeah, they might lose the farm. If they can't pay off their debts, then they'll have to sell the land."

"How much do they owe?"

"I don't know. Your dad didn't tell me."

"Maybe my college fund won't be enough." She pushes off me and moves over a little. "If it's not, they'll have to get a loan. They hate banks, and I know it would be taking on more debt, but right now they have to pay their bills."

"They already..." I don't finish the thought because I don't want to tell her.

"They already what?"

She wants the truth so I need to tell her. "They already have bank loans. And they haven't been able to make the payments. The banks won't loan them any more money."

She leans forward and covers her face with her hands. "How did this happen? Everything was fine a year ago. So what happened?"

"I'm not sure. But maybe everything *wasn't* fine last year. Maybe they've been in trouble for a while and just never told anyone."

"I don't know what this means. I'm so confused right now. And panicked. I can't go back to school in the fall. My parents need my college money, and if they refuse, I'll force them to take it. But then what? What do I do? Get a job? Live with my parents?"

I move so that I'm facing her. "You'll figure it out. You don't have to have all the answers right this second." I hold her chin up so she'll look at me. "You didn't let me finish what I was going to say earlier. The reason I got back together with you? It wasn't for any of the reasons you said. It was because I love you, more than anything. I don't want to go another day without you in my life. I've never given up on us, Willow. The timing was just wrong the first time. But as for *us*? There was nothing wrong about us. Then, or now. I know that now more than ever. And together, we can get through this."

"It's over, Silas." She pushes me away and stands up. "I can't do this anymore."

I jump up. "Willow, don't say that. You're just angry. I know this is hard, but I'm here for you, for whatever you need."

"I need you to go." She walks to the door, holding it open. "And don't come back."

"Willow." I meet her at the door. "Of course I'm coming back. I love you. I'm going to be here for you."

"I don't want you here. I don't even want to be friends with you anymore."

I stare at her, shocked that she's saying this. Just minutes ago, she was hugging me, clinging to me like she didn't want me to leave. And now she's kicking me out? Ending our friendship?

"I know you don't mean that," I tell her. "You're just mad. Mad at your parents. Mad at me. Mad at the situation. And I totally understand. But we can get through this. I promise."

"You lied to me, Silas. You've never lied to me, not even about something small. And this whole time you knew this huge secret and you wouldn't even tell me!"

"Because your parents—"

"Stop! I don't want to hear it." She looks at me with hate in her eyes. She's never looked at me that way. "I don't want your excuses. I trusted you. I get why my parents lied. I don't agree with it but I get it. They're just being parents, trying to protect their child. But you're my best friend. You always have been. And best friends tell each other the truth, even if the person doesn't want to hear it."

I'm getting angry now, because Willow kept the truth from me for years.

"Have you always told me the truth?" I look her in the eye.

She glances down. "Yes."

"So when you said you didn't love me anymore when you broke off our engagement, was that the truth? Because just last week, you told me you never stopped loving me. So which is it?"

I see her lip quiver and hear her shaky breaths, but she doesn't answer.

"Which is it, Willow? Do you love me? Or was that just a lie?"

She keeps her head down, but I see the tears drip from her face as she whispers, "Please. Just go."

I walk out the door and she closes it and locks it behind me. I stand there a moment and hear her sobbing as her body slides against the door onto the floor.

My chest is burning, aching, desperate to help her. I want to hold her and tell her everything will be okay, but that would be a lie, and I'm done lying to her. Besides, right now, she doesn't want to see me. I thought she was just saying that, but when I saw how she looked at me, that look I'd never seen before, I knew I needed to give her time alone.

Willow is right. I've never lied to her. I've always told her everything, even things I knew would embarrass her, like if she had food in her teeth or toilet paper stuck to her shoe. We have the type of relationship where we can tell each other anything. And so I've always been open with her. Never held back. Until now.

I never should've agreed to keep this from her. She had a right to know. This affects her education, her life, her future. Her parents were wrong not to tell her, and wrong to ask me to keep this a secret. I love her parents, but right now, I'm really pissed at them.

I go to the living room and sit down on the couch. Despite Willow's request, I'm not leaving. Not until her parents get home. She might need me. Or maybe she won't. Either way, I'm not leaving.

I get my phone out and call her dad.

"Hi, Silas," he answers. "Aren't you supposed to be at class?"

"It ended an hour ago. I'm at your house right now. When I got here, I found Willow in the office." I pause. "She knows."

"I don't understand. I had everything locked up."

"She broke the file cabinet open."

"Why would she do that? Did she suspect something? Did you say something to her?"

"No. I didn't say anything."

But now he has me wondering why she did it. Why would she break open the file cabinet? She had to have known something was up. But how did she know?

"Where is she now?"

"Still in the office. I tried to talk to her but she kicked me out. She doesn't want to talk to anyone. She told me to leave, but I'm going to stay here until you guys get home."

"We'll try to get out of here. We've been really busy today. We can barely keep up. But we'll close up early and go home."

"If it's busy, you should stay there and keep selling as much as you can. I'll stay with Willow until you get back."

"Thank you, Silas. Candace and I will be home as soon as we can."

I hear people talking next to him. "You better get back to work."

"Yes. We'll see you soon."

He ends the call and I remain on the couch, not sure what to do. I don't feel like watching TV. My mind is on Willow. She's all I can think about. I want to go back in there but it's too soon. She needs more time.

I check my phone and see the text Willow sent me at the end of class. The one I didn't look at. It wasn't one of her dirty texts. It was a text that says, *You lied to me*. That's it. Just four words. If I'd read those four words before I left class, I would've known what I was walking into when I got here. Maybe I could've explained myself better. Used better words. Said something to make her not hate me so much.

"Dammit," I mumble, feeling angry and frustrated. I lean back and put my arm up on the back of the couch. My hand hits something, knocking it to the floor. I look back and see it's a baseball cap. Willow's dad doesn't wear baseball caps. Someone must've left it here. I get up and go around the couch and pick it up. It's a Raiders' hat. Trent loves the Raiders. It's his favorite team. So I guess that explains how Willow found out.

I call Trent's number.

"Hey, what's up?" he asks in his usual laid-back tone.

"Are you happy with yourself? Is this what you wanted? Because you might've just got your way."

"What are you talking about?"

"I just talked to Willow."

"Oh," he mutters.

"That's it? That's all you're going to say?"

"I didn't mean to tell her about the farm. That was an accident. I was angry and it just slipped out. I'm sorry. I shouldn't have said it."

The one good thing about Trent is that he owns up to his mistakes. He doesn't lie and pretend he didn't do it or try to blame someone else.

"Why did you come over here?" I ask.

"You're at her house right now? Where is she?"

"She locked herself in the office. She told me to leave but I didn't. I found your hat, by the way. Now tell me why you were here."

"You're going to be pissed at me but I don't care. I went over there to tell Willow to stay away from you."

"What the hell? Why would you do that? You know how much I want her back!"

"Which is why she needs to end this. You're getting way too attached to her. It's even worse than in high school. And you'll love her even more by the end of the summer. Just in time for her to rip your heart out before she leaves for college."

"Who the fuck do you think you are?" I yell into the phone. I'm so pissed at him right now, more than I've ever been. "You had no right to tell her that. Do you have any idea what you've done? Do you even care?"

"Silas, I wasn't trying to be an ass. I really am worried about you. I don't want to see you go through that again."

"Then stay the fuck away from me and you won't have to."

"Hey. Don't be ending our friendship over some girl."

"She's NOT just some girl. She's the girl that I love. And you may have just destroyed any chance of us getting back together."

"Is that what she said?" He sounds hopeful.

"Yeah, that'd make you happy, wouldn't it? Well, you got your wish. She broke up with me. But I won't accept it. She's angry and hurt and she's not thinking straight. Hopefully, in a day or two, she'll have calmed down and I can talk to her again. If not, I'm going over there and strangling you."

"I'm sorry, okay? I'm sorry about telling her about the farm, but I'm not sorry about asking her to be honest with you. And honest with herself. That's what I told her, Silas. I told her to think about what she really wants. We all know what *you* want, but does she want the same thing? Because up until now, she's made it pretty clear what she wants, and sorry, man, but you're not in her plan. So unless that's changed, there's no use doing this to yourself."

"We're done talking about this. I'll leave your hat at the front door. MY door, not Willow's. Stay away from her. And stay away from me." I end the call.

I know in his warped sense of reasoning, Trent thinks he was doing me a favor, but it only made things worse. I can't be friends with him if he keeps interfering with Willow and me.

Then again, maybe there is no Willow and me. Maybe it's over. For good this time.

CHAPTER TWENTY-FOUR

WILLOW

For the past hour I've been going through my parents' files, seeing all the unpaid pills, but not believing any of this is true. The evidence is all around me and yet I don't want to believe it.

How could they let this happen? My parents have been running the farm for twenty years and we've never had money problems. They may be liberal in their beliefs, but they've always been conservative when it comes to money. They don't buy expensive clothes. They don't eat out much. They live in a small house and only have one car. So how did this happen? Where did all their money go? Why are they in so much debt?

I toss the bills aside and lean back against the wall. I close my eyes, trying to focus on a way to fix this, but instead, I keep seeing Silas in my head and how sad and hurt he looked when I told him we were over.

But he lied to me, so what choice did I have? I had to break up with him. If I can't trust him, then we can't have a relationship. He had so many opportunities to tell me the truth. Just a week ago, I asked him if he thought my parents were having money problems and he didn't give me an answer. He let me think everything was okay. I trusted him to be honest with me and he wasn't.

I rise up from the floor, grab some tissues from the desk, and wipe my face off. My parents will be home soon and I need to get myself together before they get here. I don't want to fight with them but I have a feeling that's what will happen. They'll try to tell me I'm going back to school in the fall and I'll refuse and then we'll start fighting.

I go out to the living room and see Silas sitting on the couch. He gets up when he sees me.

"What are you still doing here?" I ask. "You were supposed to leave an hour ago."

"I'm waiting for your parents to get home. I didn't want you here alone."

"I'm fine. Just go." I walk quickly to my room but feel him behind me.

"Willow, wait." He holds my arm.

I hear the garage door opening. "That's them. You need to go."

"Are you going to call me later?"

My back is to him as I shake my head.

He comes around in front of me. "Willow, I'm sorry I didn't tell you. But don't shut me out. I want to be here for you."

"I don't need you," I mutter.

"Don't say that. It's not true."

He's right. It's a lie. I *do* need him. Now more than ever. But right now, I don't trust him. And I don't trust myself around him. When he's close to me like this, I want to touch him and kiss him and tell him I love him. But that's just leading him on. Making him think we have a future together. Like Trent said, I need to make a decision about Silas. I can't keep this going if I know it's eventually going to end.

I need time to think. To sort things out and figure out what I'm going to do. About Silas. About school. About my future. The plan I made is over. Done. Gone. And that has me in a state of panic.

Silas wraps his arms around me and pulls me into his chest. I don't even try to resist because it's what I need and what I want. But I shouldn't let him do it. Not until I make a decision about him.

He strokes my hair and whispers, "I love you." We hear my parents walking in the door as he slowly backs away. "Call me later." He softly kisses my forehead and then leaves.

My dad says something to Silas but I can't make out his words. I go into my room and hear my mom behind me.

"Honey, I'm sorry. But we just couldn't tell you."

I turn and see her standing at the door with tears in her eyes and my anger toward her suddenly fades away.

"Please don't be mad at us," she says. "We thought we were doing the right thing."

"Mom." I go up to her and hug her. "I'm not mad at you. I just wish you'd told me because I want to help."

"I know you do." She takes me over to the bed to sit down. "But your father and I didn't want you worrying about this. It's our responsibility, not yours."

My mom looks exhausted, with dark circles and bags under her eyes. She's probably not sleeping well because she's stressed and tired from having to work at that new job while also managing the farm. I never really noticed how tired she looked until now. How did I not notice this before? I see her every day.

"Willow." My dad appears at my door. He, too, looks exhausted but not as bad as my mom.

My dad has always been good at covering up whatever is bothering him. When something bad happens, he's always the rock of our family. He's steady and calm and one of those people who can convince you things will be okay, even when they're not. Silas is that way too. It was one of the reasons I was drawn to him, even when we were kids. I've always been anxious and high-strung and he's always been relaxed and laid-back. That's why I crave being around him. We balance each other out.

"Let's go talk in the other room," my dad says.

The three of us go to the living room and sit down. My parents sit on one end of the couch and I sit on the other. My dad has his arm around my mom and she's holding his hand. Just seeing them together like that makes me feel better.

Sometimes stressful situations tear people apart, but my parents are still as strong as ever. And that makes me feel better. More secure. Like maybe we can get through this.

"Do you want to ask us questions?" my dad asks. "Or should I just start from the beginning?"

"How did this happen?"

He looks at my mom, then back at me. "It started a year ago, after your mom had surgery."

Last year, my mom had back surgery. She had back pain for years, but my parents try to avoid going to doctors, choosing to rely on alternative treatments, like chiropractors or massage therapy or herbal remedies. None of those treatments worked so my mom had to have surgery.

"Our insurance didn't cover all the medical costs," he says. "The hospital bill wiped us out. It cleared out our savings and we had to take money out of the business. That put us behind on our bills. Then material costs went up at the farm, labor costs went up, sales went down and..." He continues to list all the things that led us to this point.

It sounds like everything happened at once and they just couldn't keep up. And they didn't have enough money in savings to cover their bills. They give a lot of their money away to charity or families who need it. It's great that they do that but I wish they'd saved more of it for when something like this happens. In fact, it angers me that they didn't. They own a business that's unpredictable. A bad storm or insects or disease could wipe out their entire crop at any time, so they should always be prepared. They should've saved more of their money, putting some away for medical expenses and other emergencies.

This is why I am the way I am. Always worried about the future, always planning ahead. It's because my parents aren't that way and it drives me crazy. When I was twelve I watched a show on TV about farmers and it showed all these farm families living in poverty because some plant disease wiped out their crop that year. It totally freaked me out. I thought for sure that would happen to us. I told my parents about it that night at dinner and they told me to relax and stop worrying. I was so mad they didn't take it seriously that I left the table and ran off to my room. For weeks, I had nightmares that we were one of those homeless families without any food to eat. My parents refused to take my concerns seriously and that's when I went into my obsessive planning stage, which I'm still in.

Now my nightmares have come true. My parents didn't plan for this and now we'll lose the farm and maybe the house. We'll be just like those families on TV.

"Are you selling the house?" I ask.

"We hope it won't come to that," my mom says.

"You don't know if you'll have to sell the house? How could you not know that?" I'm yelling because I'm angry. I'm angry they didn't plan better and that they still don't seem to have a plan. "Haven't you run the numbers? Calculated how much money you need to save the business? Run different scenarios?" I shoot up from the couch. "How do you plan to fix this if you don't have the information to make the right decisions?"

"Ron already ran the numbers," my mom says. Ron is their accountant but he looks like a stoned-out hippie from the Sixties so I have zero confidence in him. "We've gone over everything with him but we're waiting to see how we do this summer. So far, sales are up and my job is bringing in enough extra income to cover the household expenses."

I throw my hands up. "Ron is an idiot! You need a real accountant. You can't trust some hippie friend of yours to save the business."

"Hey," my dad says in a stern tone. "Don't talk that way about Ron. He graduated with honors from UC-Berkeley. He may not dress in suits, but that doesn't mean he's not intelligent."

"If he was so great, then how did you get to this point? He should've seen it coming! He should've had a plan in place!"

"Honey, it's not his fault." My mom reaches for me but I step back.

"What's his plan? What does he think we should do?"

"Let your mom and I worry about that," my dad says. "This isn't for you to worry about."

"Are you kidding me? Of course I'm worried about it! I'm completely panicked! We're selling the house, we have no money, and I have to drop out of school!"

My dad stands up. "You are NOT dropping out of school."

"There's no way I'm going back to school, knowing how much we need the money."

"Which is why we didn't want you to know," my dad says. "We knew you would react this way. But we are still your parents and you are going to school, even if we have to drag you there and drop you off."

"Why would you do that? You need that money and you need it now! It's an emergency. College can wait."

"If you wait, you may never go back."

"You know that's not true. If I want to do something, I do it."

"Yes, but not if we can't afford it. If we use your college money, we may not be able to replace it."

"Then I'll get a scholarship or financial aid. I'll find a way. But you're taking that money."

My parents look at each other, frustration on their faces. My dad turns back to me. "I think we've talked enough for now. Silas asked me to tell you to call him when we're done, so go ahead."

"I can't. I um...I broke up with Silas."

"Willow, no," my mom says. "You can't blame Silas for this."

"He lied to me, Mom. He kept this from me when he knew I'd want to be told."

My dad comes up in front of me. "Listen to me. Silas has done a lot for us and you need to thank him for that, not punish him. He's been working on the farm since the day he got back into town. When Diane told him what was going on, he was at our doorstep, practically begging me to let him help. He

241

refused to take any money. He's been working for free this entire time."

I swallow hard. "I know. But he still should've told me."

"He wanted to, many times, but I told him not to. I told him it was my job to tell you, not his, and he respected that. He's given up a lot to help us, Willow. He even dropped two of his summer classes so he could work for us. We're damn lucky to have him. He gets twice as much done as my other employees and he won't accept a dime. So don't you dare punish him for this. He did as I asked and kept quiet."

"I don't want to talk about this. I'll be in my room." I turn and walk down the hall, feeling my parents' eyes on me. I know they're mad at me for breaking up with Silas but it's not their decision.

When I'm back in my room, I check my phone and see some texts from Silas, asking me how I'm doing and telling me to call him. But instead, I lie on my bed and end up falling asleep. I don't wake up until I hear my mom knocking on my door.

"Come in," I say, sitting up.

My mom walks over and sits next to me on the bed. "We're having dinner soon."

"Okay. I'll be there in a few minutes." I check my phone and see more texts from Silas.

"Are you going to call him?" my mom asks.

"I'm not ready to."

"Willow, you're being unreasonable. He did what your father asked. If it had been up to Silas, he would've told you."

"He didn't have to listen to Dad."

"No, but the fact that he did shows that he's respectful of your father and me, and that says a lot about his character."

"But he wasn't respectful of me. Are you saying that doesn't matter?"

"Willow, you know Silas respects you. Stop trying to make him the villain here. He begged us to tell you about this every day since you got back. This hasn't been easy on him. In fact, just last week he told your father he couldn't keep this a secret any longer."

That explains his behavior. All last week Silas kept giving my dad these looks but I didn't know what they meant. And then I'd catch him talking to my dad, looking really serious, but as soon as I approached him, he'd smile and act like everything's fine. So I guess he really did want to tell me but wasn't willing to do so without my dad's approval, which still makes me angry. His loyalty should be to me, not my dad.

"It's not just that," I say.

"Not what?"

"It's not just the fact that Silas didn't tell me. That's not the only reason I broke up with him."

"What's the other reason?"

I pause, my eyes tearing up. "I just...I don't want to hurt him again. I don't know if I see a future with Silas, and if I don't, then I need to let him go. For good this time."

"Willow." My mom rubs my arm. "What have I always told you?"

"To go with my heart. But that's not good enough for me. I can't be with him just because I..." I look down.

"Love him?" she asks softly.

I don't answer.

"Honey, that's enough of a reason to be with him. Love doesn't come along very often, and if you let it go, you may not find it again."

"That all sounds good when you say it, but it doesn't always work that way in real life. Silas and I may love each other, but the fact remains that we still want different things in life. If we stay together, one of us will have to give up what we want."

"Willow." She moves my hair behind my shoulder. "No matter who you end up with, you'll have to make sacrifices. That's part of being in a relationship."

"But this is more than a few sacrifices. Being with Silas means changing where I live and what I want to do." I pause. "I guess that's not true anymore. I have no idea what I'm going to do now."

"You're still going to college," she says in the same stern tone my dad used earlier. "If we can't afford Camsburg, you'll go to school somewhere else, but you're not quitting college."

So she's finally admitting that I may not be going back to Camsburg. I knew it was a possibility, but hearing her say it made it a thousand times more real. This is really happening. I'm not going back to Camsburg in the fall. I've wanted to go there since I was a kid, and I did. I made it happen. And I have friends there. Best friends. But now it's over. It's all ending.

Tears fall before I can stop them.

My mom hugs me. "I'm sorry, honey. I know this is hard. Your father and I hate disappointing you like this and we'll do everything possible to try to keep you at Camsburg."

"It's not going to happen. It's way too expensive."

"You can always take out loans. I don't like the idea of you taking on all that debt but it may be our only option."

"You have to do it, Mom. You have to use the money to save your business and the house."

She nods. "It hasn't come to that yet, but if things get worse, then yes, we may need to borrow from your college fund to pay our bills."

I'm glad she's finally agreeing to it, but also sad, because it means I need to find a new college and won't see my friends anymore.

She sits back. "Let's go have dinner. And then you need to go talk to Silas."

We go to the kitchen and I set the table while my dad tells us some funny story he heard on the news. He's acting like our problems don't exist. Trying to keep my mind off them. My mom is doing the same, laughing at his story in an attempt to keep the mood light.

My parents are much better at dealing with setbacks and uncertainty than I am. They always believe things will work out. So does Silas.

But me? I need more than a belief. I need proof that things will work out. And since I don't have that, I'm left feeling confused. Lost. Unsure how to move forward.

CHAPTER TWENTY-FIVE

SILAS

I've texted and called her at least twenty times since I left and haven't heard a word from her. By now, her parents have talked to her and explained that they basically ordered me not to tell her, but Willow will still say I should've told her. I'm angry with her parents for putting me in that position. They knew she'd find out eventually so why hide it from her?

My phone dings with a text. It's from Willow, asking me to come outside. It's ten o'clock. I'm surprised she's here this late.

I go downstairs. My mom and Martin see me and both look at me like they're afraid to say anything. When I got home earlier I was on edge and snapped at them when they asked me what I wanted for dinner. I ended up skipping dinner and listening to music in my room, falling asleep for a couple hours.

"Sorry for earlier," I say as I pass by my mom and Martin.

"Where are you going?" my mom asks.

"I'm not sure," I answer, because I'm not. I don't know if Willow wants to talk here or go somewhere. I don't know why she wants to see me. Does she just want to talk or is she going to try to break up with me again?

When I get outside, she's standing by my truck, wearing denim shorts, a white tank top, and flip flops that show off her bright pink toes. She looks adorable, but also hot. Her tank top fits tight against her body and when my eyes lower, I can see the outline of her navel ring.

"Can we go somewhere?" she asks, bringing my eyes back to her face. Her eyes look puffy, like she's been crying.

"Where do you want to go?"

"Anywhere but the farm."

I walk over to my truck and she steps aside as I open the door. It's the driver's side door, so she looks confused when I lift her up into the truck and set her down on the seat.

"I'm driving? I don't feel like driving."

"You're not driving. Now scoot over."

She's staring at me, surprised that I'm ordering her around like this. She probably thought I'd let her take the lead, but I can't be that way with her. Not now. Whenever she feels like things are out of control, she needs someone to step in and take over. It makes her feel safe and calms her down.

"Where are we going?" she asks as I take off down the street.

"To get some dinner. I haven't eaten since this morning and I'm starving. Did you eat already?"

"Just a few bites of pasta. I wasn't hungry."

We ride in silence during the ten-minute drive to the restaurant. I'm not ready to get into whatever she wants to tell me and she doesn't seem to be either. We'll get some food, then find a quiet place to talk.

The restaurant I take her to is a local fast food place that's open until midnight. You order at the window and eat outside. Willow and I used to go here a lot back in high school. Tonight the place is empty, probably because it's cool and breezy and people don't want to sit outside. I park, then go around to Willow's side, open the door and lift her out.

"Why do you keep doing that?" she asks as I set her down.

I ignore her question. It's part of my take-charge approach, as is my taking her hand and walking her to the order window.

Larry's working tonight. He's the owner; an old fat guy with thinning gray hair and a ketchup-stained t-shirt. He always pretends to be grumpy, but he's actually a nice guy.

"We'll have two number threes, one with everything, the other with one squirt of mustard, two squirts of ketchup, four—"

"Yeah, yeah. Four pickle slices and a very thin slice of tomato." He waves his order pad at us. "Where have you two been? Haven't seen you in years."

I can't believe he remembers us, and remembers Willow's hamburger order. That's one damn good memory.

"I was away at college," Willow says. She points to me. "And he was volunteering overseas."

He punches our order into his ancient cash register. "You married yet? Got any kids?"

I smile at Willow and yank her into my side. "Not married, but we just got engaged. Kids are a couple years off, but Willow wants at least three, don't you, honey?" I lean down and kiss her forehead.

She nudges my side and whispers, "Stop it."

Ruth appears beside Larry. "Those will be some good looking kids." Ruth is Larry's wife. She's not as grouchy as Larry. She's heavy-set with gray hair that's styled like a beehive on her head. "So when's the wedding?"

"Next May," I say. "It's going to be an outdoor wedding. I'm growing the flowers for her bouquet."

Ruth smiles. "Oh, how nice." She winks at Willow. "He's very romantic. You're lucky." She hitches her thumb toward Larry. "That one's idea of romantic is going a night without belching."

"It's $8.76." Larry holds his chubby hand out the window.

"We also want a chocolate milkshake."

"With three cherries on top and a spoon?"

"Yeah." I smile. "How do you remember all that?"

He shrugs. "It's some kind of disorder. I remember weird shit."

"Larry." Ruth pokes his belly. "Don't swear in front of the customers."

"Dammit, Ruth, you made me screw up," he says, pointing to the register.

She sighs and says to me, "Just go with the $8.76. The milkshake is on us. An engagement gift."

Larry huffs. "You can't be giving stuff away like that!"

"Get back to the kitchen." She shoos him away.

He walks off, shaking his hand.

"Thanks." I hand her a ten.

"This is why I don't let him run the register. He has no people skills." She hands me the change. "It'll be ready shortly."

Willow finds us a table and as soon as we sit down, she says, "So do you want to explain your little performance back there?"

"What's there to explain?" I set some napkins in front of her.

"That was embarrassing." She says it like she's mad, but I can see a hint of a smile. "Now they think we're engaged."

"So? Why do you care? It's just Ruth and Larry."

She glances back at the window. "I wonder how long they'll keep this place."

"Probably as long as possible. I can't see them retiring. They'd kill each other if they were home all day together."

She takes a napkin and folds it in half, then does the same to the next one. She likes her napkins folded. "It's funny how you go away for a while and come back and some things are the same and some things totally change."

"Is that a bad thing? That some things are the same?"

"No." She keeps her eyes on the napkin, running her finger over the fold.

There's something she's not saying but wants to. Before I can ask, Ruth appears, holding a tray.

She sets our sodas down. "Your burgers will be right out." She puts the milkshake between us, assuming we're sharing, and points to Willow's hand. "Where's your ring?"

"Um, I—"

"She left it at home because we were at the beach earlier," I say. "It's a one-of-a-kind ring so she didn't want to risk losing it in the water." I smile at Willow. "Although if she did, I'd just make her another one."

Ruth gasps. "You made her engagement ring?"

"I did." I keep my eyes on Willow. "I designed it and used a stone Willow found in the sand."

"That's so romantic." Ruth fans herself like she's going to pass out.

"Ruth!" Larry yells from the window. "Order's ready!"

She rolls her eyes. "I guarantee *he'll* never make me a ring. The only thing Larry's ever made me is a burger." She gets our food and brings it to the table. "If you need anything else, just let me know."

When she's gone, I ask Willow, "So what did you mean when you were talking about some things always being the same?"

"It's just...I don't know." She swirls her straw in her soda. "I liked growing up here, but as I got older I couldn't wait to go away. I wanted something new, something different. I wanted change. And I had it when I went to Camsburg. That was my first step in my new life."

I wait for her to finish because I can tell she's working this through in her head as she talks.

"But then when your old life completely changes, or is about to completely change, you desperately want it back. Or at least the things you're familiar with. The things that haven't changed. Like this restaurant." She picks up the milkshake and takes a sip. "See? It tastes the same as always." She slides it over to me. "Thanks for taking me here. I needed this."

"Maybe we'll come back tomorrow," I say casually.

She doesn't agree to it, but just eats her burger. I take a sip of the milkshake, but let her have the rest. She needs it more than I do. She can't handle uncertainty and that's all she has right now. I hadn't even considered coming to this restaurant would make her feel better, but once she explained it, it made total sense. So when we're done eating, I take her to another place that hasn't changed. A place we used to go.

"Are you going to our make-out spot?" she asks.

"It's just a field."

"That we made out at, like a million times."

I park the truck in our spot. "It wasn't a million. Maybe a hundred."

We're at an open field close to her old high school. As she said, we used to come here late at night and make out. We always parked next to a tree, thinking it would somehow hide us from the cops if they happened to be driving by, but they never did.

"Silas, we need to talk."

I undo my seatbelt and turn toward her. "Go ahead."

She undoes her seatbelt as well, and faces me. "First, I want to say that I really appreciate everything you've done. Working for my dad. For free. I can't believe you're doing that. And that you dropped two classes so that you could. You shouldn't have done that."

"To me, it was the right decision. School can wait. Saving the farm can't."

"This is what I mean. The way you're able to just drop everything and change your plans without worrying about it? I admire that about you. I always have. But it just shows how different we are."

"Willow, we don't have to be the same people in order to have a relationship. We can still make this work."

"Let me finish." She looks down at her hands. "I'm angry at you for not telling me what was going on. I understand you only did it because my parents told you to, but by doing that, I feel like you took their side instead of mine. Like you betrayed our friendship. You've never kept secrets from me before."

"Willow, I begged your dad to tell you, and he said he would, but he kept putting it off. He didn't want you to worry. He thought if he gave it more time, he might be able to turn things around and not have to tell you."

"They're too far in debt to turn things around, unless they use my college money. And it sounds like they've finally agreed to do that."

So she's not going back to Camsburg in the fall. Shit. She loved that school. I had a feeling she wouldn't be going back but was hoping it wouldn't come to that. Even though I love the idea of having her here in town, I want her to be happy, and she was happy at Camsburg.

"I'm sorry, Willow." I reach over and slip my hand around hers.

She's quiet and I'm not sure what to say, so I say nothing.

The silence continues and then she lifts her head. "What do you think I should do?"

I'm surprised she's asking me that. Willow prides herself on being independent and making her own decisions. But now she's asking me for advice, not as her boyfriend but as her friend. I've given this some thought, so since she asked, I'll give her an answer.

"I think you should take next semester off, do what you can to help your parents save the business, then go back to school in the spring and summer to catch up."

"Where would I go to school?"

"UC-Berkeley. I know you wanted to get away from here but Berkeley's a really good school and I did some research and they have a great business program. And Martin could help you with the application process. He's friends with people in admissions. Plus going to Berkeley would be cheaper because you could live at home. Or with me." I threw that last part in just to see how she'd react. It's no secret I want to be with her so I might as well put it out there.

"You're moving out of your parents' house?"

"I need to save up some money, but yeah, that's the plan. Actually, Trent's uncle isn't coming back after the summer like he'd plan to, so he's looking for someone to housesit. Trent asked if I wanted to live there after he goes back to college in the fall."

"You should do it. That's a really nice house."

"We'll see. Trent and I aren't exactly on speaking terms right now."

"Because of me," she says. "So you know he came to my house."

"Yeah. He shouldn't have done it."

"He was just being your friend. He doesn't want you to get hurt again." She pauses. "Neither do I. Which is why we can't continue this, Silas. I can't keep doing this, knowing it's just going to end."

My temper flares, angry that she's making this decision now, when she's not thinking straight. She's panicking, and right now, this is the only decision that makes sense to her. It's just like when she broke up with me last time. She made the decision based on fear. Fear that she wouldn't accomplish her goals if I was in her life. Now it's her fear of the unknown causing her to push me away. She's uncertain about the future and doesn't want to keep dating me if there's a possibility she might break up with me later when she figures out what to do.

When she gets like this I can't convince her to change her mind. She has to do that on her own. So I'm not going to fight her on this. Instead, I'm going to spend my time being her friend, reminding her how good we are together. Showing her that no matter how much she fights it, she'll still love me, and I'll love her. She'll try to keep her distance from me, but that'll be hard to do given that I live down the street from her and work for her dad.

"Okay." I let go of her hand. "Anything else?"

She looks confused. "Don't you want to talk about this?"

"What's there to talk about? You broke up with me. I got it. But we're still going to be friends."

"I don't know if that's a good—"

"You need a friend right now. And since you don't seem to have any others, I'm it."

"I have friends," she insists.

"You haven't spoken to your high school friends in over a year, so I'm guessing they're probably not your friends anymore."

She doesn't respond, which means it's true. Her friends in high school weren't close friends, so I'm not surprised she didn't stay in touch with anyone.

I lean back in my seat, facing forward and lacing my hands behind my head. "So what else do you want to talk about?"

"It's late. We should go."

"I'm not ready to go." I reach behind the seat and grab the sleeping bags and blankets. "Come on."

I open my door and step out.

"Silas, no. It's cold out. We're not going back there."

"I am. If you don't want to come with me, then I guess you'll just have to wait here until I'm ready to go." I close the door and go to the back of the truck and lay out the sleeping bags and blankets.

"Silas, this isn't funny!" I hear her voice, then see her climbing up into the truck bed. "We're broken up. We're not doing this."

"Not doing what?" I lie down, gazing up at the sky.

She sits beside me. "You know what I'm talking about."

"Hot, uncontrolled, mind-blowing sex that makes you scream my name?" I smile. "Yeah, we're not doing that. Sorry, but if you want that, we have to be dating. I'm not some manwhore like Trent. I do have standards."

She laughs and punches me. "You're such a liar. If I asked, you'd do it right this second."

I turn my head to look at her. "Go ahead and ask."

She laughs again. "Okay, but this is just a test. If you say yes, we're not really going to do it."

"I'm waiting."

She leans down and says in a sexy voice, "Silas, would you have sex with me?"

"No," I say, gazing up at the sky.

She thinks I'm kidding so she says, "Please. Just one more time?"

"Nope." I yawn. "I'm gonna take a short nap. This fresh air is making me tired. Wake me up in an hour."

I close my eyes but feel her staring at me. She's not used to me turning her down. It's never happened. And even though I told her we weren't doing it, she's still surprised I didn't at least try to take her up on her fake offer. She'll take that as a challenge.

I smile when I feel her lips on mine. I know her so well. She hates being wrong. She was so sure I'd give in to her, but I didn't and it's driving her crazy.

"Willow."

"What?" she says, kissing me.

"What are you doing?" I open my eyes and see her face above mine. "No kissing. We're friends. Friends don't kiss."

"I know." She backs away. "I was just testing you."

"Did I pass the test?"

"Yes." She sits next to me, hugging her knees.

"Are you cold?"

"A little."

"Come here." I hold the blanket up.

She hesitates. "We shouldn't do that."

"Why not? I just told you we're not having sex."

"But I just broke up with you. Aren't you mad at me?"

"Doesn't matter. I still want you in my life. So if we're not dating, we'll just go back to being friends."

"I don't know if I can do that. It's too hard to be around you without..."

"Taking advantage of me?" I pull her down next to me. "I am pretty irresistible."

She laughs. "And conceited."

"I made you laugh so that's a reason to keep me around."

She lays her head on my shoulder. "Silas?"

"Yeah."

"I feel like such a mess right now. Like I have no direction. No place to go."

"Just take one day at a time." I rest my arm over her and we stare up at the sky.

After a few minutes, she bolts up. "I can see it!"

"See what?"

"You and me. In the stars. I couldn't see it last time but now I do."

I've been looking at it this whole time but didn't think she'd notice it. So does the fact that she sees it mean something? Now that her plan is gone, will she start to see things differently? I hope so, because that's what she needs to do in order for us to have a chance.

She lies down again. "I wish the answers were up there in the sky. Like some kind of sign telling me what to do."

There are signs all around her but she doesn't realize it. The star formation is a sign telling her we should be together. And maybe her parents' business problems are a sign telling her to stay here and reevaluate her life. Maybe it's a sign that she was headed down the wrong path. I don't like bad things happening to people, but I do believe things happen for a reason. Unfortunately, Willow doesn't see it that way.

CHAPTER TWENTY-SIX

WILLOW

What am I doing? I came here to break up with Silas and now I'm in his arms, lying in his truck, looking up at the stars. This is wrong. It *feels* right, but I don't act on feelings. I act on facts. And the facts tell me I shouldn't be with Silas.

"We have to go." I move his arm off me and stand up.

"Why? What's wrong?"

"I need you to take me home." I jump over the side of the truck and get in the front seat and wait for him.

"What just happened?" he asks as he gets in the truck.

"I told you. I need to go home."

"Willow." He holds onto my wrist as I click my seatbelt in place. "Tell me what's wrong."

"I can't keep doing this to you."

"Doing what? Being friends with me?"

"This relationship. You know it's more than a friendship. We have too much history for it to be just a friendship. It's too hard to be friends with someone you...love."

"If you love me, then don't break up with me."

"It's not that simple."

"It IS that simple."

"Trent was right. If we keep this going, I'll end up hurting you again. I'm sorry, Silas, but I can't do this unless I'm committed to you. And right now, I can't commit to anything. I'm too lost. Too confused."

"Which is why you need me now more than ever. And as for Trent, are you seriously taking dating advice from someone whose idea of dating is a string of one-night stands?"

"I know, and I normally wouldn't listen to him, but in this case he was right. I'm not going to repeat the past."

"Willow, look at me." When I do, he says, "I'd rather risk getting hurt than lose you completely. I'm just asking for this summer. If at the end of August, you decide you don't want this, then we'll go our separate ways. But until then, just give us a chance. I can handle whatever happens. I'm not going to fall apart if you break up with me."

I look away from him. "I'm sorry, but I can't do it."

He waits for a moment, then starts the truck and drives off. We ride in silence until we get to my house.

"I don't need help getting out," I say, when I see him undoing his seatbelt.

"I'm still walking you to the door."

I step out of the truck and he walks with me to the house.

"Goodnight," I say.

He looks at me, pausing before saying, "Goodnight."

I go inside and watch out the front window as he drives away. He didn't seem angry or even sad. I don't get it. Is he just accepting this is over? That easily? Even *I* can't accept it. I didn't want to let him go, but I don't have a choice. I have to get myself together and figure out what I'm going to do before I even think about letting Silas back in my life.

The next day, I don't see or hear from Silas. I miss him so much. I tell myself that empty feeling in my heart will go away but I know it's a lie. For two years I tried to get over him, but the emptiness remained.

My phone rings and I smile when I see it's Lilly calling. "Hey, Lilly. How's your summer going?"

"Great, although I miss Reed."

"How long's it been since you've seen him?"

"I was there last week, so it hasn't been that long but I still miss him. It's hard not seeing him every day."

I'm happy for Lilly and Reed, but also jealous of their relationship. Why is it so much easier for them than for Silas and me? Am I making this too complicated? Should I just be with Silas and not worry about the future? I wish I could, but my stupid mind won't let me.

"So how's Silas?" Lilly asks. "You guys looked so cute in that photo you sent. You make a great couple."

My emotions hit me like a freight train and I break down crying. "I broke up with Silas last night."

"Willow!" she says in a scolding tone. "Why did you break up with him?"

"It's a long story. And to make matters even worse, I won't be going back to Camsburg in the fall." I sniffle and grab a tissue from my nightstand.

"Wait, what? Hold on. Go back and start from the beginning."

I tell her everything, from my parents' financial problems to my break-up with Silas. I'm crying so much it takes almost an hour to get it all out.

"You're really not coming back?" she asks.

"I can't. My parents need the money."

"Maybe...I mean, my dad could maybe—"

"No. I'd never ask your family for money. It wouldn't feel right and it would mess up our friendship."

"I'm sorry, Willow. I wish I could do something to help. Maybe my dad could give your parents some business advice. Or would that offend them? I only offered because you said they're not very good with business stuff."

"I don't know. I'd have to ask them."

"I still don't understand why you broke up with Silas. If you're staying there in the fall, then you guys could keep dating."

"That'll just make us closer."

"Yeah? So what's wrong with that?"

259

"I don't want to stay here forever. I may have to finish college here, but then I want to leave. Move away. Start my career. I still want to run a company someday."

"And what does Silas want to do?"

"He's thinking of going into graphic design, but that could change. I told you, he's a free spirit. He takes one day at a time."

"Maybe you should do the same."

"Lilly, you know I can't do that. I'm not like that. It's not my personality."

"People can change. You can be however you want. The old Willow had to plan everything out, but maybe the new one doesn't. This is like a fresh start. You can do anything you want now, including being with Silas."

I smile. "Okay, you're stressing me out with all these options."

She laughs. "Options are good. That's why they have that saying to keep your options open."

"Hey, are you coming up here this summer?"

"I'm not sure. My dad might be giving a speech in San Francisco, and if he does, I told him I'm going with him. He can drop me off in Berkeley."

"I hope you can make it. I miss seeing you."

Lilly is my closest friend at Camsburg. She's what I'll miss most about it. She listened to me talk about Silas for most of last year. I didn't think I talked about him that much, but a few weeks ago she told me I talked about him constantly. I didn't even realize I was doing it. It just shows what a big part of my life he is, even when he's not around.

By the end of the call I feel a little better. Even if I don't go back to Camsburg, Lilly and I agree that we'll still be friends. She's not that far away so we can still see each other and we can talk on the phone all the time.

The next week I spend at home, working on a plan to save the farm. I start by going through my parents' bills. Ron, their hippie accountant, had already made spreadsheets and run different scenarios for paying off their debt. It's all well thought out and much better than I would've done. Now I feel bad for saying Ron was an idiot. When did I become so judgmental? People used to judge me for having hippie parents and I hated it, yet here I was, judging Ron's competence based on how he dressed.

If my parents use my college fund, they could pay everything off right away. Or they could use just part of the money and pay off their debts in increments, using money from the farm as well. The farm has been profitable so far this year, but we need to get more income out of the land. After doing some research, I found that flowers are the way to go. Silas originally came up with that idea and it was a good one. The profit margin is much higher on flowers than on vegetables. Silas already planted some but we need to plant more.

Next, I work on a plan for marketing. Silas finished the logo last week and it looks great. It's fresh and modern and fits our brand. We're going to start using it on signs and on the product labels for the beauty products my mom and I are developing. Based on our success at the vendor fair, we've decided to sell more soaps and lotions. And I've convinced my mom to charge more for her homemade granola. She was practically giving it away before.

On Saturday, I go to the farmers' market with my parents. I haven't worked at our booth since last summer and I've kind of missed it. I like seeing people get so excited about our products. And now we've added our all natural beauty products, which were a huge success. We sold out in the first two hours. I couldn't believe it. Now I can't wait to go home and make more and come up with new varieties.

This past week, I've barely slept and I'm not even tired. Working on this plan to save the farm has filled me with energy. And by developing this new line of beauty products, I feel like I'm actually making a difference. Seeing my efforts paying off is exciting and makes me happy. The only thing that would make it better would be if Silas were around.

I haven't seen Silas since last Saturday night when we said goodbye at my door. He hasn't called or texted or stopped over. He's doing what I asked, leaving me alone to figure out what I'm going to do with my life. But God, I miss him. It gets worse every day. I've almost called him about a million times. And I keep walking by his house but won't let myself go up to the door.

This was supposed to get easier as time went by but it's only getting harder. I've been thinking that maybe I should take him up on his offer and just date him for the summer. But if I did that, I wouldn't ever want it to end.

Something's changed between Silas and me. We're different than we were back in high school. We've changed and grown and after two years apart, we both realized how much we missed each other. If we continue our relationship, I have a feeling it'll be for good this time. And although I like the idea of that, it also scares me because I won't accomplish my goals if I'm in a serious relationship. Like my mom said, I'd need to make sacrifices, and at the age of 19, I'm not willing to do that.

As we're closing up the booth at the farmers' market, I see Silas at the booth across from us, helping his mom pack everything up. He's wearing a light green t-shirt and faded jeans, his skin a dark golden brown from all the hours he spends in the sun. He picks up a box, his arm muscles flexing, and it conjures up a heat inside me. He turns to me and smiles. A sly, half smile that says I've been caught. I quickly glance away.

I hear my mom beside me. "Why don't you go say hi?"

"To who?" I start taking the tomatoes out of their cardboard containers.

"To Silas. You haven't seen him all week."

"Because we're not dating." I line the tomatoes up in a neat little row on the table.

"You could still say hello. You're clearly too preoccupied to work."

"I'm not too—" I stop when I see that I've just unpacked the tomatoes that I was supposed to be packing up to take home.

My mom's smiling at me. "I'll finish up here. Go ahead."

I slowly walk over to Diane's booth and go up to Silas. "Hi."

"Hey, Willow." He gives me a smile but continues to pack up the jewelry.

"So, um, how have you been?" I feel nervous. Why am I nervous? It's just Silas. Yet it feels different when he's not my boyfriend. Maybe because I know he's single now and any girl could have him. What if he's already dating someone? Is that why he's ignoring me?

"I'm good," he says. "And you?"

"Fine. I've been at home all week, working on some new products and coming up with marketing ideas. That logo you did is really amazing. You captured the tone and feel of the business perfectly."

"Thanks." He stacks one of the boxes on top of another.

I notice Diane watching us out of the corner of her eye as she gathers her receipts, pretending to sort them.

"So how was class today?" I ask.

"Boring. I've decided accounting's not for me. I'm going to sign up for graphic design classes in the fall."

"Silas, that's great!"

"Yeah." He picks up three big boxes. "Hey, I'll see ya later. I have to take these to the truck."

"You need some help?" I scan the booth for anything I could take, but the only items left are the table and two folding chairs.

"I can handle it," he says.

"I'll take these." I grab the folding chairs.

He laughs a little. "Okay. Follow me."

I'm making a fool out of myself, but I don't care. I miss Silas and I just want a few minutes with him. Actually, I'd like to spend the rest of the day with him but that would be leading him on.

When we get to his truck, I hand him the chairs.

"Thanks," he says, setting them in the truck bed. The place where we had sex. Multiple times a night. Almost every night we were back together. The best sex I've ever had.

I'm heating up again, my heart racing being this close to him.

"I should tie these down," he says. "Could you grab the ties in the truck? They're on the floor in the front seat."

"Sure." I open the driver's side door and climb in the truck. As I'm picking up the ties, I notice a sweater in the back seat. A bright pink sweater. A girl's sweater.

He found someone. Silas is dating someone. Maybe it's that hairdresser. She really wanted to go out with him. Or maybe it's someone else. Maybe someone Trent set him up with.

My stomach clenches and my throat burns as I fight back the tears. I knew this would happen. I knew he'd find someone, but it still hurts.

"Willow, did you find them?" he calls out.

"Yeah." I hop out of the truck and give him the ties. "I need to go, but it was good seeing you."

"Yeah, okay." He seems confused by my sudden departure, but I scurry off before he can ask me about it.

"Ready to go?" my mom says when I get back to the booth. "Or is Silas taking you home?"

"Why would Silas take me home?" I ask harshly, now angry that he's dating someone. I know he's single, but couldn't he wait a few weeks before finding a new girl?

"I just asked, honey. I didn't mean anything by it."

I shake Silas out of my head. "Sorry, Mom. I'm just in a bad mood today, I guess."

"You weren't earlier. Did something happen with Silas?"

"No." I grab a box. "I'll go take this to the car."

As I'm walking to the vendor parking lot, I see Silas leaning against his truck, talking on the phone. He's smiling as he talks and I'm sure it's because he's talking to his new girlfriend. The box slips out of my hand and tomatoes spill out on the ground.

I quickly pick them up, hoping Silas doesn't see me and see how flustered I am. He doesn't. Even when I'm walking back to the booth, he doesn't seem to notice me.

The loss I've felt without him the past week becomes even worse now that I know he's moved on. It's what I told myself I wanted. What's best for him. But my heart refuses to accept it. Why can't my damn heart get in sync with my brain? Why are they fighting each other like this? And why does my heart keep winning the battle? Filling my thoughts with Silas? Making my chest ache from the loss of him? It's so damn frustrating, and painful, especially now that he's with someone else.

The next week I put all my energy into making more lotions and soaps. I create some new body scrubs with sea salts and essential oils. If I wasn't so heartbroken over Silas I'd be loving every second of this. I'm having so much fun. I've never let myself be this creative before. I didn't even know I *was* creative until now. But I'm not skilled in art and design so I could use some help designing the labels for all these new products. That's Silas' expertise, and although he might say no, I figure I might as well ask, so on Thursday night I decide to call him.

"Hey, Willow," he says in a casual tone, as if the past two weeks didn't even happen. As if we've been friends this whole time.

"Hi," I say nervously. Seriously, why am I nervous? This is ridiculous. I take a calming breath.

"Did you need something or were you just saying hi?"

"I um...I was just wondering if you'd help me out with something. You don't have to but—"

"Sure. What is it?"

"I made some new body scrubs and I was wondering if you could design the labels."

"Okay. Just email me the details and I'll get to work on it. Do you need it for Saturday?"

"Yeah, but that's not much time so I'll just plan on using plain labels this Saturday."

"I might be able to get it done. I can't work on it tomorrow night, but I can tonight. Send me a description of what you need and I'll see how far I can get."

"Okay. Thanks."

"Yeah. Talk to you later."

He hangs up and I drop the phone on my nightstand and lie down on my bed. Why does this hurt so much? Just hearing his voice made me miss him even more.

I was hoping we could meet to go over the labels but he wants me to email him instead. And he said he's busy tomorrow night. Friday night. Date night. He'll be out with his new girlfriend.

I want to be mad at him about that but I can't. He tried to make it work between us and I ruined it. And now I feel like I ruined any chance of us ever getting back together.

CHAPTER TWENTY-SEVEN

SILAS

It's been over two weeks since Willow and I broke up. My initial plan to get her back was to just be her friend until she figured out what she wanted. But when she told me she didn't think we should even be friends anymore because of where it might lead, I decided to do as she asked and leave her alone. I know that's not what she really wants, but I can't tell her that. She needs to figure that out for herself. And I think she's starting to.

I've only seen her twice the past couple weeks, and both times she seemed nervous. Whenever she's around me, she gets all flustered. I've never seen her act like this. It's like she thinks I've moved on and now she wants to get my attention but is worried it might be too late. I can see why she'd think that. I've basically ignored her, not calling or texting or stopping by her house. It's been hard to do that because I miss her and want to talk to her but I'm doing what she asked, and until she tells me differently, I'm going to stay away from her.

But that hasn't stopped me from keeping tabs on her. I care about her and need to know that she's doing okay so I've been asking her dad for updates. He said she's been doing really well. He said he's never seen Willow show so much enthusiasm for the farm. She's developing new products. Creating a marketing plan. Finding new venues to sell at. She's determined to save the business and, according to her dad, she's loving every second of it.

The only thing bringing her down is the fact that she and I are no longer friends. I explained to her dad that Willow asked me to stay away and he just shook his head, as frustrated with his daughter as I am. He told me how much she misses me. He said he can't even mention my name without her tearing up and running off to her room.

I've seen her walk by my house a few times. She goes really slow like she's hoping she'll run into me. I could've gone out there and talked to her, but I decided not to. She needs more time to make a decision about us. I want her to be sure of it this time and not doubt it. So I'm going to stay out of her way and not try to sway her decision. Besides, she knows how I feel.

Now that Willow's not around, I've had a lot of free time. Aside from working on the farm, I've spent the past few weeks researching what types of jobs I could have as a graphic designer. I think this is something I want to do, so I picked out some classes to take this fall. I also got some new design software and I've been teaching myself how to use it. I used it to design the labels Willow wanted for the new products she made. When she called me, asking me to make them, I could hear the disappointment in her voice when I told her to email me the details. It was a good sign because it shows how much she misses me. But she doesn't miss me enough to take me back, and until then, I'm going to keep my distance.

"You gonna pass the ball or just stand there?" Trent asks.

We're at the park, playing basketball. I've been hanging out with Trent again. I've forgiven him for what he did. It ended up being a good thing he told Willow the truth. It finally got everything out in the open and now it's forcing her to think about her future with me.

"What's the rush?" I toss it to him.

"I got shit to do later," he says, shooting the ball and bouncing it off the backboard.

"What shit do you have to do?" I retrieve the ball and sink it into the basket.

"None of your damn business." He's hiding something. Something he doesn't want me to know.

I take the ball and hold it. "Does this have to do with Leah?"

He holds his hands out. "Give me the ball."

I laugh. "You're still going out with her, aren't you?"

He sighs. "We're friends. That's it. Now give me the damn ball."

"What's it been? Like two weeks now?"

"Three," he mumbles.

"It's been three weeks already? I guess I lost track."

Trent's been dating Leah, the girl who made margaritas at his pool party back in June. The margaritas that got Willow drunk. I like Leah. I went out with her and Trent for dinner a couple weeks ago and afterward he kept asking me what I think of her. He never asks for my opinion on the girls he dates, so that was my first clue that this relationship might actually go somewhere.

Then there's the fact that Leah doesn't put up with his shit. She calls him out on stuff when he's being an ass and she never phones him or texts him. If he wants to see her or talk to her, he has to track her down. The hard-to-get approach is working. He can't seem to get enough of her.

I've become friends with her because she's having me design the logo for her new business. She and her friend are developing a line of signature cocktails that she hopes to sell to bars and someday get into stores. I've met with her several times the past week about the logo, but she hasn't even mentioned Trent. I assumed they broke up so I didn't ask.

"Don't be giving me shit about her," Trent says, grabbing the ball from me.

"Who? Your girlfriend?" I kid. Trent hates the 'girlfriend' label. It sounds too serious.

"You better not let her hear you call her that. She'll freaking punch you."

I laugh. "She doesn't want to be Trent Kincaid's girlfriend? I thought that was every girl's dream."

He throws the ball at me. "Shut up, asshole."

"So you're saying she's just like you? Only in it for the sex?"

"Yeah." He lifts his baseball cap and turns it the other way, the flap in the back.

"That's what you wanted, right? Just sex? No strings?"

He shrugs. "I guess."

It's clearly bothering him that she won't be his girlfriend, which is completely shocking. The whole time I've known him, he's never wanted a girlfriend.

"So are you going to keep dating her?" I ask.

"Why wouldn't I?"

"You've already gone past your two week limit. Isn't it time to break up with her?"

"It's a lot of work finding someone new." He glances off to the side. "I think I'll just keep this going."

He's such a liar. He'd have no problem finding someone new. He just likes Leah too much to give her up.

"By the way," I say. "Your girlfriend left her sweater in my truck."

"So that's where it went. She kept asking me if I'd seen it."

He didn't even correct me on the girlfriend label, which means he already thinks of her that way. That's a huge deal. Before he met her, I couldn't even get him to consider the idea of having a girlfriend.

"Come get it." I motion him to the parking lot. "I've gotta get going."

"You got plans tonight?"

"I'm designing a new logo for my mom's business."

"You're really getting into this design stuff," he says as we walk to my truck. "It's good you found something you like."

"Yeah. I think I finally figured out what I want to do." I open the door and grab the sweater and toss it to him.

"So what about Willow? You two still aren't talking?"

"We talk when we need to. Other than that, no."

"I can't believe you've been able to stay away from her."

"If I want her back I need to give her space. And if she decides she doesn't want me in her life, then I'm starting to accept that. I love her, but I'm done playing these games. Either she wants me or she doesn't. And if she doesn't, it's time to move on."

"Good for you, man. I like Willow, but the girl needs to get her shit together." He walks over to his car. "Call me tomorrow. Maybe we'll go golfing...if Leah doesn't wear me out too much." He smiles.

"Yeah, see ya."

I'm jealous. I wish I had a girl to hang out with tonight. And not just any girl. I want Willow. I miss her like crazy and I want her back. What I told Trent isn't entirely true. I'm not ready to give up on Willow. I need to convince her we belong together, and if giving her space doesn't work, then I'll have to find another way, although I'd rather have her come to that conclusion herself.

But like I told Trent, I'm starting to accept the fact that despite my best efforts, Willow and I may not end up together. I love her and want a future with her, but I can't force her to feel the same way. And I can't keep playing this game of back and forth. By the end of the summer she needs to make a decision, and if she decides not to be with me, then I have to move on, even if it kills me to do so.

The following week, Willow shows up at the farm. She's working in the fields again, but only in the mornings, and then she goes home in the afternoons to make more soaps and lotions. When she's at the farm I leave her alone, but I keep catching her watching me. I've been watching her too, but she hasn't caught me yet.

It's now Friday, and almost three weeks since our break-up. Tonight will be yet another Friday night when I should be out with Willow, but instead will be home, working on logos. Trent invited me to go out with him and Leah to an outdoor concert

271

but I didn't want to be a third wheel, or worse yet, have him ambush me with a blind date. I think he knows better than to do that after the incident earlier this summer, but with Trent, you never know.

"Silas!" Willow yells.

I'm way back in the lettuce fields and see her walking toward me. "What do you need?"

"It's lunch time," she yells back.

"Yeah, I'm not hungry."

"You have to eat. You've been out here since six this morning."

How did she know that? Her dad must've told her. Since the break-up, I haven't slept well so I've been getting to work early every day.

"Come on. I have everything set up." Willow's in front of me now, dressed in one of her sexy farm girl outfits; denim cut-off shorts with a tiny white t-shirt and her red cowboy boots, her long dark hair tied back in a loose braid. I'd like to grab that braid, tug it back, and plant my mouth on hers.

"Silas?"

"Yeah." I wake up from my fantasy and toss my cutting shears in the bucket. "I didn't bring a lunch today. I forgot, so I'm just gonna skip it."

"You're not skipping lunch. Come on." She takes my hand, then freezes, like she didn't mean to do that.

I grip her hand, letting her know it's okay, and smile at her. "Are you saying you brought me lunch?"

She smiles back. "I didn't just bring it. I made it."

"What did you make?"

"Fried chicken." She swings our arms a little as we walk through the fields.

"You made fried chicken? Isn't that hard to make?"

"Yeah, and it's messy. Grease splattered all over the walls."

"Then why did you make it?"

"I've been watching these cooking shows on TV and I saw them making fried chicken one day and thought I'd try it." She pauses. "And, well, you really like fried chicken."

Is she saying she made it just for me? She's never cooked for me. I've cooked for her many times, but she's never made anything for me, other than cold sandwiches.

"It's been in the cooler," she says, "so it's not hot, but the lady on TV said cold fried chicken is how you eat it in the summer. I also have potato salad but I bought it at the store. And I cut up a cantaloupe that my dad picked this morning. I was going to make brownies but I didn't have time."

I tug on her hand, stopping her. "Why'd you do all this?"

She shrugs, her eyes gazing down. "I just haven't seen you much lately and I thought maybe if I brought you lunch, you'd spend some time with me."

"Willow." I tip her face up to mine. "I'll spend time with you whenever you want. But you told me to leave you alone, so that's what I'm doing."

"I didn't say to leave me alone. Or if I did, I didn't mean that. I just—"

"You said you didn't want to be friends. You said it was too hard to be around each other." I look her in the eye. "Have you changed your mind about that?"

She holds my gaze for a moment, then glances away. "We should eat before the bugs get all over the food." She starts walking off.

God, this girl frustrates the hell out of me. Why won't she just say what she's thinking? I can tell she wants to, but she won't. Just now, some thought entered her head and the happy mood she greeted me with turned sad and almost regretful. But why?

I follow her to one of the picnic tables. The other workers are already eating lunch, two tables down. They glance at us, then return their attention to their phones. I spot Willow's dad standing by the trailer, watching her and shaking his head. I think he's just as confused by his daughter's actions as I am.

"You even set the table," I say, noticing the red checkered tablecloth, plates, and silverware.

"Since I went to all that work to make the chicken, I thought it should be served in a nice way."

"I like it." I smile at her. "Thanks." I lean down and give her a peck on the cheek.

She looks surprised by the kiss but smiles back. "You're welcome."

As we have our fried chicken, she tells me what she's been up to the past few weeks. Her dad is right. It's like she has this new energy about her. I've never seen her like this. When she talks about all the products she's been creating, her whole face lights up. It's good to see her this happy. Even if we don't get back together, this is what I want for her. To be this happy about whatever it is she ends up doing.

When we're finished eating, she starts putting our dishes back in the picnic basket.

"Need some help?" I ask.

"No, I got it."

"Thanks again for lunch. It was really good." I stand up. "I better get back to work."

"Silas?"

"Yeah?"

She hesitates. "Are you, um, going out tonight?"

"No. I'm working on a logo for my mom."

"Really?" Her brows rise. "I thought maybe you'd go out. I mean, it's Friday." She smiles nervously. "That's date night, right?"

I smile. "I guess, but I don't have a date."

"What about your—" She stops and shakes her head. "Never mind. It's none of my business."

"My *what*? What were you going to say?"

"I just..." She sweeps the crumbs off the tablecloth in short, quick strokes. "I thought you'd be out with that girl."

"What girl?"

"The one you're going out with." She sets the picnic basket on the ground and whips the checkered cloth off the table.

"Willow." I hold her wrist so she'll stop moving. "I'm not going out with anyone."

She looks up at me. "Silas, you can tell me. It's okay. I assumed you'd start dating again."

I release her wrist. "I'm not dating anyone. Why did you think I was? Did someone tell you that?"

She folds up the tablecloth. "I saw her sweater in your truck. I didn't mean to, but it was right there."

Her attempt to hide her jealousy is a complete fail. I can hear it in her tone. And on her face I see the hurt she's feeling over thinking about me with someone else.

I take the tablecloth from her and set it down. "Just stop for a minute and listen to me. That was Leah's sweater. Leah, as in the bartender who makes your favorite margaritas. She's dating Trent, and one day I had to give her a ride and she left her sweater in my truck. I'm not dating her. I'm not dating anyone."

"Oh." Willow's shoulders relax and she gives me a hesitant smile. "Okay. Well, do you maybe want to have dinner with me tonight before you get to work on your logo?"

I cross my arms over my chest, a grin on my face. "Are you asking me out?"

She bites her lip, avoiding my gaze. "Maybe. I don't really know."

"Well, I need you to know. So when you figure that out, ask me again." I turn and walk back to the fields.

"Wait." Willow catches up to me, but I keep walking. "Could we maybe try being friends again?"

I stop and face her. "Just friends? Or more than that?"

"Just friends. For now."

I almost tell her no because I'm afraid this will just lead us back to where we were a few weeks ago. Friends with benefits and nothing more.

"If we do this, we're just going to be friends. It's strictly platonic. Unless you've decided something about us. But I get the feeling you haven't."

She nods. "Okay. Strictly platonic."

Dammit. That was her chance to tell me she wants us to get back together, but instead she chose the friend option. So frustrating.

"I'll be home around six," I say. "So just call anytime after that and we'll figure out dinner."

"Actually, I'm staying here this afternoon. I'm going to plant flowers where the broccoli used to be. Do you want to help me?"

"I need to finish the lettuce first, but after that, yeah, I can help."

"Then I'll see you over there." She leaves with a big smile on her face.

I swear, I can't figure her out. She wants to spend time with me but she doesn't want to date me. She says she loves me but won't commit to being in a relationship with me.

I've been trying to stay positive, but I'm starting to think this summer isn't going to end well.

CHAPTER TWENTY-EIGHT

WILLOW

I'm convinced I'm going through Silas withdrawal. I was completely addicted to that boy, and still am. Ever since we broke up, I haven't been able to stop thinking about him. Wanting him. Craving him. It's bad. So bad. I have dreams about him. Naughty dreams. And if that's not bad enough, I keep embarrassing myself, trying to find ways to be around him.

I'm like a pathetic lovesick teenager. Technically, at 19, I still am a teenager but I like to think I'm no longer pathetic or lovesick when it comes to guys. But it turns out that's exactly what I am when it comes to Silas.

It's a good thing I've had work to keep me busy so I'm not constantly thinking about him. I'm starting to really like working in the family business. Actually, I love it. I'm surprised I'm even admitting that because for years I told myself I had no interest in the farm. I'd help out every summer but I had no interest in doing anything beyond that. My dream was to run a large corporation. I even imagined what my office would look like, with a big desk and floor-to-ceiling windows that look out at a city skyline.

But just last week, as I was sitting in my parents' office, I imagined myself running a small business. I even imagined running the farm someday, transforming it into something bigger but still keeping that homegrown family feel. I'd expand the prepared food line with jams and jellies and salsa, and maybe even get them into retail stores. And I'd do the same with the soaps and lotions and other skincare products.

Last night I wrote all my ideas down and had so many I didn't finish until two in the morning. Now I'm actually considering doing this. I might do like Silas said and take next semester off and go to UC-Berkeley in the spring. I'll miss being at Camsburg, but I'm not as sad as I was about not going back because I have other options. Options I might even like better than my old ones.

"Thanks for dinner," Silas says as we're driving home. I took him to the barbecue place he likes.

"You should thank my dad. It was his money."

"You still invited me. You could've gone with someone else."

"Well, apparently I have no friends other than you," I say kiddingly.

"Willow, I didn't mean it that way. I know you have friends."

"I did, but they've all moved on. Or some moved away. I called Kami last week and she's working at a summer camp in Portland. And Anna got an internship in San Diego."

He nudges my arm. "So that's why you wanted to be friends again? You had no other options?"

"No. It's because..." I pause. "Because I missed you. I really missed you, Silas."

He smiles at me. "I missed you too." He pulls the truck into my driveway. "Have a good night."

"Oh. Okay." I hear the disappointment in my voice.

"Is something wrong?"

"I guess I didn't know we were done." I undo my seatbelt and put my hand on the door handle. "I'll see you later."

"Yeah. Bye."

I start to get out but then stop, turning back to Silas. "Would you care if I came over for a little while? I know you have to work, but it's Friday night and I'm not quite ready to go home."

A slight smile appears. "Sure. You can come over."

I close the door, relieved that he agreed to it. Dinner only took an hour and I want more time with him. I freeze when I feel his arm reach over me for the seatbelt.

"Gotta buckle up." His hand brushes against my chest as he pulls the belt over me and clicks it in place. I'm burning up inside from just his brief touch, which is completely ridiculous. Just a few weeks ago, I was having sex with him several times a day, and now just the feel of his hand on me sends sparks flying? This guy has way too much power over me, and yet I like it.

"So what do you want to do?" he asks on the short drive to his house.

"Maybe just hang out in your room," I say casually so he doesn't read anything into it. He's being very strict about this platonic rule and although I know why he's doing it, I find it frustrating because it makes me want him even more.

Once we're in his room, he sits on his bed, tempting me once again. But I fight the temptation and go sit at his desk.

"Can I see what you've been working on?" I ask, turning to face his computer.

"Yeah, I can show you." He comes up behind me, leaning over me to wake up his laptop. His scent surrounds me. The scent that belongs only to him, and that I love and find comfort in. "So this is what I've been working on for my mom." He clicks open several files, each with a different logo. "These are just some rough drafts. I have a lot more work to do."

I look over his designs. "Silas, these are so good."

"You really think so?"

"Are you kidding?" I turn back to face him. "They look like they were done by a professional design firm."

"Thanks." He smiles and our eyes lock. He's still leaned over me, our faces so close they're almost touching. Before I can stop myself, I kiss him. Almost. He backs away before our lips meet.

I feel my face heating up as I quickly turn back toward the computer. "Sorry. It's just a habit. I'm so used to..." I don't bother finishing the thought. He knows I wanted to kiss him.

"Don't be embarrassed," he says low and soft by my ear. My pulse races at the feel of his breath. "You know I want you, Willow. I want you so fucking bad."

I freeze, my breathing fast and shallow from my racing heart.

His lips brush over my ear as he says, "But I won't let myself have you until I know that you're mine. For good this time. Understood?"

I swallow, then nod.

He raises up and points to the laptop. "So those are the designs I'm working on for Leah."

He just goes back to normal, while I'm left with my heart beating out of my chest, heat burning up my core, my head filled with images of Silas ripping my clothes off and taking me right here on his desk.

"You're designing logos for Leah?" I sit up straighter, trying to regain my composure.

"Yeah. She's starting a business with her friend and they needed some design work done."

I try to focus on the laptop screen and set aside what just happened. And yet I can still feel Silas' warm breath by my ear, and I can still hear his words, telling me how much he wants me. Holy shit, that was hot. I'll definitely be replaying that scene in my dreams tonight.

"What do you think?" he asks, referring to the logos.

"Your designs are great. I mean it. You need to start doing more of this. You could pay for college doing this."

"I don't know what to charge. I'm doing it for free right now, just to get some experience."

"I can help you figure out what to charge. And I could work on a plan for getting clients. Oh, and I could—"

"Willow." I hear him laughing behind me. "I don't need to figure this all out tonight." He shuts the laptop. "Why don't we grab a soda and go out back?"

"Okay." I get up from the chair and follow him to the door. "Silas, I just have to say how impressed I am. I was always impressed by your jewelry designs but I had no idea you were hiding all these other talents."

"And I had no idea you'd ever get so involved in your parents' business," he says as we go down the stairs. "You've really done a lot in just a few weeks."

"I guess, but I feel like there's so much more I could do."

As we sit on the back patio, I tell Silas some of the ideas I have for the business. The more I talk about it, the more I want to make those ideas happen. I think I really want to do this. I think that's my new plan.

After two hours, Silas says, "I'd like to talk longer but I have my final for accounting tomorrow and I should probably study."

"Final? Your class is over already?"

"Yeah, it was an eight-week class and tomorrow's the last day. I'm not doing that great but I haven't put much effort into it. Once I decided to study graphic design, my accounting efforts dropped off. I'm sure I'll flunk this final tomorrow." He gets up. "You can stay out here if you want."

"I think I will. My parents are out tonight and I don't feel like being in an empty house."

"I'll see you later."

"Yeah, bye."

A few minutes later, I hear the door open behind me. I turn and see Martin there, holding a book. "Oh, sorry, Willow, I didn't know you were out here. I'll read inside."

"No. Come on out. I can go. Or, actually, do you have a minute?"

He checks his watch and smiles. "You're in luck. I actually have more than a minute."

Martin's wearing plaid Bermuda shorts, a wrinkled white button-up shirt with the sleeves rolled up, and thick black socks that go up to his knees. His gray wiry hair is sticking up everywhere and his beard needs to be trimmed. He always has that disheveled look, but it fits him. He calls himself the nutty professor, and he is kind of nutty, but in a good way. He's funny, and has always been nice to me and a great stepdad to Silas.

"What should we discuss?" Martin asks, sitting across from me. "World peace? Stock prices? The energy crisis?"

I smile. "Those are kind of heavy topics. Let's save those for another day. For now, tell me about UC-Berkeley."

He grins, knowing exactly why I asked. He goes over the basics, then answers all my questions and tells me to apply now if I'm really serious about going there.

An hour later I go back to my house and get to work on my application. I can't believe I'm doing this. Just two months ago, my life was headed down a totally different path. Now it's all changed, and instead of panicking, I'm happy about it.

On Saturday I help my parents at the farmers' market. With all the new products, we end up making more money than we've ever made. Some of the flowers we planted were ready to sell and we sold out within the first hour. We didn't have a lot to sell, but I was still surprised they sold out that quickly.

In the afternoon, I call Silas to see if he wants to do something, but find out he went surfing with Trent. Silas loves surfing but he hasn't gone all summer. And I haven't been in years. We should go surfing together. I'm adding that to my list. I've started a list of all the things I want to do with Silas, leaving off the dirty things in case my parents see it.

I started the list because I've made the decision to be with Silas. For years, I told myself that Silas and I couldn't be together because my life would never be what I wanted it to be if I stayed with him. But the truth is, even if I were CEO of the biggest company in the world, I wouldn't be happy knowing the person I love is out there but not being able to be with him.

So in the end, there was really no decision to make. My heart decided this a long time ago. I just had to get my head to agree to it. And it finally did. And now, I have no doubts. I know what I want.

I want Silas. The boy who made me a report card so I wouldn't transfer to a different school. The boy who memorized how I like my hamburger and isn't embarrassed to order it that way. The boy who kept calling me from thousands of miles away, even though I never answered his calls. And the boy who made me the most beautiful engagement ring I've ever seen.

Being with Silas doesn't mean I'm giving up my dreams. I can still have a successful career. I've just changed how I define success. It's not about a job title or a big salary. It's about finding something I really want to do. Something I feel passionate about.

And I've already found that, in the place I least expected it. My family's business. It's been there all along and I never even considered it, but now I know it's exactly what I want to do. I've already talked to my parents about it and we decided that I'd take over the organic skin care products as if it were my own company. So basically, I'm already a CEO. The one and only employee of a company I hope to make a huge success someday. And I want Silas there every step of the way.

It's now Sunday afternoon and I'm going to tell Silas what I've decided. He's at the farm, so that's where I'm headed. It's the perfect place to tell him this. Silas and I have so many memories there, and hopefully will have many more in the years to come.

I park next to his truck. Every time I see it, I think about what we did in it. I'm dying to do it again, which is why I'm wearing a short cotton sundress with tiny straps that can easily be undone. But we may have to wait and do it later when it cools off. It's brutally hot out today, which is unusual because the temperature here is generally more moderate.

"Silas!" I yell as I walk through the fields. He said he'd be picking blackberries but I don't see him. Maybe he's kneeling down to reach the low branches. "Silas, are you out here?"

I fan myself as I trudge through the fields. It's so hot I'm already sweating.

"Silas?" I keep calling him but he doesn't answer. I'm now standing between the rows of blackberry bushes, looking up and down the field, but I don't see him. I turn to go back, but then spot something on the ground in the next row over. It's a work boot. Silas' work boot. I shove the bushes aside and see him lying on the ground.

"Silas!" I race over and kneel beside him. "Silas!" I turn his face toward me. His eyes are closed. "Silas, wake up! Please! Wake up!" His face is wet and clammy. "Silas!"

He's not responding, no matter how many times I yell his name.

CHAPTER TWENTY-NINE

WILLOW

I yank my phone out and call 911. The operator tells me the ambulance is on its way, then asks me a series of questions, but none of them explain what's wrong with Silas. As she hangs up, I hear the ambulance sirens in the distance.

I cradle Silas' head in my arms. "Please Silas. Please be okay." I'm so scared I'm shaking. I'm trying to be strong, trying to stay focused, trying not to break down crying, but that's nearly impossible to do when the person you love is lying unresponsive in your arms and you have no idea if he'll wake up.

"Silas, I love you." I'm crying now as I hear the sirens getting louder. "Please be okay."

Finally the ambulance arrives and I frantically wave them over. The paramedics surround Silas. I don't know what they're doing. I ask, but they don't answer. They load Silas on the stretcher, and only after I beg and plead do they agree to let me go with him to the hospital. On the way there, I call Diane and tell her what happened. She's as freaked out as I am and I hear Martin in the background trying to calm her down. I call my mom next and she tells me she'll meet me at the hospital.

When we get there, they take Silas away, leaving me alone in the crowded waiting room. Minutes later, Diane and Martin arrive, along with my parents. Diane finds a nurse who takes her down a hall.

"He'll be okay, honey," my mom says, sitting beside me and rubbing my back.

"We don't know that," I say, my voice cracking. "We don't know what's wrong with him. It could be really bad."

"Or it could be something minor," my dad says, sitting on my other side. "Low blood sugar. Dehydration. You know how Silas never drinks enough water. And when he gets busy in the fields, he forgets to eat."

I nod. "Yeah. He does."

My dad puts his arm around me and I lay my head on his shoulder.

A few minutes later, Diane returns and I race up to her. "Is he okay?"

"Yes. They say he was dehydrated and had heat exhaustion but that it could have quickly turned into heat stroke." She hugs me. "Thank God you got there when you did. His body temperature was rising fast, and if it kept going, his brain and organs could've been damaged."

I pull away from her. "Are you sure he's okay? Did you talk to the doctor? Where's Silas? Can I see him?"

She smiles, knowing my nonstop questions are because I love her son so much.

"They're cooling him down and pumping fluids in him," she says. "They're going to keep him overnight."

"So can I see him?"

"Not yet. They'll let us know when we can go in there."

The wait is excruciating. I need to see for myself that he's okay. Finding him lying there, unconscious, in the fields, I've never been so scared in my entire life. In that moment, I realized that nothing else matters. Where I go to college. What I do for a job. Where I live. None of it matters if Silas isn't there beside me.

Two hours later, the doctor finally tells us we can see him. Diane and Martin go in first. When they come out of his room, they tell me he's sleeping, but I go in there anyway. I need to see him and be with him and make sure he's okay.

I sit next to him on the bed and kiss his cheek. "I love you, Silas," I tell him even though he's asleep. "I've loved you since we were kids. I loved you even when I broke up with you. I wish I hadn't done that. I was just scared and stupid and thought we'd be better off without each other." I sniffle. "But I was wrong. We're so much better together." I rub his hand. "You need to wake up, Silas, because I need to tell you something. I need to tell you that I want us to get back together. For good this time."

I close my eyes and take a breath, wishing he could hear me because I don't want to wait another second for him to know this.

"You're admitting you were wrong?"

I hear his voice and lift my head to see him smiling at me. That famous Silas smile. I hug him. "You're awake!"

"I was awake since you came in here."

I pull back. "Why didn't you say something?"

"Because you started talking and I wanted to hear what you had to say."

"So you heard what I said?"

"Every word."

"And what do you think?"

"I'm thinking I can't wait to get out of this hospital so I can start living my life with the girl that I love." He reaches behind my neck and pulls my face to his and kisses me. "I also can't wait to do other things with you. Things I've been dying to do for weeks."

I smile. "Me too. You would not believe the dreams I've had."

"Oh, yeah? I'd like to hear about these dreams."

"You will, but not in the hospital. Let's wait until you get home." I lower my voice to a whisper. "Someplace where we can act them out."

He nods at the door. "Go ask the nurse if I can get out of here."

I laugh. "I don't think so. You need to be healthy for what I've got planned for you."

His brows rise. "Okay, seriously, Willow. Get the nurse. I've gotta get out of this hospital."

"You will." I kiss him, then sit back and notice a bracelet on the table next to his bed. "What's that?" I point to it.

"Oh, that's for you. I had it in my pocket and it fell out when they moved me to the bed."

I pick up the bracelet. It's a black leather cord with one of Silas' handmade silver charms threaded on it. The charm is a flat rectangular piece of metal stamped with a design.

"You made this?"

"Yeah. Can't you tell? It's a Silas original. I even stamped the back with my name."

I turn it over and see 'Sparks' carved on the back. "That should be the name of your company. Spark's Designs."

"I didn't know I was starting a company."

"You will. You're going to be famous someday, Silas Sparks." I hold up the bracelet. "Why did you make me this? And why were you giving it to me today?"

"When you said you were meeting me at the farm, I had a feeling you'd made a decision about us. Even if you'd decided not to get back together, I still wanted you to have this to remember this summer."

I hold up the bracelet again, looking closer at the design on the metal charm. It's a star formation. The same one we saw when we went to the farm that night and gazed up at the sky. The one that looks like Silas and me lying together in the back of his truck. At first, I couldn't see what Silas did. I saw the stars but I didn't see the pattern, the shapes, or what they meant. But then it all came into focus. And I finally saw what Silas did.

Now I'm seeing more than that. I'm seeing what Silas saw all along. With us. He knew we were meant to be together years ago, and now, finally, I do too.

"Silas, this is perfect. I love it." I slip it over my wrist. "Will you tighten it for me?"

He pulls on each end of the leather cord until it's snug against my wrist. "How's that?"

"Good." I hold it up. "I'm going to wear this all the time." My eyes go back to the design and it's almost like it changed. Now it looks like a house with Silas and me and...two kids? That's weird.

"Is something wrong?" He's got a sly look on his face like he has a secret he's not sharing.

"For a minute there I thought I saw something else in the design."

"A house?"

"You saw it too?"

"Yeah."

"With you and me and—" I stop, not wanting to mention the kids.

He smiles. "Let's just pretend we see you and me in the truck for now."

"I like that plan."

"Hey." He pulls me down to lie next to him. "No more talking about plans. Your plan is what got us off track in the first place."

"But now my plan includes you. In fact, I was thinking I should make a whole new plan with—"

He kisses me before I can finish. "No more plans. We're taking each day as it comes."

"But—"

"Willow. Trust me. I've been doing it for years."

"And it doesn't stress you out?"

"Never. It's awesome not knowing what's around the corner."

"That would stress me out."

He runs his finger under the tie strap at the top of my sundress. "Then it's a good thing I know how to relieve your stress." He tugs at the strap, releasing it, and exposing part of my chest.

"Silas!" I hurry to retie the strap.

"You weren't planning on that, were you?"

"Planning on you undressing me in your hospital room? No, definitely not."

"But you liked it," he whispers in my ear.

I bite my lip. "Yeah."

"So stop planning everything and just take what life gives you. It's a hell of a lot more fun."

Maybe he's right. After all, I never planned on getting back together with Silas this summer. When he picked me up at my dorm room, I was determined to keep him away. But plans have a way of falling apart when love comes walking into your life. For me, that came in the form of a tall, muscular, messy-haired, laid-back surfer boy named Silas.

Soon my plans got thrown out the window. Things got messy. Complicated. But like Silas said...things also got a lot more fun.

CHAPTER THIRTY

Five Months Later

WILLOW

It's been five months since Silas and I got back together and I'm happier than I've ever been. Silas and I moved in together last September. When Trent went back to college, we moved into his uncle's place to housesit because his uncle is on sabbatical this fall. He's even paying us to watch his house. Between that and not having to pay rent, Silas and I have been able to save up some money. In a couple weeks, Trent's uncle will be back and then Silas and I are moving into an apartment.

In January I start classes at UC-Berkeley but I'll continue to work for the family business, managing the organic beauty products. I've grown that business substantially the past few months, to the point that we might break it off into its own company. I've been able to get our products in hair salons and spas in the local area, but word's spreading fast and now I'm getting requests from retailers as far away as L.A. and Seattle.

I never dreamed it would take off like that. I also never dreamed this would become my career, and yet it's exactly what I want to do. I realize now that working for some massive corporation I had no connection to was never right for me. I have to believe in what I'm doing and feel like I'm making a difference. I sound just like my hippie parents. They said the same thing to me when I asked why they were organic farmers. I used to think I was so different than them, but the truth is,

I'm really not. I may dress differently than them and eat burgers and junk food, but when it comes down to what we want out of life, I'm finding I'm more like my parents than I thought I was.

My parents are finally out of debt. They used most, but not all, of my college money. The farm was doing well enough that they were able to use some of that income to pay off the rest of their bills. Now they're back on track, making money and even putting a little into savings. And luckily, they didn't have to sell the house. My mom still works at the real estate company but she's going to quit in January and go back to working full-time at the farm.

Silas just finished his fall semester at the community college. He liked his graphic design classes and decided that's what he wants to do, but as a freelancer, not in the corporate world. He's not a nine-to-five guy and he'd go crazy being stuck in a cubicle. He'll do better on his own. He already has several paid projects he's working on and people are starting to recommend him.

"Nice night," Silas says as we sit in the back of his truck, our legs dangling off the end as we lean back and watch the sun set over the farm.

"I love being out here at night. It's so quiet and peaceful."

Silas glances at me. "It wasn't that long ago you wanted to live downtown L.A., which is basically the opposite of quiet and peaceful."

I shrug. "What can I say? I've changed. I'm not that girl anymore. I haven't even planned anything for months."

He nudges me. "Willow, be honest."

"What are you talking about?" I ask innocently.

"I found your notebook. The one with the lists? And I'm pretty sure I saw a timeline in there."

I sigh. "You weren't supposed to find that. I swear it's more of a list of ideas than actual plans. And the timeline was just—"

He kisses me. "You don't have to explain. It's who you are. You can't help yourself. But at least you're not as obsessive about it as you used to be." He sits back. "And actually, I was going to ask you if you'd like to plan an event I have coming up."

"What is it?"

"It's a party. And it'll probably have a dinner. I'm not sure about all the details yet. I need your input on that."

"When is it?"

"I need your input on that too. It could be months from now. Or years."

"Months or years? What are you talking about? That doesn't make sense."

He laughs a little. "It makes perfect sense."

"Silas, you need to explain yourself. I can't help you unless you tell me what exactly this party is and why you're having it."

He hops off the back of the truck and turns to me, holding my hands, his eyes on mine. "The party will only happen if you agree to it."

"Is this for my birthday?"

"It's not a birthday party. It's not even really a party. It's more of a celebration with family and friends." He pauses. "That typically follows a ceremony."

My heart thumps harder as I realize what he's talking about it.

He picks me up from the truck and places me on the ground, then steps back and takes something from his pocket. Tears form the second I see it. It's my ring. The ring he made me two years ago. My engagement ring.

He takes my hand and gets down on one knee and smiles. "I know we've done this once before, but we're older now and I think we both finally know what we want. At least I do. And what I want is to be with you forever. I love you, Willow. Will you marry me?" He holds out the ring.

"Yes!" I smile so wide my cheeks hurt, then jump into his arms.

He lifts me up and kisses me. "You know you can't change your mind this time."

"I won't change my mind. I promise. I want to marry you."

He sets me down, but keeps his arms around me. "So now that you know more about this party I need you to plan, when do you think it should be?"

I stop to ponder it. "I think May would be a good month. Is that okay with you?"

"It's great, but that doesn't give you much time to plan."

"I don't need much time. It's going to be a simple wedding." I look out at the fields. "Right here on the farm."

He puts his arm around me. "That's exactly what I wanted too."

"Then I guess we have a time and a place. I'll work on the other details later."

We watch the sun go down, then I turn to Silas and say, "So are you going to give me my ring or what?"

He laughs. "Yeah. Sorry." He'd stuffed it in his pocket when I hugged him. "Here." He takes my hand and slips it on my finger.

I gaze at the ring, remembering the last time it was on my finger. I was so different back then. I thought I had it all together, when in reality I was lost. Confused. Unsure of myself.

"Willow, I'll get you a better ring. A real ring. With a diamond. I just need to save some more money."

I look up at him. "Silas, I don't want a diamond ring. I want *this* ring. The one that you made me. It's beautiful and one-of-a-kind." I smile. "A Silas Sparks original."

He brings my face to his and kisses me, and we kiss our way into the bed of the truck, then make love under the stars. *Our* stars. The ones that showed us where we needed to be. Right here. Together. In the place we grew up. The place we'll get married.

The place we fell in love.